IMMORTAL MERI

CW00536926

FLOODGATES

EMMA SHELFORD

This is a work of fiction. Names, characters, places, and incidents either are the product of the author's imagination or are used factitiously, and any resemblance to any persons, living or dead, business establishments, events, or locales is entirely coincidental.

FLOODGATES

Kinglet Books
Victoria BC, Canada

Cover design by Deranged Doctor Designs

ISBN: 978-1989677155 (print)
ISBN: 978-1989677070 (ebook)

www.emmashelford.com

First edition: November 2018

DEDICATION

For everyone with a little bit of magic in their hearts.

CHAPTER I

I breathe deeply when I exit the glass double doors of the history building on campus. My class in this summer term is over for another day, and the sky is a cloudless, beckoning blue. How shall I spend this beautiful afternoon?

"Excuse me."

I turn. A middle-aged woman stands on the sidewalk. I would assume her to be a professor, except she is attired too formally in a crisp navy pencil skirt and matching jacket, the blouse underneath an immaculate white. Her graying hair is neat in a cropped style that frames her strong chin and ascends above her neck at the back. Her face creases in a warm smile, but her eyes are too intense for a casual greeting. Deep burgundy lauvan swirl calmly around her torso and head.

"Can I help you?" I reply.

"It is Merry Lytton, isn't it?" When I nod, she puts out her hand. "I know of you through a common acquaintance. May I introduce myself? My name is March Feynman. I am the founder of Potestas."

That gives me pause. I take a moment to examine her. Potestas is the organization that is searching for the spirit world. They tried to trigger a volcanic eruption in the spring, and a rogue member attempted to murder me a few weeks ago. Why is their leader approaching me?

"Pleased to make your acquaintance," I say slowly and grasp her hand firmly in my own. She takes it with a strong grip. "I must say, I am astonished that you are speaking to me. Your organization's aptitude for secrecy is almost as impressive as its talent for mayhem."

March's smiling expression turns to one of concern.

"Yes, that is why I am here. I feel you are owed an apology,

1

and an explanation. Can I buy you a coffee?"

The leader of Potestas wants to answer my questions? I am all ears, if we sit in a public space where she can't cause trouble.

"Certainly. My class is finished, so I'm free for a while. The best coffee is this way."

We start to walk. March looks around at the milling students around us.

"You're an instructor, are you? What do you teach?"

"Please don't insult my intelligence, Ms. Feynman. You clearly know much more about me than I do about you. You knew enough to find me at the university, for example."

She glances at me sidelong with a half-smile.

"I will cut the pretense, then. And it's March, please. No need to stand on ceremony." She nods in thanks as I hold the door of the café open for her. "I will explain all once we're comfortable."

After we order our drinks, March leads the way to a quiet corner where we are unlikely to be overheard. We settle into our seats, and I gaze at her expectantly. She's not what I expected, given the actions of her associates. I anticipated an evil overlord, not a well-heeled businesswoman. She looks back, unfazed.

"Dr. Lytton," she starts.

"Merry."

"Merry. On behalf of Potestas, its followers, and all we stand for, I would like to sincerely apologize for the actions of Drew Mordecai. His attempts on your life were not sanctioned by the organization, but for our part in providing him with the means to attack you, we are truly sorry." She leans forward in her earnestness. "I am truly sorry. His actions should not have gone so far unrestrained, and I hold myself to blame for that. Attacking innocent bystanders? Without provocation? That is not what Potestas is for."

I gaze at her with interest while she delivers her apology. Her lauvan swirl with bland smoothness, so I can't get the measure of her true sincerity. How much did she really know about Drew's plans? Was the whole thing orchestrated by Potestas to test my abilities, or was Drew truly a rogue, intent on killing me for his own purposes? From March's words and lauvan, I can't yet tell.

"Drew would argue that I wasn't an innocent bystander." I choose my words carefully and watch March for a reaction. She sighs.

"You refer to the business at the volcano. I'm afraid Drew was unbalanced and unable to look at the facts logically. I had no idea Drew was acting against my instructions. Honestly, Potestas is more of a group of truth-seekers than a hierarchical organization. For obvious reasons, I've tightened my involvement in org activities."

"What role do you think I play in all this?" I ask. No point in being coy. Let's see how much March knows or is willing to tell me. "What do you think I know?"

March takes a sip of her coffee before she answers. Her eyes never leave my face.

"You had a dalliance with Anna Green in Wallerton, and somehow discovered the plans to erupt the volcano there using Potestas' connections with the spirit world. Your special abilities, which I know little about, allowed you to pause those plans. Those abilities also saved you from Drew's attacks. Your connection with the spirit world is unlike anything I have ever encountered." March's eyes grow hungry for a moment before she composes herself.

"What makes you think I have these special abilities? Perhaps I've been lucky, at the right place at the right time." I swirl coffee in my cup. This conversation with March is both enlightening and tense. We're pacing around like lions, sizing each other up.

"Knowing how to stop the volcano erupting at Wallerton took some special knowledge," March says. "As well, you managed to defeat Drew, despite his connection to an air spirit. No ordinary person would have stood a chance."

"Where is Drew now?" I'd like to know if I should be watching my back.

"He's at the same facility you dropped him off at," says March. "Rehab is the best place for him right now. He needs help with his addiction, and the facility can provide that."

A hopeful man would hear that March is concerned about her former acquaintance. A cynical man would hear that Drew is no longer useful to the org, and is a liability best kept out of the way. I've been around too long to avoid cynicism.

"I would like you to get to know us a little better, if you're interested," says March. "With your special abilities, I think you will find what we do intriguing. And perhaps you may, in time, find it in your heart to forgive us the actions of one when you meet the many who wish you well." March takes a sip. "In fact, you might be able to help us in our quest. Be assured, the rewards of membership in Potestas are not trifling."

"Rewards?" I want to hear more about this. What are they getting out of this connection with the spirit world? March waves her hand.

"Every member of Potestas will eventually be connected to a spirit. That connection will give them powers over the physical world, senses that we can't imagine." March smiles with a glint of enthusiasm in her eyes. Her cool businesswoman demeanor is only a façade that covers the power-hungry soul underneath. "Come to a meeting at Potestas and we will tell you more."

I can probably imagine those senses. I watch her lauvan

twist around her, only slightly affected by her fervor. How is she so calm? Why can't I read her? Are the reactions of her lauvan being dampened under the influence of a spirit connection?

I have so many questions, but I won't receive answers in this café. March's vagueness is a ploy to entice me to Potestas headquarters, a ploy I'm only too willing to fall for. This is an opportunity I hadn't expected. My hunt for information about Potestas has been fruitless so far, and March promises to drop answers in my lap. Answers about the spirit world, how they connect to it, the nature of it...

I must feign reluctance. It might be suspicious if I jump too readily in with my would-be murderer's colleagues.

"I have to say that I'm intrigued. But how do I know that another member of your group isn't waiting to take me out when I arrive? I stopped your plans at the volcano. I'm sure Drew isn't the only one sore at that."

"No one is unstable like Drew," March assures me. "Everyone else is simply excited to experience the promised changes. They do not have murder in their hearts. I promise, it will be clear that you are under my full protection and that no ill will toward you will be tolerated."

"The promised changes?" That's an intriguing phrase. What does she mean by that? March only smiles.

"This isn't the place to discuss such things. Come to a meeting and find out."

I shrug.

"I'll think about it."

"Good." March pulls a business card from her pocket. "Stop by this address at seven, tomorrow evening. There will be a gathering—you can meet the group, tour headquarters, ask more questions."

March stands and extends her hand. We shake, her palm

cool and smooth against mine.

"I think we can help each other immensely, Merry. I do hope you consider putting the past in the past and coming to visit the group. We look forward to it."

I nod but don't commit myself to anything. She places the business card on the table then walks with quick steps out of the café door. I lean back in my chair and exhale. I have an invitation to the elusive, dangerous, intriguing Potestas.

I'm in.

CHAPTER II

Dreaming

We sit at the breakfast table. Uther's cook brings us bread with ale, and I help myself to liberal portions. I'm used to taking advantage of the opportunity for food when it presents itself, in my nomadic existence. Arthur stuffs his mouth as only a growing boy can, and Uther sips small ale. Morgan fidgets with a piece of bread in her hands.

"Father," she says in a hesitant tone, then her voice strengthens. "Father. Since Merlin is here to teach Arthur, might he teach me also? My duties don't take the whole day, and there are so few diversions or company nearby. He might as well."

"I see no need for that," Uther says. He picks up a chunk of bread. "What do you need an education for? Unnecessary."

"But, Father—" Morgan opens her mouth to say more, but Uther cuts her off.

"If you're bored, there is plenty to sew and spin. Ask cook for ideas. A woman has no need for education, so that's the end of it. Merlin, can I offer you some ale?"

"Thank you." I hold out my cup. Morgan casts her eyes down, but her shoulders shake with anger and frustration. My lips thin, but I say nothing to my new employer. In the north, where I was brought up, women are treated with more equality than in the south. The Roman way of treating their women like property has not reached the hills yet, the mountains where worship of a goddess is still prevalent. I have no issue teaching Morgan as well as Arthur, but Uther has made it clear where he stands. I wait a few moments before I speak.

"Well, Arthur, I have a mind to teach you herblore today,

followed by tracking. Let's start in the meadow near the river."
I glance at Morgan as I say it. She meets my gaze with defiant
eyes, then looks startled when I twitch my head to speak
without words.

"All right," says Arthur.

"Excellent notion," Uther says with approval. "I will be
leaving in the afternoon for a few days, but I trust that all will
carry on as usual while I'm gone."

"Of course," I say with a bland expression. Morgan meets
my glance with a secret smile.

In the meadow, Arthur sits on a rock in front of a bank of
bushes that grow between him and the villa. I stand to face him
and the bushes.

"Herblore is one of the first things I was taught on Eire.
Herbs can be used for medicine, of course, and to flavor food,
but also…"

A free-floating lauvan drifts past my hand, and I reach for
it, hiding my motion in a gesture while I speak. It's a ruby-red
one that crackles with excitement. I suppress a smile. Morgan
watches us, as I had hoped. I don't trust Arthur not to spill the
news to his father inadvertently, so I don't call Morgan out.
Instead, I conduct the rest of the lesson in a louder voice,
careful to always face Morgan's way.

Now that I have wordlessly invited Morgan to eavesdrop
on our lessons, I must accept that she will find out about my
special abilities. Luckily, I have something on her. After
explaining the various uses of herbs in the meadow, I dust my
hands.

"Arthur, care to go for a run?" I ask. He jumps up, his short
curls bouncing in his excitement.

"Yes!"

I grab his lauvan, twist the correct ones, and knot them
loosely. Arthur dissolves into a young buck, tiny tips of antlers

budding from his forehead. His hooves prance delicately on the grass.

"Go on, I'll be right behind you." I smack his rump and he bounds forward to follow the river. I wait until he is out of earshot.

"If you want to keep learning, Morgan, you will kindly keep this to yourself."

There is silence from the bush, but I don't expect an answer. I gather the necessary lauvan and transform. I toss my antlered head, then tense powerful haunches to spring after Arthur.

Morgan doesn't appear until dinner, after Uther has departed for his journey. Arthur lounges before the fire and pets the two dogs there, tired after our long day out. I relax in Uther's wood-backed chair with one leg over the armrest and whittle a small piece of wood with my knife. Morgan enters the hall, and her eyes are drawn to me immediately. She twists her hands together.

"Hi, Morgan. I'm starving," says Arthur. He jumps up. "I'll see if cook's ready yet."

Morgan takes a seat on a bench by the fire but doesn't speak until Arthur disappears out of the door.

"Are you a sorcerer?" she whispers. I continue to whittle but glance at her face to gauge her mood. She is tense, waiting, ready to flee.

"I don't know about that. What is a sorcerer, anyway? I was born with some different abilities, and I use them when I feel like it. Does that make you afraid?"

"No," she says quickly. Her chin rises. "Does my father know?"

9

"Certainly not. I have a comfortable position here for the winter. Why would I jeopardize that? Most react with fear."

"Why did you tell me, then?" Her brows knit in confusion. I sigh.

"Because my abilities are an integral part of my lessons with Arthur, and I want you to be there if you wish. You Romans treat your women as chattel, for the most part. Chattel or spun glass. I see no reason why you can't learn if you wish."

Morgan looks into the fire, but her eyes are moist.

"Thank you, Merlin. There is nothing I wish for more."

"Then it's settled," I say. "I will teach you, either in secret or with Arthur, if you believe he won't tell Uther. And you will stay quiet about my abilities."

"Yes. It's settled." Morgan smiles, a slow smile that grows from the upturned corners of her mouth to a full grin. "And I'm not Roman."

"As good as, the way you live." I grin back, since Morgan is clearly not offended. A thought crosses my mind.

"Would you care to learn the harp? While Uther is away, of course."

Morgan's mouth drops.

"I—I don't—truly?"

"Why not?" I lay down my knife and reach across for my harp case. "Another musician in the house will give my fingers a rest."

CHAPTER III

A pigeon wakes me early this morning. Its soft cooing burrows into my dreams, fragmenting them into shards of ice, melting them into formless thoughts that cannot withstand the light of a summer morning's day.

The pigeon stares at me with beady eyes when I twitch back the curtains.

"Good morning to you, too," I say. "I am sorry, were my dreams disturbing you? How ill-mannered of me."

The pigeon ignores my sarcasm and bursts off the windowsill in a flurry of beating wings and floating feathers. I stretch my arms above my head and breathe deeply. The day is fresh and still cool. I'm suddenly hungry, starving. I slip on loose-fitting pants and amble to the kitchen. Nothing in my fridge or cupboard calls out to me.

Wienerbrød, or danishes as they're known here. That's what I need right now. Flaky, buttery, jam-filled *wienerbrød*. My stomach agrees with a rumble. Nowhere in this city makes them the way I like them, though, with a raspberry filling and a dash of nutmeg. If I want it done right, I'll have to do it myself.

Butter out of the fridge, flour in a bowl, nutmeg seed shaved using my trusty kitchen knife. My stomach rumbles again and I recall making these with my fourteenth wife Josephine, during my stint as a pastry chef.

My phone rings. Who would call at this hour? I answer it with flour-dusted fingers.

"Hello?"

"Oh good, I was hoping you'd be up this early," Jen says. She's in Paris currently on a job, which explains the crack-of-dawn call. There's a pause, then, "What are you doing up this

11

early?"

"Baking danishes." I squish butter between my fingers, deftly breaking it up into neat discs within the flour. "I can't find a reliably good source in this city, and I had a craving."

"I didn't know you could bake. And danishes, those sound tricky."

"Jen, haven't you figured out by now that I know how to do everything?" I pour milk in a steady stream into the bowl while I stir with a spoon. Jen laughs.

"Of course, of course. Although I'm a little miffed you've never baked anything for me."

"There are plenty of good bakeries in Vancouver. I'm not a masochist—I make enough money to buy the baked goods I want, if someone is willing to make them for me. But if you like, I can certainly whip up something for you when you return. What's your pleasure?"

"Can you make…" Jen thinks for a moment. "Croissants?"

"Mais oui. Were you trying to find something difficult, or are you anticipating a croissant withdrawal once you leave Paris?"

Jen laughs again.

"A bit of both. Hey, I should probably get going, I'm in the Louvre at the moment, there's a new exhibit of Jean-Honoré Fragonard. They recently found a bunch of his paintings in someone's attic, and everyone is super excited over here. I popped by on my way to the airport to check it out."

"Fragonard, huh? I quite enjoy his work." I was good friends with him, too, back in late-eighteenth century Paris.

"I just wanted to ask you, does your family come from France?"

"Odd question. I sincerely doubt it. Why do you ask?"

"Because there's a man in one of these paintings who could be your twin."

I stop folding the dough and it spreads out stickily on the counter. How can this be? I forbade Fragonard to paint me, and he always held true to his word. Or so I thought.

"That's odd," I say, stalling for time. "How interesting. What's the painting? Can you describe it?"

"It's a scene of a dinner party, which is strange because he tended to paint outdoor scenes. The man is sitting at the edge of the painting, at the table. He's looking out at the fourth wall, with that annoying all-knowing smirk on his face just like you get sometimes."

"What smirk?"

"Have a look in the mirror some time when you think you're right. You'll see it." She giggles.

"So, have a look any time."

"Ha, ha. There's a woman draped over the man in the picture, too. Dark hair, curly. I think she's quite pretty, but her face is shadowed and in profile, so it's hard to tell."

My eyes close in remembrance, the dough long-forgotten on the counter. Celeste, my thirteenth wife. The right side of her face was badly burned, and although Fragonard often used her as a model, he always painted her in profile. And Jen's right—she was beautiful indeed, especially to me.

How did Fragonard hide this from me? Why did he paint me? Bastard, getting the last laugh, and now I can't even berate him.

"Merry?" Jen says after a pause. "Are you still there?"

"Yes, yes, I'm here." I try to make my voice sound brisk, although my mind is still miles and centuries away.

"So that's weird, isn't it?"

"Very. Could you buy me a poster of the painting? I'm interested to see my doppelganger. And this annoying smirk which you apparently love to hate."

"For sure. I'd better fly—I'll buy the poster before I head to the airport. See you tomorrow."

"Safe journey."

I hang up the phone, then stare at the wall in a daze, lost in memories. When I finally drag myself back to the present, my dough is beyond repair—partially risen and entirely stuck to the counter. I scrape it into the garbage. It doesn't matter—I've lost my appetite anyway. Coffee will have to do, then a shower and off to the university for my morning class. It feels so distant from Fragonard and Celeste.

Alejandro finally wakes up and enters the kitchen, yawning and stretching, from his nest on the living room couch.

"Good morning, Merlo," he says thickly. "Were you talking to Jen? When is she coming back?"

"Tomorrow, I believe." I open the cupboard and pull out two mugs for the coffee that brews on the stove. "Coffee?"

"Yes, please." Alejandro rubs his face to wake himself up. "Where are you going this morning? Could I have a ride?"

"Normally, the answer would be yes. But my car still is in the shop, and the mechanic informs me that it will be out of commission for a few weeks while they order parts." I pour the coffee and hand it to Alejandro. "Until I get around to renting a car for the interim, you'll have to take the bus."

"Of course." He sips his coffee then looks confused. "How will you travel to work?"

"I could take the bus, I suppose, but flying is so much easier."

Alejandro laughs.

"I guess it is."

He rummages in the fridge for something to eat while I

finish my coffee, then turns to me with a jar of jam in his hand.

"Can I pick up the rental car for you? I'll be out today and can stop by, if you like."

"That would be very helpful. Thank you." I drain my mug and set it in the sink, then pass him my driver's license. "For the rental. I'll call in the credit card. Where are you off to today?"

"Oh, just a few errands, some exploring," Alejandro says with a vague wave of his hand. He pauses for a moment, then says, "I'll be leaving your couch soon, don't worry. If I stay too much longer, I will dent it permanently."

I'm surprised by the disappointment that flushes through me. It has been a delightful change, having Alejandro around. I live alone from necessity, not choice. Having another body around alleviates the loneliness that threatens to overwhelm when the apartment is silent for too long. And Alejandro is good company. His enthusiasm for life is refreshing, and his conversation is peppered with insights that show his thoughts run deeper than the superficial.

I don't show my disappointment. Instead, I reply with careful nonchalance.

"It's a tough couch, I wouldn't worry about that. Are you going back to Costa Rica soon?"

"I'm not sure yet." Alejandro moves to the hallway. "I'd better get ready. Have a good day, Merlo."

Alejandro closes the bathroom door. I am left with a forlorn sense of loss.

15

CHAPTER IV

We're discussing the concept of courtly love in the Middle Ages in my morning lecture. I pull out a few examples, and the students ponder the difference between romantic ideals of yesteryear and today.

"Don't forget," I say. "These were lofty ideals from the literature at the time. It was as indicative of their daily life as the actions of a typical romcom is to your life. Somewhat influential, but not something you tend to emulate."

The class chuckles. I split them into discussion groups and let them talk among themselves while I wander around, ostensibly eavesdropping, but really thinking of other things. Love, for example, and how Celeste liked to surprise me with my favorite chanterelles from the market. The nobility and chivalry of courtly love were all well and good, but what did it do for the lady if her knight was gallivanting off on quests all the time? And the ideal courtly love was often unconsummated, which I could never condone.

I watch the lauvan of my students. Those of the engaged speakers are tight and lively, and those of the disinterested students are sluggish and drooping. Threads of connection fan out from each person, fading into invisible lines from each student to some unknown person of importance to them.

I compare their closely swirling lauvan to my own, which drifts in a loose cloud around my body. It's scarcely connected to me anymore. I would worry, but it's been that way for the last three centuries at least, and I'm still alive and kicking.

What is more interesting is the fact that my lauvan appear to be thinning. There are distinct strands that are slenderer than the rest. I first noticed it centuries ago, and for a while I was convinced of my approaching death. They haven't grown worse, though, so my concern was short-lived.

I try to concentrate on the conversations around me and pitch in from time to time. When the students have had enough, I clap my hands.

"All right, pack it up. We'll continue next day. Make sure you do your readings, otherwise don't bother to come."

The students shove their belongings into backpacks and shuffle to the door. One girl remains behind.

"Dr. Lytton, I have a question about the essay you've assigned." She flips glossy black hair over her shoulder.

"All right, spit it out." I'm only half-paying attention. My thoughts are still in eighteenth century Paris, walking along the Seine with Celeste.

"Umm, for my topic, do you think I should focus more on the grammatical use of kennings, or the meaning behind them?" She bats her eyelashes at me.

It finally clicks. She's trying to flirt with me. She picked the wrong day, I'm afraid. Celeste fills my mind, and this peppy student in tight shorts does not even cross my radar.

"Whatever you think you can write the most eloquently about." I pick up my satchel. "I'll see you next class."

Despite my age, I am more prone to action than philosophy, so my upcoming meeting is a welcome diversion to my thoughts of death. Wayne Gibson, a colleague and initiate of my lauvan secrets after our battle with Drew Mordecai and his air spirit, has invited me for a sparring session at his gym during lunch.

"It's just off campus," he said last week during our lunch break. "And you're good, but everyone can always use practice."

I'm looking forward to it. Modern life has a dearth of fighting. While it's probably for the best—peace is usually the aim of any right-thinking people—I miss the adrenaline rush of battling for my life. I'm so good at it, too, that it seems a shame to waste my skills. No matter. Wayne is providing an opportunity, and I won't waste it.

The gym is unassuming, entered through a frosted glass door behind a bicycle repair shop. Inside, the smell of sweat and dust fills my nostrils. It's a big room, with a central padded foam floor surrounded by painted gray walls and punching bags. On one end is a fenced octagon. Wayne is lifting free weights in the corner but hails me when he spots me enter.

"Merry! Glad you could make it."

Others glance at me briefly, then continue to punch bags or run on treadmills. One duo grapples on the floor, and I watch them with interest as I walk to meet Wayne.

"Thanks for the invitation, Wayne. What's the plan?"

"In about five minutes, the session will begin. It's an informal group a few of us started for lunchtime fighting practice. We do two-minute bouts and cycle through. Do you need to warm up?"

I half-heartedly roll my shoulders and stretch my arms over my head. My body rarely gives me the aches and pains that I hear others complain of, mainly because I can massage my lauvan into their correct orientation before tightness becomes a problem. I don't need to boast about that to Wayne, though.

"I have news," I say to Wayne. He looks at me with interest. "Potestas approached me. The leader herself. She extended an olive branch and invited me to their secret headquarters."

"Wow." Wayne's eyebrows shoot up in surprise. "After all our digging, to no end, they ask you to waltz in? What are you going to do?"

"Go, of course. Will I ever get another opportunity like this again? I plan to ingratiate myself, worm my way in as deep as I can, and figure out exactly what they are doing and why. Finally, I might have some answers."

A man behind us takes a long slurp out of the water fountain. I shake my head when a bevy of voices start whispering wordlessly in my ear. It sounds like a crowd of people, but there are perhaps eight here, maximum. They stop abruptly.

"Merry? I asked whether you want backup. I don't know if this was an exclusive invite, but you might not want to go in alone."

"Thanks for the offer," I say. "I don't want to drag you into this more than you already have been, and I don't know if they would welcome someone else. Don't worry about me, I'm an excellent actor. They'll have a hard time seeing the truth. And it's nice to know that someone is on the outside to call the authorities if I don't show up for work." I say this last bit as a joke, but Wayne doesn't crack a smile.

"All right, if you're sure. At least you'll have some recent sparring practice, hey? If they try anything funny, punch them and run."

I laugh. The voices start again, more insistent this time.

"Merry! Are you okay? You seem off. You've got to be on your toes with this bunch."

"I'm fine, thanks. Don't worry about me." Is someone's music on too loud? I don't know what I hear, but it will take more than a few bodiless voices to throw me off a fight.

"Everyone up!" yells a man on the floor. His arms are filled with ropy muscles and a liberal sprinkling of tattoos, and the expression on his square face means business. "Let's get this show on the road. Gibson, you start today. Choose a partner. On the bell, do what you do best."

"Come on, Merry." Wayne claps me on the shoulder and grins. "You're up. I hope you're ready." He leads me into the cage, then turns and frowns. "No funny stuff, right?"

"Please. I don't need it."

"Is that so? I'll believe it when I see it."

DING.

At the bell, Wayne and I circle around each other. I watch Wayne's movements and lauvan for hints of what he will try first.

Swift as a bird, Wayne throws a punch at my right shoulder. I narrowly dodge it and we circle again. I throw my own without warning, and Wayne blocks my fist with a forearm. My next fist jabs in quick succession, and I fling my leg around in a powerful kick before dropping to the ground in a sprawl. Wayne's retaliation takeout flies harmlessly over me.

Before I can keep my advantage, Wayne rolls me onto my back and starts to punch. I block his jabs and wrap my legs around his torso to force him in, then pull his neck to my chest and squeeze my legs together. Wayne flails in futile defense, but I have him trapped.

The voices start again, soft but insistent. What is that? What are they saying? My eyes grow dim and I lose focus.

When the voices stop, I find myself facedown, cheek smashed against the mat with my arms pinioned behind me. I kick my foot to tap out, and Wayne releases me. He holds out a hand with a grin.

"Good match, Merry."

I smile weakly back. Wayne didn't seem to notice my momentary lapse. I hope it doesn't happen again. What is wrong with me?

I stay for the duration and fight twice more with no more lapses before the group wraps up. I'm bruised and sweating but grinning widely. It feels so good to fight again.

"Thanks for getting me out," I say to Wayne on our way out the door. "That was great."

"Any Thursday, you're welcome to come. That move you did to trip up Chang, you'll have to teach me that one. Very effective."

After a shower in the staff washroom, my exercise-induced euphoria fades and is replaced by concern. It's difficult to maintain concentration with whispers in my ear. I must check the lauvan around my head when I next find a mirror—hearing voices can't be healthy. I want to be on top form when I visit Potestas tomorrow.

CHAPTER V

Dreaming

The skirmish on the borderlands of Caer-Gloui left too many casualties. While Arthur and the others remain behind to chase down enemies who escaped, I follow a wagon filled with wounded men to a safe house where Guinevere and others of Arthur's household are staying for a few weeks this summer. The wounded will live or die there in as much comfort as they can hope for.

I've been tasked to heal as many as possible without alerting suspicion to my interference. I've quietly stopped the bleeding of the worst of the men's wounds, but I can't do more until we stop. The wagon jolts along, slower than a comfortable walk, and with every hole in the earthen track that it bumps over, the men inside gasp and groan as one.

After a long journey, during which a third of the wounded faint from their pain, we reach the safe house. It's a Roman villa like Arthur's with a tiled roof and numerous outbuildings. Our arrival causes the inhabitants to stream out the main door from their supper table.

Guinevere picks up her skirts and runs nimbly to me, her round-cheeked face creased in worry below her braided blond hair. She puts a hand on my forearm in greeting then peers over the edge of the wagon, her eyes searching.

"Arthur's fine," I say. She slumps and passes a shaking hand over her face. "A few minor cuts, nothing I couldn't handle. But these lot are in desperate need."

"Of course." Guinevere smooths her skirt to collect herself, then turns to the others waiting.

"We need hot water, my bag with herbs, and—" Guinevere

22

turns to me and hisses in Saxon. "What's the word for bandages?"

"Bandages," I call out. The others scurry to comply, and the stronger of the women and old men help me lift each man from his perch in the pile of wounded. Groans, screams, and curses accompany our work, and it's a relief to carry the immobile weights of the fainted.

Finally, sweating from exertion, I lay down the last man on a waiting blanket in the great hall. Guinevere is already in charge, her Brythonic becoming more broken under the strain, but also more commanding. Servants hurry to do her bidding.

"Aife, stir poultice on fire," she orders. "Newlyn, bring my bag. We must make drink for pain. And where are bandages?"

She waves to me when a servant delivers her the drink.

"Merlin, who is worst?"

I point to a man nearby, whose face is contorted with pain. He clutches his side, where his clothes are stained with blood.

"I tried to staunch the bleeding but wasn't very successful," I say. "And I'm certain the organs are damaged. He doesn't have long if I don't get to him."

Guinevere nods with determination.

"I will distract, you work."

She kneels at the head of the man and carefully lifts his head enough to put the cup to his lips.

"This is for pain. Drink," she says gently. The man grimaces with the movement but opens his mouth enough for Guinevere to tip the contents slowly into it. The man's eyes are half-closed, so I get to work.

The snarls and knots of sand-colored lauvan above his abdomen are extensive. I massage out the largest ones first and tease out strand after strand, but still there are more.

"What is your name?" Guinevere asks the man. She accepts a wet cloth from a passing servant and wipes the man's face.

23

He closes his eyes in relief from the drink, my ministrations, and the knowledge that he is being cared for.

"Atty," he whispers. "From Lot's household."

"You are well here, Atty," Guinevere says. "We take care of you. You see the sun again soon."

The man lets out his breath and nods with his eyes still closed. Guinevere looks at me.

"I've almost done enough," I answer the unspoken question. "He will live, and there are others. Ready?"

Guinevere beckons to a passing servant.

"Clean wounds and make comfortable. I must see others." Guinevere lays the man's head gently on the blanket and we move to the next wounded man in dire need.

The hall is busy with servants heating water, noblewomen bandaging wounds, and old men hauling wood for the fire. Only one person spares a second glance at my handwaving above the patients we visit. I feel eyes on me and lift my head. A servant girl watches my hands pass over the man's leg with wide eyes, a bucket of water on her hip. I give her a small smile, as if inviting her into a secret, and she reddens and turns away with haste.

She may tell someone, but it isn't likely. A servant accusing a lord of witchcraft? Her potential punishment would be severe. And I made no effort to cover my movements to her, which she will hopefully interpret to mean that my actions are known to those that need to know. In any event, we won't be at this house for much longer, and she can put me from her mind.

We've left the ninth and final man until the end because his thigh wound was severe, but I managed to suppress the bleeding before we left the battlefield. He's in a lot of pain, but little danger of dying quite yet. Guinevere sits beside his head as with the others, and I kneel at his legs. It's only then that I feel the wetness on my knees.

The red blanket conceals the spread of blood, but one look at the man's ashen gray face tells me what has happened. My fix has failed, and he is slipping away from us.

"He's lost too much blood," I say. I untangle knots in a frenzy of motion, not caring who may be watching. For every knot that I massage back into place, another one tangles itself below my fingers. The man's eyes close and his head slumps to one side. Guinevere props it up again and whispers to him frantically in Saxon, nonsense words meant to wake him. She slaps him lightly on the cheek, but there is no response. The lauvan knots form faster than I can remove them, until the wriggling mass stops its incessant movement.

The man dies. I sit back and watch his lauvan depart his body, where they drift away into transparency and leave his mortal body untethered. My shoulders drop, and I sigh.

Guinevere sees the end of my untangling and her face crumples.

"No!" Tears run down her cheeks as she carefully places the man's head on his blanket, then she covers her face with her hands. I shuffle over to her and wrap an arm around her shoulders. She turns into me and muffles her sobs in my shirt.

Eventually, her tears stop falling and she sits up again.

"We can't save everyone," I say in Saxon. Guinevere nods.

"I know. But with you, I forget that. We were so close." She sighs then takes my hand. "I'm glad you are here. I don't know if any of these men would have lived without your help. And for me, too—it's so good to see you again." She gives me a sweet smile through her reddened eyes. "I missed you. You and Arthur are my favorite people, and when you're gone, the sun doesn't shine as brightly."

I stroke her cheek.

"Don't worry, soon enough it will be winter, and I'll be

25

pacing around your hall, complaining of the weather. You'll
wish me away soon enough."

Guinevere laughs.

"Never. Even when you're complaining."

CHAPTER VI

Alejandro is out this morning, and I have no classes to teach. The sun streams in my open balcony doors, accompanied by a fresh breeze, and I decide that the time is ripe for a little music. I pull out my harp from beside my bookshelf. It was a present from a well-known seventeenth century harpist and a good friend of mine. My fingers stroke the smooth, waxed wood of the frame in greeting then pluck the strings to tune them. I make only a few adjustments then launch into an old drinking song in the Mercian dialect of Anglo-Saxon. This song was a favorite of King Offa when I entertained his court in the late eighth century in England. He often requested it after his fifth goblet of ale.

It's rousing and lively, a far cry from the harp tunes most modern folk are used to. My voice, a vibrant tenor well-honed after centuries of practice, rings out in the small apartment and floats away through the balcony door. After the drinking song, my fingers pluck a few strings at random until a new song announces itself to my mind.

It's a lay of Tristan and Iseult in Breton that I composed in the twelfth century. My seventh wife, Marie, adored it, and she even wrote her own narrative version which is still read today. It's plaintive with a lilting melody that moves from one verse to the next with a current that always reminds me of a flowing river. There is no historical basis to the couple—at least I never knew them—but the story was a popular one at the time.

I'm halfway through the fourth verse, which describes Tristan's exile from Cornwall, when I hear a thump and then a "Shush!"

I frown, then transfer the small harp to my hip while continuing to play with one hand and sing. I walk toward my

27

front door, and only stop playing when I round the corner.

Jen is there, as well as Gary Watson, my neighbor from next door. They are frozen in the doorway, their faces caricatures of guilty dismay. I laugh aloud.

"You don't need to sneak around if you want a concert. I'll play any time you ask."

"I didn't know you could actually play that harp," says Jen. "I thought it was there for decoration."

"Because the décor in my apartment is so chic and artfully placed." It's a joke between us how sparse my apartment is. I have no pictures on the walls, and the only items that are not furniture are a few mementoes on my bookshelf.

"Sorry for listening in, Merry." Gary looks abashed. "I heard the music when I came in the elevator, and your friend here opened the door." He picks up his bag of groceries. "I'd better get these to the missus. Are you still interested in a game of chess this afternoon, Merry?"

"I'll come by at three," I say. Gary shuffles off and Jen enters my apartment.

"Welcome back," I say, and give her a swift hug. "Come on in. Coffee?"

"Please. I still feel weird from jetlag, but it's nice to be home." She reaches out and plucks a string of my harp with light fingers. "You have a really nice voice, by the way. What language were you singing?"

"Breton. An old lay from France." It's the truth—let her make of that what she will. I place the harp back in its home beside my bookshelf, then move to the kitchen to put the kettle under the tap. The rush of water is accompanied by a different sort of hiss, like the sound of a theater of people whispering before a concert. What is this noise that keeps occurring? I turn the tap off and the sound stops.

"Oh, I brought you something." She rummages in her huge

purse that lounges like an overweight cat on my countertop and extracts a roll of paper in a thin plastic bag. "A poster of that painting. You know, the one with your double."

I reach for the roll, intensely curious to see Fragonard's work, and take the poster to the dining room before I spread it on the table there.

"See?" Jen points at a figure in the bottom-left corner. "It could be a mirror."

It's a portrait of myself, smiling close-mouthed at the viewer, a knowledgeable glint in my eye. Celeste leans over my shoulder and reaches for a shiny red apple on the laden table before us. Her curly brown locks cascade over my shoulder and her cheek touches my ear. There is a long table in the center of the painting, and I sit at one end. A wing of poultry and a bunch of grapes languish on a pewter plate, as I hold a full glass of wine. The other revelers gesticulate, laugh uproariously, place their arms around each other's shoulders—one couple is clearly singing in the background—but I alone gaze out at the viewer.

"The kettle's boiling. I'll make the coffee." Jen moves to the kitchen. The sound of clanging mugs follows.

I lean closer to examine the picture of Celeste. I painted my own portrait of her—it's in my sketchbook—and while I'm an accomplished artist, Fragonard brings a vivacity to his work that I have never mastered. This picture is priceless to me. My finger gently strokes the hair of Celeste until I realize that Jen stands silently beside me with a mug in each hand. My arm falls to my side and I straighten.

"Remarkable similarity. How much do I owe you?"

Jen looks at me with narrowed eyes but doesn't comment on my actions.

"It wasn't much, don't worry about it. Here's your coffee." She hands me a mug and we sit at the table. "It must be a distant relation. The painter lived in the late eighteenth century, so it has to be."

"Perhaps."

"Where is your family from, again?"

"My mother was from Wales, but I know nothing about my father." I take a sip of my coffee and wonder how this conversation will progress.

"He must have been French. That's the only explanation. Unless you are the last in a long line of clones."

"You found me out."

"But seriously, you never met your father?" Jen looks at me over her mug with inquisitive eyes.

"No. It was a one-night stand for my mother. It's not something I asked her about in detail, and now she's in no condition to be asked." I smile to show that Jen doesn't have to be concerned about bringing up potentially fraught subjects. Hopefully she doesn't take that as an invitation for more questions.

"I guess it will have to remain a mystery." She gazes at me expectantly. I sip my coffee and meet her gaze.

"For now."

Her eyebrows raise.

"When?"

"Soon." I will tell her soon. I've almost decided how to tell her. I'm dreading the day and am putting it off for as long as I can. Jen heaves a deep, long-suffering sigh but doesn't push further.

"Oh, I almost forgot to ask you," she says. "What are you doing Sunday night? Care to be a plus one for my cousin's wedding?"

"Well, of course. But what happened to dearest Cecil? Shouldn't he be escorting you to these things?"

Jen puts her mug down and twists it between her hands.

"I, uh—I broke up with him." She glances at me quickly, then back to her coffee. I feel strangely happy at this news but try to paste on a concerned face for Jen's sake.

"I see. Any particular reason? Did he snore?"

A laugh escapes through Jen's nose.

"No, nothing like that. Honestly, Merry. Surely no one is that shallow." She narrows her eyes at me in question, and I shrug. She says, "No, I just didn't feel like we were connecting. He was into me way more than I was into him, and it didn't seem fair to him. I've been feeling it for a few weeks, really, but I've been too chicken to say anything until now." The coffee mug spins and spins. "It just didn't feel right to give up on him, since—well, he was my first." Her eyes flicker briefly to mine, the barest butterfly brush of gaze, before the empty mug gets her full attention once again. Her golden lauvan swirl tightly around her body. "You must think that's a silly reason. And that I'm so old for firsts."

I finish my coffee before I answer.

"Why would it be silly? Sex can create a powerful bond." The lauvan that appear after intimacy last for days, even with the most fleeting of connections. "But I'm glad you figured out what is best for you. Life is far too short to waste time on relationships you don't want." I lean back in my chair. "You waited for someone who truly struck your fancy. Not a big deal."

"How old were you when you first had sex?" Jen looks up at me finally. I give her a tight-lipped smile.

"Fourteen." Jen laughs before I continue. "It was forced. I was homeless, and someone took advantage. I'm glad to hear you were in control for your first." I gaze at her calmly while I recall the past. I had left my uncle's house after my mother died and was wandering the hills, alone and friendless, grubbing in the bushes for berries and peeling bark off trees to

31

fill the incessant gnawing of my empty stomach. When I came across a settlement, I banged on the first door I could find. The man put me to work chopping wood for my supper, but he passed out after dinner from too much ale. The wife, who was far younger than her husband and who had been eyeing me all day, told me it was into her bed or out of the door. I was afraid, of the cold and the night and the hunger. I left before dawn.

Jen looks appalled.

"That's horrible, Merry."

"It was so long ago, I can scarcely remember. Honestly, it's far in the past. All I wanted to illustrate to you is that I think it's fine Cecil was your first. And, yes, I am happy to suit up and escort you to this wedding."

"Thank you." She gives me a look as if she's delivering bad news. "It's black tie. The bride went super formal."

I grin.

"I'll manage. Just tell me what time. We'd better take your car. Mine is still in the shop."

"I'll pick you up at four." Jen reaches out and rubs my arm. "Thanks for sharing, Merry."

"You know me, always saying too much."

Jen laughs and takes our mugs to the kitchen. She puts the mugs in the sink and turns the water on.

"Do you have a dish cloth?" She rummages in the cupboard. "Honestly, I don't know how you manage. You are seriously lacking in kitchen equipment. You have, what, one knife to do everything with?"

I open my mouth to answer that most kitchen activities can be handled with a good knife, but a sound stops my breath. The hushed voices are back, louder this time. I strain to hear what they say and where they come from. I almost catch a word, here, there—perhaps they say...

"Merry! What's wrong?" Jen shuts off the water and stares

at me. "You totally zoned out. You look worried. What's up?"

I gaze at her in confusion. The voices have stopped now, and I shake my head from the trance they induced.

"Nothing, sorry." I rub my face. "I suppose the coffee hasn't kicked in yet. Everything is fine." Hearing voices is never reassuring, and I don't like worrying Jen. She does that frequently enough without me adding to her burden.

"Well, if you're sure." Jen still stares at me with concern in her eyes, but then she checks her watch. "I have an appointment. I have to run. But I'll pick you up Sunday, okay?"

"See you then." I wave her off, and she heaves her purse over her shoulder and departs. The door clicks softly behind her. I ponder for a moment the details of our conversation, then pull out my phone to text Alejandro.

Jen has stopped dating Cecil. Her favorite coffee is a mocha. Good luck.

Fridays are a lazy day for me lately, with no classes, but I should clean myself up sometime. Once Jen leaves, I shower and am shaving in the steamy bathroom with a towel around my waist when the outer door clicks open.

"Alejandro!" I call out and push the bathroom door open with my foot. "You were out early this morning. Having fun?"

Alejandro appears in the doorway.

"Yes, thanks." He doesn't elaborate. He's been less forthcoming the last few days, and I'm not certain why. His lauvan cling to his torso as if hiding something. I expect he'll tell me when he's ready.

"Do you really shave with a straight-edge?" Alejandro

notices my razor.

"I've done it for centuries, why stop now?" I run the blade along one cheek, and he stares with amazement and envy. Then he shakes his head.

"I cut myself enough with a safety razor. There's no way I would trust myself with that. Anyway, I met a new friend while I was—downtown. His name is Liam. He invited me for drinks with his girlfriend and their friends. Do you want to come along? He's a great guy."

"I appreciate the invite, but I have plans tonight."

"A date?"

"It's exciting, but not in that way. I've been invited to Potestas headquarters for a tour."

"What?" Alejandro looks flabbergasted. "How? When? Why?"

"Who? Where?" I reply. "Let me answer. The leader of Potestas, March Feynman, approached me on Wednesday to apologize for one of her people almost killing me, and she invited me to a Potestas meeting tonight for a meet and greet. As to why, she thinks we can help each other. She'll provide answers about the spirit world, and I'll somehow help her with my 'special abilities,' as she terms it."

Alejandro whistles through his teeth.

"Into the pit of vipers. You might get answers, but at what cost?"

"She has assured me of my safety. For what it's worth." I run the blade down my throat and contemplate what the evening has in store. For once, I'm not sure.

"Let me come with you," Alejandro says. "Maybe I can help. Watch your back."

I smile into the mirror. Alejandro's reflection is determined, perhaps a little fierce.

"I appreciate the offer, but I don't believe it was an open

invitation. Don't worry, through long practice and necessity, I am an excellent liar and actor." I glance at Alejandro. "Please don't take offense, but I can read you like a book most days."

Alejandro grins, unperturbed.

"I know. I try, but it's terrible. Keeping your secret is the hardest thing I've ever done in my life."

"Just as well I'll tell Jen soon. She's likely to guess from your facial expressions alone."

"When will you tell her?"

"Soon. Very soon."

"How do you think she'll take it?" Alejandro searches my face. I shrug, but my stomach clenches at the thought.

"I can never tell. We'll have to see." I flash him a pleading glance. "I might need your help in the aftermath, if it doesn't go well. Perhaps help her come to terms with it." I go back to shaving. "If worst comes to worst, I will leave town immediately. I hope it won't come to that."

"Is that what you do?" Alejandro gazes at me with pity. "It's hard to have a life if you leave like that."

"Don't I know it. But my secret can be dangerous in the wrong hands. Dangerous for me. I was almost burned as a witch in the sixteenth century. Do you know how hot a bonfire can get?"

"Hotter than you want."

"Precisely. Not that anyone will burn me today, not here. But it's simply easier to leave."

I splash my face with warm water from the tap. The voices start again, faint but growing in volume.

"Alejandro, can you hear that?"

"Hear what?"

"Those voices." I look around. "Do you have the TV on?"

"No." Alejandro stares at me in concern. "Hearing things again, Merlo?"

"I suppose not." I turn off the tap and the voices stop. I turn it on again and they return—off, they stop. What is going on?

"Oh, Merlo, I almost forgot." Alejandro digs into his pocket and extracts a set of keys. "I picked up the car today. It's in the visitors' parking right now."

"Thanks, Alejandro. That's great." I take the keys, then look at the insignia on the keychain with suspicion. "What kind of car did you get?"

"There wasn't a lot of selection," Alejandro says with diffidence. "Really none. The man said there were lots of rentals for summer vacations. It's a Prius."

I groan.

"A Prius? There's no power in that thing. They really couldn't do better?"

"I'm sorry, Merlo. It's not your Lotus, I know. And—well, the color isn't typical."

"What does that mean?"

"It's yellow." Alejandro winces. I stare at him in disbelief.

"It's a taxi. I'll be driving a taxi."

Alejandro shrugs in apology, then he perks up.

"Jen approved of it being a four-seater, though."

"Oh, well, if Jen approves of the taxi, I suppose it must be the best." That's interesting. What was Jen doing chatting to Alejandro? I smile to myself as I pull on my shirt. "At least it's wheels. I suppose."

After an early dinner with Alejandro, we part—him to meet his new friend Liam, and I to my rendezvous with the infamous Potestas. The Prius is a bright, glaring yellow, and only misses the sign on top to complete the taxi look. It hums to life and I suppress a growl of annoyance.

The address March gave me is for the cupcake shop I visited while trying to find Drew a few weeks ago. It's not far and the streets are quiet, although I receive three waves for rides. I gun past each with grim satisfaction.

Parking is more troublesome. A block away, I pull the car into a loading zone and turn off the ignition. I check my reflection in the rear-view mirror and pass fingers through my hair. I must decide how I want to present myself to these people. Do I want to come open and eager to learn, or do I want to appear knowledgeable, as if I hold secrets they need? That might be safest, if I appear indispensable.

Unfortunately, March has already met me, and Anna knows far too much, both from our dalliance in Wallerton and from our reconnection a few weeks ago. I can't appear other than what they have already seen. And who knows what Drew has seen or guessed, and how much he told March.

I must be vigilant. This whole situation may be as straightforward as March made it appear, or it might be a trap. Spirits and lauvan are the order of the day, so if any strange lauvan attaches to me, I must be ready to remove it.

I step out of the car. Although the loading zone sign has no lauvan of its own, being affixed to the ground with little ability to fall and therefore no potential energy, it is a simple matter to change the wording. I tear off a few leaves from a nearby tree planted beside the sidewalk then wrap the lauvan around the pole and over the sign. A few people glance with curiosity, but no one bothers to stop. A couple of judiciously placed knots, a tug here and pull there, and the sign is blank.

Assured of my parking spot, I stride briskly to the cupcake shop, Sweet Thing. Its blindingly neon green sign stands out from the shops surrounding it, so it's not hard to find. The storefront is closed, but March's instructions on the business card she gave me state that the door will be unlocked. I reach for the handle without hesitation—I don't want to look like I'm breaking in—and the door swings open without resistance.

Chairs are stacked upside down on tables, and the light is dim. Refrigerated cases stand empty, waiting for a new day to be filled with tiny cakes covered in frosting. I slide behind the counter and walk into the kitchen. March's instructions indicate that the entrance is through here. I spy a door marked "plumbing" tucked behind an industrial-size oven and reach for the doorknob. A brief pause, a deep breath, and I turn the handle.

CHAPTER VII

A buzz of relaxed conversation greets my ears, and warm light streams through the open door. I step inside and look around. A large open space is filled with comfortable couches and low tables with bright lamps, and an open kitchen sprawls against the right-hand wall. Large double-doors stand closed in the center of the far wall, with hallways at either corner that lead to a row of other doorways. The couches are filled with people of all ages and descriptions. Two young women converse with animation on a loveseat nearby, and an older man with unkempt dreadlocks waves his hands in conversation with a middle-aged woman whose cropped pink hair nods as she knits a fuchsia-colored scarf. A man in a suit with his tie relaxed helps himself to pizza from one of the open boxes on the kitchen counter, and others chat over the sink and on other couches. When they see me, a hush falls over the group.

I suppose they don't see newcomers often. I'm surprised by the cozy conviviality at Potestas headquarters. After my encounter with Drew Mordecai, I expected something far more sinister. I wonder what to say but am spared from speaking by a voice I recognize.

"Merry. I heard you might be coming."

Anna Green walks toward me with swaying hips and an unhurried air. Subdued chatter picks up again behind her, but most eyes remain on me.

"Anna. I'd say it is a pleasure to see you again, but I dislike lying unnecessarily."

"Oh, don't be like that." She pouts, then smiles with a mischievous twinkle in her eye. "I, for one, am happy to see you. I knew you'd come around. Just wait, you'll see what we do here, and you'll be won over."

"I'm interested, I won't deny. Show me around?"

"I'd love to, but March has requested to do that herself. I'll show you to her office. Chat later, though?" She looks at me with hopeful eyes. I paste on a serviceable smile.

"Of course."

Anna leads me down the right-hand hallway to the second door on the right. She knocks and turns the handle.

March sits at a polished oak desk, looking quite at home in a crisp white blouse behind a laptop. She stands when we enter.

"Merry. So good to see you." She comes out from behind her desk and shakes my hand. "I'm pleased you decided to join us."

"I'll be in the common room when you're done, Merry," Anna says with a quick smile, then withdraws.

"May I give you the tour? It's small, but I think you'll find it interesting," March says.

"I would like that."

"This way, please." March waves me to the doorway. In the hall, she ignores the first door. "Just a supply closet. Ah, in here is our amulet acquisition room. As you may have guessed, amulets are fundamental in harnessing the power of the spirits. In a few days, we will have a ceremony to prepare an amulet for spirit connection. You might be interested in joining us for that."

I nod noncommittally, but I am certainly interested to see that process. The amulet acquisition room is sparsely furnished with a small table and a row of bookshelves, filled not with books but with a strange assortment of things. Necklaces, rings, bracelets, books, crosses, menorahs, singing bowls, and other items lay quietly on the shelves, but each is so thickly wrapped in multicolored lauvan that I can scarcely make out what each item is. These so-called amulets have been deemed special at one point in their existences, and threads of belief have collected on each. I wonder if the members of Potestas can somehow sense the increased lauvan on these items, or whether they have simply collected precious belongings with a history of worship.

A middle-aged man wearing a ratty shirt and thick glasses peers at a ring on the table. The tools of his trade lay before him—a small brush, a carver, a magnifying glass—and he picks up the carver to scratch a design onto the ring. He looks up at the sound of the door.

"Good evening, Arnold," March greets him. "How are you progressing?"

"I've almost completed the insignia on this ring. With any luck, it will be finished tonight." Arnold holds the ring up for March to see. Through the swirling lauvan, I manage to make out a carving of a wave on the wide gold band.

"Beautiful work, as usual." March smiles at him, and he beams back then bends to his work again. March says to me in a low voice, "Arnold is our head of amulet acquisitions. He owns an antique store on Commercial Drive, and he has a remarkable knack for choosing those items that have the strongest aura. The stronger the aura, the less we have to build it up, and the quicker we can create a connection."

"How do you build up an aura?" I ask. "And can you tell me more about connecting to the spirit world?"

"In a few days, when we have our ceremony, it will be much clearer how we build an aura. As for the spirit world, we can discuss that later. All in good time. Let's focus on our tour for now."

March ushers me out of the amulet room. I let myself be guided, disgruntled but not surprised. I will be shocked if it is easy to extract all the answers I want from Potestas. March appears forthcoming, but I sense she has a much tighter rein on goings-on here than she says. For example, there is clearly a hierarchy in this organization, if she has a "head of acquisitions." I wouldn't be surprised if lower-ranking Potestas members were not privy to certain information.

There are no doors on the left-hand side of the hallway. When March sees me looking, she explains.

"Our meeting room is in the center. Here, come see the room of reflection."

"That's quite the name."

March smiles.

"And yet, very apt." She knocks gently, and a voice calls out.

"Enter."

March opens the door. Inside, it is very dim, and the only light comes from a standing lamp with a beaded shade that casts red and gold streaks of light on the room. There are no hangings on the walls, and the only furnishings are the lamp and numerous tasseled cushions that are strewn across the carpeted floor. I'm not sure if I'm in an unadorned Thai restaurant or a fortuneteller's lair.

A young woman with wide trousers and a flowing peasant-style top sits cross-legged on a purple cushion with her eyes closed. Her long blond hair is loose and drops in a sheet down her back. She opens her eyes slowly once March shuts the door behind us.

"Fiona. I hope we aren't disturbing you." March's voice is pitched low and quiet.

"Not at all," Fiona says in a dreamy voice. "I was simply calming myself. Barry requested a reading later this evening, and I wanted to prepare myself for the clearest vision possible."

I refrain from raising my eyebrows with effort and look Fiona over for lauvan other than her own teal-colored strands. Nothing is evident, but around her neck is a golden chain that

42

descends into her shirt. I would bet my broken car that she wears an amulet covered with spirit lauvan.

"Has he made any progress?" March asks Fiona. To me, she says, "Fiona specializes in searching for visions of past lives. We have discovered at least three of mine. It's quite fascinating."

"Barry's past is still hidden in the mists," Fiona says. "But I have hope that the light of our searching will pierce the clouds for us tonight." She turns her slow gaze onto me. "Your aura is most interesting. Would you like to attempt a reading?"

I don't think I could handle knowing that I am even older than I know.

"Not tonight, thank you."

"Merry is new with us, Fiona. I'm giving him a tour. We won't disturb you further. Best of luck with Barry."

Fiona raises a hand in farewell and closes her eyes as March shuts the door behind us.

"Two rooms left," March says in her normal voice. "One is our central meeting room, not much to see other than chairs. But this one," March turns the corner into the final hallway. At the end is the common room, but beside us is the only door in the right-hand wall. "This is the library."

She pushes the door open and allows me to enter first. I walk into a brightly lit room lined with floor-to-ceiling bookshelves, crammed with books ancient and modern. Some are so old that their leather bindings are crumbling into dust, and some display glossy, colorful spines. Several comfortable armchairs with nearby reading lamps are clustered in the center of the room. I run my finger along the closest bookshelf and read titles aloud.

"*Spirituality for Daily Life, The Path Uncharted, The Unseen, Beginner's Guide to Tarot.* And the theme of this library is…"

"Anything and everything to do with spirits: their manifestation in the physical world, legends and religious texts that describe them, ways to contact, anything. Trevor and Gail are our chief librarians. They aren't here tonight, but they generally spend their time combing the books for scraps of information and compiling it for the rest of us to peruse." She waves at two large notebooks on the nearest side table. "They jot their findings in these books, and the rest of us read through and look for connections."

I itch to explore the library and those notebooks without March breathing down my neck. I try not to show my fascination too overtly.

"It's quite the collection." I turn to her. "Thanks for the tour. What's the history of Potestas? I'm curious."

"I started the org a few years ago," says March. "I'm in business, hardly someone you might expect would be interested in this type of thing." She smiles and raises an eyebrow at guessing the basis of my question. "But I've seen too many things to not know that there is more in this world than we currently understand. I started Potestas to collect like-minded individuals in the pursuit of truth."

"Why the secrecy?"

"I dislike the judgement of the world at large. It's bad for business, for one. And it provides a measure of security for our members, to know that their actions won't be scrutinized and mocked."

Scrutinized, indeed. I wonder how quickly the authorities would shut them down if they knew of Potestas' involvement with the volcano. But then, who would believe it?

March moves to the door and opens it. It's a clear signal that question-time is over, although her smile remains. I walk through, content with my observations thus far. I will certainly be back. The ceremony sounds enlightening, and that library is begging to be explored.

"I must apologize, I have some business in my office to attend to. But please, feel free to have some pizza, introduce yourself to the other members here tonight. My aim is to make this a safe space for all Potestas members, so please make yourself comfortable."

"Thanks for the tour, March." I extend my hand. "It was enlightening."

"Thank you for giving us a second chance, Merry." She shakes my hand firmly. "I do hope you will join us for the next meeting. Tomorrow at seven, if you're free."

"I'll do my best."

She walks back around the U-shaped hallway to her office, and I proceed to the common area. Anna chats to another woman in a blue blouse who looks like she came here straight after work, but when Anna sees me, she excuses herself from her conversation and comes over.

"All done your tour?" she says in greeting. I nod.

"Yes. I understand now how all those spirit necklaces cropped up in little old Wallerton. Your amulet room is full of them."

"Hey, there're no hard feelings between us, are there?" She looks at me with wide eyes. My eyebrows raise.

"What, that you told a strung-out murderer how to find me?"

"I didn't know that was his plan. I thought he was still working with us." She looks contrite, then reaches for my hand to hold. "I'm sorry. Maybe we can still be friends?" She strokes my fingers with her other hand.

I look her over. Her long auburn curls drape over her shoulders, and her kissable lips smile in anticipation. But the bloom is off this rose, at least for me.

"Fool me twice, shame on me. Acquaintances, perhaps.

Friends, unlikely. Lovers? Never again."

Anna drops my hand and sighs.

"It was worth a try. If you ever change your mind, let me know. And for the record, I always liked you. I hope this won't affect your membership in Potestas. I really think you'll fit in here." She jerks her chin toward the pizza. "Help yourself. Maybe you'll find someone else to talk to who you can tolerate better."

"Perhaps, but not tonight." I have no desire to mingle with the members congregated here, although I'm sure it would be informative to find out why they are here and what they know. But I have much to think about, and I plan to come back tomorrow. It will wait until then. "I'm off."

"Will we see you tomorrow?"

"I expect so."

CHAPTER VIII

The next day is gorgeous and sunny, and I climb into my taxi and head for the hills. It's been a while since I've hiked. I miss the trees and fresh air, and I've been cooped up in my apartment for too long. I invited Alejandro, but he is running another mysterious errand this morning.

Wind whips in the open window and through my hair as I zoom across the bridge to the North Shore. I'm heading beyond Whistler, to where grow some of the oldest trees within easy driving distance of Vancouver. It's a spectacular place to spend a summer's morning.

I pull onto the logging road. After a bumpy few minutes, I park the car on the side of the road and strike out on a favorite trail of mine. Within half an hour, I am surrounded by cedar trees that are hundreds of years old, some almost a thousand. Their massive trunks sink deep into the loam and soar into the canopy above, straight as arrows and solid as rocks. I lay my fingers on the bark of one. It is rough to the touch and deeply grooved with indentations that could house a whole universe of insects. I close my eyes and breathe deeply. The scent of the forest fills my nose with dust and green and cedar and sun.

I like to visit these trees. Sometimes they feel like the only creatures who might understand me, ancient as they are. They have seen hundreds of years of quiet growth, the arrival of Europeans on this coast, the changes from forest to metropolis and all the stages in between. They are still young compared to me, but I feel an affinity with their unchanging nature.

I give the tree an affectionate pat before I carry on down the path. It leads me over wide planks of wood that span a creek, almost dry at this point in the summer. A hushed sound of voices begins, and I turn my head to look for a group of hikers on my heels.

The forest is empty, yet the whispering remains. Is it the wind? I look up, but the breathless forest does not stir. Words almost pierce the unintelligible muttering, and I strain to catch them, but their meaning vanishes with my listening.

It must be the sound of water against stones in the tiny creek. I shake my head and continue down the path.

The trees thin as I hike up a slope, and the sun pierces the canopy in shafts of light that dazzle with motes of dust. A feeling of entrapment overtakes me in a rush, and I long to leap among the trees and over fallen logs, as light as air. Sometimes I tire of this body of mine, stuck always the same, unchanging for centuries. I wish I could slough it off and soar through the trees.

Changing form is the next best thing. My mind races through the possibilities. I consider my merlin falcon form—always a favorite—but the shape of a deer beckons me. It was the first animal I learned to transform into, and there are few things so freeing as bounding through the woods on cloven hooves.

It's decided. My heart quickens, and I feel for the necessary lauvan. It's been so long that I struggle with the combination, but my fingers remember and weave themselves into the correct conformation. I pull, hard.

Breathless nothing. A squeeze. Then, my eyes open to a world of blues and greens, the loud twittering of birds, and a powerful scent of dusty earth. With a recoil of powerful hindquarters, I leap high in the air and run as if a cougar gives chase.

Much later, my energy nearly spent from running and the sheer joy of transformation, I let my lauvan revert to their usual position and gasp as I reform into my human self. I collapse onto a rocky outcrop overlooking a lake and lay my head on a scraggly bit of dry moss until my breathing calms. Clouds drift in wispy tendrils across the achingly blue sky above. A strand of my chocolate-brown lauvan snakes overhead, and I glance at the disparate threads that float around me in a loose froth.

They are so spread out, so formless compared to the lauvan of everyone else. They were not always so. Up until a few centuries ago, they flowed around my body, tight and close. Slowly, they have been falling away from my physical form, and now they sway far from me. I feel as though I'm unraveling, and I don't know what it means. How much farther can they go? Will they float away from me completely? With anyone else, lauvan leaving the body signifies death. When my lauvan spread too far, will I die?

I know no answers to these questions and have no way to find out. I let myself ponder for a few minutes, but wallowing in unanswerable questions is fruitless, so I heave myself off the rock and begin my descent to the car. I've run farther than I meant to, and it's a long way back. I'm too tired to hold a deer form now, so plodding on human feet will have to do.

A stream that I bounded across in a single, graceful leap as a deer, I must now wade through. Halfway across, I am knee-deep in water when a gentle tugging pulls on my calves. I look down. Nothing is there at first glance, but upon further inspection, I see that my lauvan are caught up with water lauvan in the swiftly flowing current. I shuffle my leg forward, and the water strands resist the movement with a stickiness I've never noticed before.

A hushed whisper begins, as from the muffled chatter of a thousand people far away. I push my other leg forward, but it's like stepping through a pool of molasses. The whispers grow louder and more excited but are still unintelligible. I strain my ears, wanting to know the meaning of this mystery, but am distracted by the resistance in the water. I force my way through, and the water lauvan release my own strands with reluctance.

I stumble out of the stream, and with every step away from the water's edge the voices grow fainter. My feet carry me out of range of the whispers, and I am not sorry to leave them behind. I don't know what is going on, but I am keen to put as much distance between me and the sticky water as possible.

Perhaps I will read about water lauvan in my old friend Braulio's notebook when I get home. He left his research findings to me when he died, and his insights into the spirit world have proved useful recently. The notebook may have some answers for me now.

It's Saturday evening, which means that it is time for my second Potestas visit. The cupcake shop is once again closed, but I let myself in through the unlocked door and enter the kitchen. Once the door marked "plumbing" swings open, a barrage of chatter engulfs me. There are far more people here today than last time—it must be a meeting for everyone in the org.

I didn't talk to anyone last time except March and Anna, so I make it my mission to mingle before the meeting. The food table is always a great icebreaker, so I head directly to the kitchen area. A smattering of people has collected around a platter of pastries, so I take a napkin and a muffin and turn to the nearest person.

She is a woman in her fifties with dark black hair with gray roots and makeup too kohl-heavy for her age. She is swathed in colorful scarves above sensible sandals. She gives me a wide smile.

"You look new. Allow me to introduce myself. My name is Esme."

"I'm Merry. Pleased to meet you."

She leans toward me and speaks in a loud whisper.

"Esme, short for Esmeralda. My stage name, you know. But it's a bit of a mouthful for everyday use."

"Stage name? What theater do you play at?"

"Regional markets and fairs, mostly." She smiles with fire-engine red lips. "I'm a fortune teller."

"Ah, I see." I wonder if March has found any genuine spirit-sensitive people, or whether they are all frauds. But with the help of a special amulet, Sylvana from Wallerton read my fortune correctly, back in the spring. Perhaps with enough help, even Esme can do the same. "That makes sense why you were drawn to Potestas."

"Drawn? No, I was invited. Potestas keeps a low profile, as I'm sure you're aware. I was approached during a fair last year. Ben here was the same." Esme tugs on the sleeve of a young man in a hooded sweatshirt and blue jeans. His shaggy brown hair falls into his eyes. "I was just telling Merry here how we were invited into Potestas. What's your story, again?"

"I was taking a theology class," says Ben, clearly fond of an audience for his tale. "And I guess I was asking too many questions, getting too mouthy. I was *questing*, man, trying to get answers to the big questions. Isn't that what we're supposed to be doing? Anyway, someone overheard, and the next thing I knew, I was pulled aside in the hallway after class and asked if I wanted some real truths. Well, duh. I came here, a few months ago now, and never looked back." He nods at me. "What about you, new guy?"

I wonder how much to reveal. Keeping a low profile is surely in my best interest, but nothing was ever gained by playing safe. The more one reveals about oneself, the more others are willing to reciprocate. They will know about me soon enough—might as well leverage what I have for my own gain.

"I have an ability to—" I pause and search for the right word, and Esme and Ben lean in closer. "Detect auras. The energy around a person, their mood, emotions, whatever you like to call it. I suppose I was approached for that."

"Wow." Ben looks impressed. "With no help from an amulet? Just born like that?"

"Yes."

"Well, I never," says Esme. "Could you read my aura right now? What am I feeling?"

I study her lauvan. Her moss-green strands are lively and open, swirling with interest and excitement. There is a small knot at her shoulder.

"You're a cheerful, open person," I say. "Not much to hide. You're excited about the ceremony tonight, although apprehensive as well. You also have a shoulder injury, a significant one by the looks of it. I would take it easy for a while, if I were you."

Esme's mouth opens in shock, then she laughs in delight and amazement.

"What a wonder you are! What a jewel to have in our organization. I'm so pleased to meet you, Merry."

"Seriously cool, man," says Ben.

"It's a burden and a gift," I say with a show of modesty, but add for the sake of my persona here, "Mostly a gift. So, who are the head honchos here? March is obviously the boss, but who is second-in-command?"

"It's not like that, really," says Esme. "Potestas is a group of individuals with a common purpose. But I suppose a few others help organize meetings and whatnot, mainly Arnold and Anna, lately."

A quick check of her lauvan tells me she is telling the truth as she knows it. I sense that Arnold and Anna have more clout and information than a simple organizational role would give them.

"Ah, Anna," I say. "I've met her before. Is she here tonight? I'd love to chat with her."

Ben scans the room, then his expression clears, and he points a finger.

"She's over there, on the couch."

I say my farewells and saunter over to Anna. When she spots me, she finishes her own conversation and turns to me with a smile. She pats the couch beside her and I sit.

"Merry. Nice to see you back."

"My tour here last time was enlightening. I thought it worthwhile to return. It's quite the facility. Do people tend to spend a lot of time here?"

"Yes, it's a home away from home for many. We have a cozy, tight-knit community, and everyone really looks out for each other."

"Too bad no one was looking out for Drew," I say. At Anna's pout, I raise my hands in surrender. "Sorry to harp on it, but it's not something one can let go of easily."

"I understand. He's much better now, by the way. He's doing well in his program, and I believe he feels bad about his attacks. We have hope that he will leave the rehab facility soon, although March isn't certain she wants to welcome him back to the fold. His actions are not something to be forgiven lightly."

"I won't argue with that. So, whatever March says, goes?"

Anna's face clears from worry over the Drew situation to affection for March.

"She's our leader, as much as she doesn't like to style herself as such. She's so modest about her role, but people

53

really look up to her. And she's so knowledgeable about the spirit world—we've come so far with her guidance. And she's so approachable, she really cares about each one of us. We're lucky to have her."

Well. Anna's devotion to March is absolute. If everyone feels the same way, I can see why so many come to clandestine meetings to be a part of this group.

"What are most people here for, truly?" I ask. "Does everyone want what you want?"

"Power over the physical world? For the most part. It's not something to sneeze at. I'm surprised that you aren't more interested." She raises an eyebrow. "Of course, you have your own abilities, don't you? Maybe the power of the spirits isn't as enticing because of them?"

I don't bother answering that. I've never felt the need to tell Anna more than she can guess, which is too much already.

"Everyone is here of their own accord? No one being coerced into joining?"

"No!" Anna appears outraged, and her lauvan stiffen with indignation. "That's not how we work. Everyone is here because they want to be, full stop."

"Good to hear." I offer an apologetic smile, which Anna eventually returns. I only asked to see the reaction of Anna's lauvan, which convinced me that she tells the truth. Now, it's time to talk about the other reason I'm here.

"What do you know about me?"

"What do you mean?" Anna says with studied calm.

"You know I have some different abilities, but I think there's more. You know something, don't you? What aren't you telling me?"

"Not a lot. I'd love to know more, though." She leans in closer. "Any time you want to spill your secrets, I have a willing ear. But, not at this moment, since I need to help with meeting set-up." She pats my thigh and stands. "See you in a minute."

That was an evasive exit if I've ever seen one, but it gives me a chance to wander off myself. I stand with a casual air and make my way to the far side of the room. No one gives me more than a cursory glance, and I slip into the empty hallway with ease. The library door is unlocked.

Inside, cozy armchairs and warm lamps infuse the air with comfort. I settle into an armchair and pull one of the notebooks toward me, the ones in which Trevor and Gail jot down findings from their research.

It truly is a notebook. Lined pages are filled with bullet points written in different colored pens. Some notes are tidy and methodical, and some are a dashed scrawl as if the writer couldn't scribble thoughts onto paper fast enough. I skim through the notes.

Spirits in a different world, or maybe another plane of existence?

The Rusalki were water nymphs associated with fertility before nineteenth century tradition turned them into malevolent undead beings...

Hapi, Anuket, Khnum, Satet, Sobek, Tefnut—the Egyptian pantheon covered all aspects of the Nile...

Before the Romans came to Britain, spirits walked the Earth...

Wait a minute. I read further with a quickened heartbeat.

... in the guise of men, prompting tales of otherworldly beings, as reported by a Roman governor in a second century report.

Spirits walking among us? It sounds like what Potestas hopes for. I wonder what is left of the human after the spirit takes over. I read more and stumble across writing in a different hand.

A note from Fiona: When I was seeking for Ahmed's past lives, the spirits contacted me from my amulet. They wanted to know when the son would come. It was unclear, the words were messy and indistinct, but then they said the father was dead, the new father was born, and the son must be found. Meaning? I'll bring it up with March, but it's late and I wanted to write it down, so I didn't forget.

My reading is interrupted by the click of the doorlatch. I tear my eyes away from the page. March is in the doorway with a smile, although her usually sedate lauvan contain a hint of agitation. Is it about the upcoming meeting, or does she not like to see me lurking in the library?

"Good evening, Merry. Please, join us for the meeting. We're about to start."

She stands aside and holds the door open. I am clearly expected to go through. I sigh inwardly and place the notebook on a side table. Perhaps next time I can read more, but I don't want to alert March to suspicious activity on my part. But did Fiona truly hear something? I need to come back, to find out more from this library. Braulio's notebook now seems lamentably mediocre compared to the wealth of knowledge sequestered in this room. What answers could I find here, answers to questions I haven't yet conceived? I must come back.

"What a fascinating collection you have here," I say with a smile. "I congratulate you on your findings."

"It is, isn't it," March says with no elaboration.

The central room is almost full when we enter. Chairs stand in rows between bare walls. The only break in the monotony is a pedestal at the front. It appears to be carved from white marble.

I slip into an empty seat, next to a large woman in shorts and a tee shirt with a shock of blue hair. March closes the doors behind her and walks to the front of the room. The quiet murmuring hushes when she turns toward the audience.

"Good evening, everyone. Thank you all for coming tonight. And what an excellent turnout! I am constantly amazed by the strength of our organization, both in numbers and the quality of people in it. We are destined for great things, and I am honored to walk this path with you."

The woman next to me beams, and her expression is mirrored on the others' faces in the audience. From the looks of it, March knows how to inspire loyalty and devotion. She continues her speech.

"As you know, we are constantly in search of items to create amulets. Well, we have recently discovered the location of an artifact of great power, one which will aid us greatly in our quest. Have you all heard of the grail? The legendary King Arthur's goblet, reputed to have the power to bestow eternal youth, happiness, and abundance?"

The grail. I'd forgotten about that legend. The cup with that name that crops up throughout history was never Arthur's, but it's been around long enough to gain a following and stories of its own. I saw it once, or one of the versions of it. Even through the thick lauvan, I could tell that it was nothing Arthur ever drank from. There were rubies encrusted along the edge, something Arthur never had, despite his status as war chieftain of Gwent.

"We have painstakingly researched its whereabouts, through rumor and hearsay and legends in the historical literature, and finally traced its most recent owner to one Mr. Collington, a rich collector on the run from gambling debts in California in the eighteen seventies. The records state that he loaded his most treasured possessions in a ship called the *Minerva Louise* and sailed for Canada in the hopes of running from his debtors. They hit a patch of rough weather off the coast of Vancouver Island, and the boat sunk along with all its crew and passengers.

"However, that means that the most likely location of the grail is on a shipwreck. We have located the wreck of the *Minerva Louise* on an uninhabited stretch of land, north of Port Renfrew on Vancouver Island. It is miraculously preserved, so I suspect we will be able to search for the grail with ease. It's so remote that we will have to access it by water, although the ship itself is happily situated less than eighty feet from the surface, so we will be able to scuba dive there."

March pauses and gazes around the room before delivering her next statement.

"There is one unfortunate issue. Because of the immense aura that surrounds the grail, its location in a tidal region, and the length of time it has lain there, it is possible that collecting the grail from its resting place will set off a tsunami that will affect Vancouver Island and the coast of British Columbia. Possibly even as far as Hawaii." March attempts to look contrite. "It should only rise two meters, which will affect at maximum three hundred meters inland in the very low-lying areas. However, collecting the grail is vital to our mission, and we may have to suffer a few casualties to bring about the promised changes."

I glance around at my fellow audience members. There are a few worried looks, but most faces show determination. The woman next to me has tightly coiled, jittery lauvan, a sure sign of her excitement at the thought of the grail, with no regard for the consequences.

I have never seen lauvan-covered items intertwine with elemental lauvan and cause natural disasters, but I can imagine how they might. It doesn't take much tweaking of the earth's lauvan to disrupt balance, just as a few severed lauvan on a body can be catastrophic for the health of a person. If elemental lauvan were ripped apart from the forcible removal of an entangled object, it's not impossible that a tsunami could occur. And Potestas seems to be well-informed on all matters spirit—I can believe they know something that I do not.

"I wished to warn you," March continues. "If you can find higher ground during our expedition, I would recommend it. We will contact you when we have chosen a date for retrieval of the grail. Anna will hand out maps when you leave, showing the maximum possible wash zone."

The audience mutters, but not in disapproval. Can everyone truly be accepting of this venture? No one will stand up and oppose March's plan to possibly flood the coast?

I wait for a moment, but no one stirs from their seats. Should I volunteer? On the surface, it seems like an immediate no. Why would I help Potestas find new ways to contact the spirit world? But if there really could be a tsunami created from this retrieval... I can scuba dive, and the lauvan disentanglement would be a simple task for someone of my abilities. I really am the only one who can prevent this, since March seems determined to carry on despite the cost.

I stand.

"I'd like to volunteer to help collect the grail. I have my diving certificate."

A sea of faces turns to me and gazes with surprise. March lifts her brows.

"I appreciate your offer, Merry, but I don't think it will be necessary."

"This is a slice of history, isn't it?" I keep my voice light. "And certainly, you will need to dive with a buddy. Safety first."

March looks at me for a moment with pursed lips, then she nods.

"Thank you, Merry. I would be honored to have you along.

Please, everyone, applause for our volunteer."

The audience applauds, and I raise my hand in acknowledgement. Anna looks at me with an inscrutable expression. I hope this was the right thing to do.

CHAPTER IX

Dreaming

Morgan plucks the strings of my harp with precision and fluidity. Her voice carries to the far reaches of the room, low and sweet. I lean back with my hands on the bench and watch her technique and her form, the way her fingers graze the strings, graceful in their assurance. Arthur plays with a dog on the hearthstones, its playful growling no match for Morgan's song.

When she finishes, she looks at me expectantly. I nod.

"Very good, Morgan. I'm impressed by how quickly you've improved. It's only been a year since you began to learn, but already there isn't much more I can teach you. Practice will be your best instructor from now on."

"It's difficult when my father is here, though," she says. "I know I should wish for peace, but his absence during battles does have its benefits."

"Will you play more?" says Arthur from the floor. "I like the music."

"My fingers are too sore. Perhaps tomorrow." Morgan rises from her bench and carries the harp carefully to me. The harp's case lies on my bench, and I hold it open for her to nestle the instrument in its soft wool blanket within. As she removes her hands from the harp, her fingers lightly touch mine. Her eyes catch my curious gaze and hold them for a moment. A moment is all I need to understand Morgan's intentions, although the ruby lauvan that twist and twine toward me also tell a story. Morgan wants me.

Now I'm intrigued. Morgan moves back to her bench and picks up a dress she is sewing, a faint flush on her cheeks the only outward indication of her state of mind. I regard her. When I first arrived, she was still a lithe girl. Now, her form has all the curves of a woman, and I realize she must have seen seventeen summers, if not more.

There is little contact with others at this remote villa. A few neighbors of Morgan's social standing are within a morning's walk, but I have never seen her interested in any of the young men of those households. It surprises me that Uther has not found a husband for her yet, at her age. She is clearly ready for the nuptial bed.

I won't pursue Morgan out of respect for Uther.

But if she pursues me, how can I say no? She is my employer's daughter, after all, and I don't have much reason to deny the advances of a beautiful woman. I'd be happy to prepare her for a husband, but I'll see what Morgan does next. I'm not worried that Uther will discover any dalliance, for we have successfully kept her lessons a secret for a year.

I will leave Morgan to her devices, but I'm very interested in what happens now.

Uther is away again, visiting a brother-in-arms at his own villa, so I don't bother to hide my midnight departure. I'm off to practice touching water lauvan in the river. I haven't played with them much before, and I find I can see them better in the light of the full moon, when they glisten and shimmer through the dark water.

The river isn't far. When I reach it, I strip off my clothes. No point in wetting my second-best shirt, especially when there is no one around. Naked, I wade into the chilly waters up to my waist, instantly awake. I decide right there that practicing water lauvan is a summer project only.

The river's current is slow, and the water lauvan flow sinuously past me, moving around my body in graceful curves. Each gossamer-thin strand is as long as my forearm, and sturdier than its fineness indicates. The moonlight is nearly as bright as day, and the threads twinkle like diamonds.

I dip my hands in and let the strands run through my fingers. They tingle with the barest sensation of movement, almost drowned out by the feeling of the cool water. I grasp a few strands between my fingertips and tug lightly. I'm curious what will happen.

Water rises on either side of my body in fluid arcs, shooting from the river's surface and pouring into it again a few handspans away. Elated, I pull my hands upward and the arcs ascend until they flow in semicircles higher than my head. Both the water and the lauvan glisten in the moonlight. I gaze at them in open-mouthed delight.

There's movement on the shore, and I twist my head around. A lone figure stands on the riverbank. Her slight body is covered only in a light shift that gleams pearly white. A faint red glow from her tight lauvan alert me to her identity, and I lower my hands to the river.

"Morgan?"

She doesn't answer, only takes a step closer to the water's edge. She hesitates, then her lauvan relax with a decision made, and she pulls her shift slowly over her head. My breath catches, and heat fills my body despite the cold river. Only a few weeks ago I decided to let Morgan pursue me, and here she is.

I push through the water to join her.

Uther is home for a spell, and we are all gathered outside to enjoy the last rays of late summer sun after our supper. Arthur kicks a ball with a servant boy, and their happy shouts linger in the still air, while Uther and I play a game of tabula at a low table. Morgan was feeding her favorite horse a carrot but approaches our game to peer over my shoulder.

"That one, Merlin." She points. I swat her hand away in play.

"I'll make my own moves, thank you very much."

She shrugs with a smile and settles herself on the ground before us. I hesitate, then make the move she suggested. Uther chuckles quietly.

"I'm glad you're here now, Morgan," he says. "I have important news for you. I have found you a husband."

Morgan stiffens and her lauvan freeze.

"What? Who?"

"Do you remember Idris, from northern Gwent? It is he."

Morgan's face shows disgust and horror.

"Idris? No! I don't want to marry him. He's a brute. And old."

"He's a brave warrior and a loyal ally. His lands are fertile and plentiful, and he commands many warriors. He is an excellent match." Uther peers at his daughter with surprise. "I don't understand your hesitation."

"I'm not interested in Idris. I don't want to marry him!" She looks at me in mute appeal.

My eyes widen. Does she expect me to speak on her behalf? Or, after our dalliance of this past month, does she expect me to ask for her hand in marriage?

I didn't think of that, at any time. I have no interest in

64

settling down with a wife. Morgan was fun for a while but nothing more.

I say nothing and look at my feet. Once Morgan realizes that I won't speak for her, her whole body goes rigid with anger. Then it deflates, and her eyes moisten. She picks herself off the ground and runs into the villa without a further word.

Uther watches Morgan with confusion then turns to me.

"I thought she would be happy to have a husband at last. She is certainly old enough and ready for one. If I don't marry her off soon, she'll find her own way."

So, Uther never guessed that Morgan has already 'found her own way,' with me. That's one good thing. I don't reply to Uther. What would I say? I feel a mix of guilt that I let Morgan down, and relief that it's over. She is curious and eager to learn in everything she does, but her intensity and drive are difficult to take. I know little about Idris, but I hope he will prove a fit match for Morgan. Few would, and I open my mouth in a rash attempt to tell Uther everything, then close it with a snap. I don't want to jeopardize my position here, not when I have well-paid work, a roof over my head, and plenty of food. I've been without all three often enough that giving them up is not something to be done lightly.

I will keep quiet and hope that Morgan will land on her feet. And that someday, she may forgive me.

CHAPTER X

"I knew I should have worn my black pumps." Jen shifts her weight from one leg to another. A lone cello plays a somber melody as a little flower girl trots down the aisle, tossing rose petals at guests' shoes. "These silver heels are cute, but murder on the feet."

"You'll forget once you start dancing." I adjust my shirt sleeve, so the cufflink is straight. "At least you are a knockout in them."

Jen bumps my shoulder with hers. Her dress is a simple sheath of royal purple with a silver chain belt that drapes gracefully from her waist. Her long legs are particularly shown off in her despised stilettos.

"Says the man who can pull off wearing anything and make it look good."

"It's not difficult in a tux."

"But you look so comfortable in it, not like Tom over there." Jen nods at a cousin of hers a few rows up, who sweats in a cheap, shiny suit. An older woman next to us with a fussy fascinator of peacock feathers jiggling on her head shushes Jen. Jen stands straight and watches the procession with rapt attention.

Poor, sweating Tom. Adaptability is my forte by necessity and by personality, so adopting a new persona is as simple as shrugging on a new set of clothes. Jen will understand one day. One day soon, I expect.

I turn my head to watch the bridesmaids and groomsmen parade down the aisle. Some look sweetly bashful, and others bask in the attention. So many weddings I have attended, some as a groom, many more as a friend. They have varied from sumptuous church affairs with hundreds of guests to clandestine ceremonies under the full moon. I would like to say that they all had a happy couple in common, but the choice of a marriage partner was often not up to the couple in question. The groom today appears nervous but happy, and I wish him well.

The maid of honor and the best man walk down the aisle together. My eyes narrow in disbelief. I recognize the maid of honor. It's none other than Dr. Dilleck, my erstwhile psychologist.

My stomach clenches in anticipation at the sight of her, and I wonder at myself. I never thought our paths would cross again. Am I happy now that they have? I thought I wanted to live in a big city to remain anonymous, but perhaps this meeting is a chance. A chance to try again under new circumstances.

Why am I interested? It's possibly because she knows so much about me, and I know so little of her. The mystery of the lauvan over her eyes, for instance. There are several strands still intact over each eye. I love a good mystery.

Perhaps tonight I'll solve it.

Dr. Dilleck glances around the room and smiles widely at the gathered guests. Her eyes touch lightly on the older woman with the peacock fascinator, on Jen, on me. They narrow in confusion then widen with recognition. She stumbles, and the best man grabs her arm more securely.

Dr. Dilleck doesn't look my way again, but from the agitation of her lauvan and her fidgeting body, she is clearly shocked at my presence. The music changes to a joyful march and the bride, Jen's cousin Cynthia, sails down the aisle on the arm of her father. She smiles hugely as if bestowing on us the gift of her benevolence. Jen mentioned that this wedding will have an open bar, so I look forward to receiving the bride's gift.

The wedding progresses as weddings do, but my mind is preoccupied with the darting blue lauvan above the maid of honor. When the bridal party exits, Dr. Dilleck avoids my gaze, but the lauvan that still connect us are taut with her tension. Jen tugs my arm when it's our turn to file down the row of seats. I squeeze past a large floral display of magenta dahlias and pink ribbons that mark the end of the row and have to dust a few specks of pollen from my trousers.

"That was a beautiful ceremony," says Jen once we exit the church and step blinking onto a lawn beside the main doors. "But I'm starving. And I would kill for a drink. Luckily, Cynthia took pictures before the ceremony, so the party starts now."

"Excellent," I say. "Lead the way."

"Oh, hey," says Jen once she closes the car door at an upscale golf club nearby. I offer her my arm and we walk toward the front entrance of the club house, which is festooned with garlands of flashy magenta dahlias. "Do you know Minnie? The maid of honor? She looked at you weirdly in the ceremony."

My mouth twitches in an involuntary smile at the name. Minnie.

"Yes. Funny story. She was my shrink for a while."

"You went to a therapist?" Jen looks flabbergasted. "Wow, I wouldn't have guessed you would ever do that. I mean, you have to—gasp—open up to someone in a therapy session."

I laugh.

"I'm a little closed at times, I hear you."

"No, I'm proud of you, really." She squeezes my arm.

68

"Why isn't she still?"

I shrug. We turn into a room decorated with an overwhelming mass of pink. Rose-colored chair covers, pink candles, bunches of bright dahlias on tables and in puffy garlands around the room give a sense of diving deep into someone's gullet.

"Wow," says Jen. "Cynthia went bold with the pink."

"You said it first," I say. "I stopped going to Minnie because she stopped offering her services. To me, anyway." We reach a table with a list of people on it. Fourth on the list is "Ms. Jennifer Chan and Guest."

"That's weird. I thought Minnie was expanding her practice." Jen's face freezes, and she looks at me with a guilty expression. "Why do I feel I shouldn't have said that?"

"It's all right," I say, but the confirmation of my suspicion stings. "I had a feeling."

"What did you do?"

I stop in the middle of pulling out a chair for Jen and frown in a show of indignation.

"Why would you assume it was me?"

"You're right, that's a terrible thing to say." Jen sits in the chair, then leans toward me. "But was it?"

"As it happens, no." I unbutton my suit jacket and sit with a sigh. "Not that I'm aware of. It's fine. I only went to see what therapy was all about. I got the gist."

Jen looks disappointed—that I don't want to keep going and unburden myself of secrets, perhaps—but is prevented by the arrival of a multitude of her cousins, who descend on her with shrieking laughs and cries of greeting. I murmur an unheard excuse and move toward the bar, open and already with a cloud of guests hovering.

I order a bottled beer for me and a Mai Tai for Jen. I deliver the Mai Tai to our table, but Jen is still engrossed in the gossip

69

of her cousins and I leave her to it. The balcony beckons. It's a beautiful late summer's evening, warm but with the crispness of approaching autumn in the distance, enough to make one appreciate the warmth all the more. I take a deep breath then a long drink and lean on the railing to admire the view. Manicured green lawns roll softly between landscaped gardens for acres and acres, with the city rising through the summer haze in the far distance. It's hard to remember the forests that once carpeted these lands. I take another contemplative sip.

"Merry?"

I turn my head sharply. Minnie stands behind me, looking lovely in her rose-colored dress of silk, which hugs her curves on top while flaring into a modest knee-length full skirt. It complements the deep blue of her swirling lauvan. They are calmer now, but twist tightly against her body in a protective way.

"Dr. Dilleck, hello." I'm stumped as to how I should greet a former female psychologist in the twenty-first century, so I settle for a handshake. When she grasps my outstretched hand, a faint blush of bemusement colors her cheeks.

"It's Minnie, please. Like the mouse." She grins. "How are you?"

"Well enough. It was a surprise to see you here. You're a friend of the bride, I presume."

I gesture at the railing in invitation. She leans her arms on the top rail.

"Since forever. We live different lives now, but Cynthia asked me to be maid of honor for history's sake." Minnie waves at her dress. "Pink isn't really my color."

"And yet it suits you remarkably well." I take a sip of my drink. Minnie blushes again. It's sweet how such a small comment can redden her cheeks.

"And you? How did you turn up here?"

"My friend's beau is a suitor no more." I bow with my hand extended. "I am the plus one on call."

Minnie laughs. The sound dances on the breeze.

"Who is your friend?"

"Jennifer Chan."

"Oh! I know her." Minnie sighs and fidgets. "This is difficult, being connected to a client's circle."

I shrug and take another drink.

"It doesn't have to be. Former client, don't forget. I didn't tell you anything incriminating, certainly nothing inconvenient about Jen."

"True." She smiles again and her lauvan dance more lightly. "It was bound to happen sometime, I suppose. Vancouver is big, but not that big."

A bell chimes from inside, and Minnie jumps.

"Dinner. I have to give a speech afterward." She makes a face, then leans in and whispers, "I didn't want to, but Cynthia insisted. She's a bit of a bridezilla, truth be told, but don't tell anyone I said that."

I put a finger to my lips.

"Mum's the word."

She gives me a parting gift of a smile and slips inside, the silk of her dress rustling against the doorframe with her passage. What a change, from a calm, collected professional to this sweet, confessional woman in soft rose. I hope she wants to continue our conversation after speeches. Perhaps I can convince her to dance.

"Where have you been?" Jen asks when I slide into my seat next to hers. Plates are already floating around the room on the arms of crisply dressed servers and descending before hungry guests.

"Mingling on the balcony. It's what one does at a wedding, is it not? Thank you," I say to the server as she places a plate

71

of salad in front of me. I turn back to Jen. "Did you have your drink?"

"Yes, thanks. You know me too well." She points at the empty glass in the center of the table. The server spies the gesture and whisks it away. "Were you talking to Minnie, by any chance?"

"Perhaps." It's difficult to keep a grin off my face, but I succeed, mostly. Jen elbows me.

"What are you smirking at? Do you like her or something?"

I give Jen a look.

"I was greeting an acquaintance, thank you. Keep your theories to yourself."

Jen giggles and pours us both wine.

"Fine, keep your secrets. I'm watching you, though." She points at her eyes with two fingers then at me with one, then giggles again.

"Are you tipsy already?" I shake my head. "You are the lightest drunk I've ever known. Give me those car keys now before you forget where you put them. And eat your supper."

Jen rolls her eyes but digs into her salad without further comment. We eat and chat with the others at the table for the rest of the meal. Talk consists of how we know the happy couple, what we do for work, and the weather. I yawn inwardly and wonder how I can spice up the conversation.

"Your purse is very unusual," I say to the young woman sitting beside me. It's a small clutch of leopard-print velvet with sparkling stones along the edge. "Is the leopard your spirit animal? I channel the spirit of the timber wolf, myself. Cliché, perhaps, but nevertheless true."

Jen overhears me and chokes on her steak. I smile blandly at the woman, who looks taken aback.

"Umm, no. I just liked it." She shoves a spear of asparagus into her mouth to avoid further conversation.

Speeches start shortly after. The fathers both speak, as well as the best man. None are trained in elocution, and their anecdotes tend to wander. My eyes glaze over and I settle into one of my trances to pass the time. I am roused by the voice of Minnie.

"Cynthia and I were together through thick and thin in our younger years back in Calgary. Although we have grown apart in recent times, I am so honored to be a part of this special day for Cynthia. New friends are silver, old friends are gold, bodies may age but hearts will never grow old. A toast to the happy couple."

Minnie lifts her glass and we all follow. She holds herself tall, and her voice was strong and sure when she delivered her short but sweet speech. If all were like hers, I might have paid more attention. I drain my glass in the hope that her speech is the final one, and my wish is realized. The master of ceremonies introduces the band, a five-piece number with fedoras and rolled-up shirt sleeves, and the lights dim. I slide out of my coat.

"I hope your feet are rested," I say to Jen. "In those murderous shoes of yours."

"Ugh, don't remind me." She pushes back from the table and examines her feet. "I think I've drunk enough to not care. Was that your way of asking me to dance?"

I don't answer. Instead, I stand and pull her out of her chair, toward the dance floor. When we reach a clear spot, I whirl Jen around in my arms and she shrieks with laughter. I lead her in a simple swing dance which she follows surprisingly well, considering I only gave her a short lesson minutes before we left for the wedding. Her smile is wide and joyful, and the beat is electric.

At the end of the dance, she pulls me off the floor, laughing and breathless.

73

"That was too much fun, Merry. We need to go out dancing sometime. Proper dancing."

"Name the day." I loosen my tie.

"Jennifer!" An aunt grabs Jen by the elbow. "Jennifer, sweetie, it's been too long. How are you?"

Jen grimaces at me. I grin and pat her shoulder as I melt away. I'm not in the mood to pander to random relatives. I'm restless after sitting for speeches, and the dance with Jen has only whet my appetite. A light touch on my elbow turns me around.

Minnie smiles at me, a nervous yet hopeful smile.

"Can we finish that conversation? I feel I owe you an explanation."

I take her hand. It's smooth and the slender fingers wrap around my own. A shiver runs along my neck.

"Only if you dance with me first."

Her grin is wide and infectious. I twirl her onto the dance floor and she clutches my shoulder tightly. The music is fast, and I lead her in a lindy hop. It's tricky footwork, and although I'm an excellent lead, the woman needs to know something of the beat to follow correctly. Somehow, Minnie does. She matches my feet flawlessly, responding to every suggestion as if I were speaking out loud, and even adding her own little stylish flair to the steps. We move as one well-oiled machine, and I can't remember the last time I've been so in sync with another dancer. When the song ends, I can't bear to stop, and whirl her into the next tune.

At the end of the next dance, Minnie breaks away. She laughs breathlessly.

"Water, I need water. Come on, a quick break before we go again."

I take her arm and lead her to the water table, then outside to the balcony for fresh air. We both sweat from our efforts, although the glow on Minnie's skin and the flush of exertion only heightens her beauty.

"Where did you learn to dance the lindy hop?" I ask. "You're a natural."

"I didn't," she says. She fans her face. "That was incredible. You must be an excellent lead, that's all."

My brow contracts in confusion. Surely, she's had some instruction. It's impossible to dance like that for the first time. But why would she lie?

Minnie takes a gulp of her water and leans against the balcony, facing me. She has a serious expression, and her lauvan have calmed from their joyful leaping of the dance to a measured swirl.

"Merry. I feel I owe you an explanation. About why I transferred you to another psychologist, why I stopped having you as a client."

I shrug, suddenly defensive. I don't know if I really want to hear why.

"You don't have to explain. I'm sure you had your reasons. I'm a big boy and can handle it."

"It wasn't you, it was me." Minnie blows air out through her lips as if trying to decide what to say. "Or, rather, it was me with you. After you started sessions, it affected me. Adversely."

"In what way?" I stare at her, mystified. She looks away from me, across the darkening golf course, biting her lips as if embarrassed.

"It started with dreams. Endless dreams. Of you and me. Over and over, in different situations and places. They were so vivid." She shakes her head as if to clear the dreams from it. "And then I started having symptoms of a condition that I suffered from as a child, the one that interested me in the human mind in the first place, actually."

"What's the condition?"

She waves my question away.

"It doesn't matter." She glances quickly at me and smiles in apology. "It's not a common condition, you wouldn't have heard of it. In any event, I started sleeping less, my anxiety was through the roof, and I deemed it best for my health to transfer you to another therapist. I'm truly sorry. I felt our sessions were very productive, and I didn't want to leave you hanging."

I join her in consideration of the green lawns, now russet in the sunset. We gaze in silence for a moment.

"Thank you for telling me," I say at last. "I wondered if it was something I said."

"That's why I wanted to tell you. As soon as you left, I felt terrible about it."

The sun sends out a long, last ray into the approaching twilight, then sinks below the horizon. A cool breeze flows over my skin.

"So, you've been dreaming of me," I say in an offhand tone. "Anything fun?" I give her a sidelong glance and her cheeks color, visible even in the fading light.

"No," she says, but her lauvan tell a different, squirming story. I smile widely and leave it at that.

"Have the dreams stopped now that I don't come to your office?"

"Mostly," she replies. "And my condition has improved."

"Interesting. I didn't realize I could have such an effect on a person. You'll give me a complex."

"In my professional opinion, you don't need an ego boost." She glances at me to see my reaction to her teasing. I laugh aloud.

"False modesty is no virtue. But after tonight, what will you do?"

"I don't know," she says, suddenly pensive. "Monitor

76

myself to see if the dreams and symptoms return. I don't know whether it is your presence in my life, or your confessions, that was the trigger."

"It will be a test. Take it scientifically. Spend a decent amount of time this evening with me and see what tomorrow brings."

She smiles mischievously at me.

"I can do that." She looks out across the lawns and points to the sky.

"Oh look, the moon is rising. It's huge tonight. Like a beacon of light, shining on the wedding." She nods at a waterfall below us. It catches the moonlight in jumping arcs of light. "Look at the water. It's a sparkling river of diamonds with the moon. Oh, for a swim in the moonlight—is there anything more dazzling?"

I gaze at her profile, highlighted by the moonlight. I hope we can get past her fear of dreams, and I can tarry with her for a little while. Physical attraction is easy to come by, but it's pleasant to have more connection in those I court.

The sky deepens from vibrant orange to a dusky violet and blue. Stars twinkle overhead and music drifts out from the open doors of the balcony. We speak of little things, drifting lightly from one topic to another, like dragonflies alighting on lily pads. She is both comfortable and alluring, all at once. I find myself inching toward her, wanting to close the empty space between us, the void that must be filled. Her lauvan reach to me, grasp mine in tight tendrils, pull me willingly forward.

A voice on a microphone from inside interrupts our conversation. I shake my head as if from a dream.

"It's cake-cutting time," Minnie says. "And the bouquet toss. Ugh, Cynthia will expect me to be there. Have you seen the cake? Enjoy eating every pink-fondant flower—Cynthia spent a fortune on that silly seven-layered thing."

I laugh and offer my arm.

"Come, let's see this towering monument to love and diabetes."

Inside, Minnie pats my arm and lets go.

"I should be with Cynthia."

"Another dance, later?" I don't want to leave here without that. I ache to touch her again, and the prospect of her leaving, even to walk across the room, distresses me. Her wide smile reassures.

"I would love that."

I join Jen back at our table, where she chats to a young woman her age. The woman kisses Jen's cheek and leaves. Jen leans back, looking drained.

"Rough evening?" I ask.

"So much family, it's overwhelming. My cousins spreading gossip, my aunts asking me why I don't have a boyfriend— after figuring out that you're not him—it's enough to wish myself without any of them."

"You don't mean that," I say quietly. Jen glances at me with a stricken look.

"I'm sorry, Merry. No, of course I don't mean that. They are a bit much at times, but I do love them." She leans forward and pierces me with an inquisitive stare. "What have you been up to all this time? I saw you dancing with Minnie, then you disappeared."

"Mingling," I say. At Jen's raised eyebrows, I amend, "All right, not mingling. Chatting with Minnie."

"Do you like her?" Jen looks interested, then frowns. "Isn't that a bit weird? She was in a position of authority, so, I don't know, aren't there rules about these things?"

"She's not my shrink any longer, she saw to that. And anyway, I never feel anyone has authority over me." I give her an impish grin and she rolls her eyes. "It does sound like it would be strange, but it's almost as if we're starting later. We don't have to bother with the dull small talk that starts an acquaintance. We can move on from that stage."

"Stage? Are you two dating?"

"No, no, I only mean..." I find myself at a loss for words, an unusual circumstance for me. What do I mean? "Well, I'm not against it if she wants to."

Jen looks over to the cake-cutting. My eyes follow and land instinctively on Minnie. Her cheeks are as pink as her dress, and pieces of her hair have fallen out of their elaborate up-do and fall deliciously in tendrils down her neck. She laughs at a comment from a fellow bridesmaid.

"Just—be careful with Minnie, okay?" Jen says softly. "She's really lovely. And she's had it tough. Both her parents died a few years ago. A car crash, I think. Your track record with women, well, you never date them for long. Just be good to her, okay?"

We both stare at Minnie. I don't know what to think. Jen obviously thinks me a cad, not surprising given what she's seen of me. What she might not have noticed is that all the women I've dated have been in the relationship for the same reasons as me—physical attraction and temporary companionship. I could always tell from their lauvan, and when we broke off relations, often it was mutual.

I don't know yet what Minnie wants. It will take more observation for that conclusion. All I know is that I desperately want to find out. I have no desire to hurt her, though.

"She has some hang-ups about me, so I don't know if anything will happen," I say at last. "But I will take care, I promise you that."

Jen puts her arm through mine and squeezes.

"Thanks, Merry." She looks back at the cake-cutting and

her face falls. "Oh no, the bouquet toss. I hate these things. If you have a boyfriend, it's awkward, and if you don't it's even more so."

"Oh, come on," I say, happy to inject a jovial note to our conversation. "You have to respect tradition. It's all in good fun. Don't worry, if you catch the flowers, I'll be sure to let your next boyfriend know what awaits him."

Jen pushes off from me with mock-disgust, and a cousin swoops her up to drag her to the dance floor. I grin and watch the gaggle of girls and women jostle each other. Minnie stands on the edge of the crowd with an uncomfortable look on her face. The bride turns, gives a few warm-up swings of her arms, then lets the bouquet fly.

It sails through the air, and a bevy of women leap to catch it, stiletto heels and all. The bouquet rebounds from hand to grasping hand, until with a punt it bounces over their heads. It hits Minnie in her startled face and drops into her unresisting arms. Minnie's surprise turns to laughter at the improbable scenario, and the bride comes over to hug her.

The band picks up again and the dance floor quickly fills. I intercept Minnie on her way to place the bouquet on the table.

"You promised me a dance." I hold out my hand in invitation.

"I did." Minnie glances at the bouquet in her hand and blushes. "Let me put this down first."

She lays it on the nearest table. I lean in to whisper in her ear.

"It takes more than superstition to make a marriage. Don't worry, dancing is just dancing."

Minnie looks at me sharply, and I wonder what she is thinking. Belatedly, I recall that she knows I was married before, and that she has me pegged for commitment issues because of it. Damn shrink. This could be more complicated than I'd bargained for. But, likely worth it.

"Then, let's dance," she says and pulls me to the floor.

It's a slower song this time, lyrical with a Latin beat. Minnie follows gracefully along with my salsa steps as if born to dance. But whereas our dancing before was flawless and fun, this is different.

Our dancing is more than simply dancing—it is a conversation. Nothing as trite as a conversation with words. It is an affirmation—*I'm here. You're here. We're here together. I know how you move, I know how we fit. I know you. I know you in a way that I could never say out loud. You know me the same way. And that's all we need. That's everything.*

Nothing exists outside the circle of our dance, and I only tear my eyes away from hers when I spin her away from me. I clutch her back quickly, not wanting to be apart for longer than necessary. Her feet never falter, and those blue eyes with the swirling navy-blue lauvan over them never leave mine.

At the end of the dance, I draw back and kiss her hand formally.

"Good luck tonight, Minnie. I hope your dreams are sweet and untroubled."

I leave quickly. Her expression is bewildered, but I can't stay for a moment longer, not without sweeping her into my arms and spiriting her away with me. I can't calm my breathing and I stride quickly toward Jen, who chats with an older uncle on the side of the room.

"Jen, would you mind terribly if I go for a walk?" I say without preamble. "You can text me when you're ready to go home. I won't be far."

She searches my face for a sign of my inner state but doesn't press for answers.

"No worries, Merry. I probably won't be long."

The walk helps. I stride swiftly over the pristine lawns of

the golf course and the night air cools my fevered brow. That dance riled me up in a way I didn't anticipate. My desire for Minnie must be stronger than I realize.

And why is Minnie haunted by vivid dreams of me? Is her attraction that strong? Perhaps it is the conversations we have had in the past. Those sessions in which I spilled my innermost thoughts must have influenced her lauvan in unintended ways, transferred some essence of me into her own subconscious mind. That must be it. The therapy sessions must have connected us in stronger ways than I expected, as strong as a much longer relationship.

I breathe deeply and try to exhale out my agitation. The pearly white light from the moon is calming. Unbidden, an image of Minnie's face in the moon's glow floats across my mind's eye, and my body warms once again. I curse and march around a pond.

When Jen texts me, I am mostly calm and appear unruffled.

"Good party?" I ask when she toddles out of the main doors.

"Food was amazing, drinks were plentiful, the band was fun, but my throat is sore from talking and my feet are killing me. Take me home, Merry."

"This way, my lady."

CHAPTER XI

Dreaming

It's early spring in Gwent, too soggy for campaigns but too nice to stay inside. I've convinced Arthur and Guinevere to come for a ride through the woods. They didn't need convincing. We've been inside too much lately in the throes of late winter storms. The poor horses need some exercise, if nothing else.

We strike out west along a dirt track that leads to the mountains. A few white wood anemones line the path, a welcome sign that spring will arrive shortly. Even the light breeze that lifts my hair is mild and gentle.

"This is a good idea, Merlin," says Guinevere. "It is very lovely out here. My fingers are tired of sewing all winter."

"I do like my new cloak, though," says Arthur, and they smile at each other.

"I couldn't spend another moment indoors," I declare. "I'm surprised I lasted the winter here. Next time I'm tempted to ride south until snow is a legend."

"That would be a long way," says Arthur. "I know you've traveled far, but surely not even you have gone that far."

"Nearly," I say.

"Look, a rider," says Guinevere. "Who would travel at this time? Beside you, Merlin."

"Yes, before the most recent terrible weather, you visited your mysterious lady often this winter." Arthur grins at me. "She must be something special to travel in winter so much."

"She is," I say absently. I peer at the rider. "It's a woman in a blue cloak. And her lauvan…" My heart jolts.

"What is it?" Guinevere looks at my changing expression

83

with concern.

I don't answer but kick my horse with a "Hah!" It breaks into a canter. It's a risky move on the hole-ridden and muddy path, but I must know who is on that horse. I'm certain I do know, and she is worth the risk.

The closer I get to the figure, the more certain I am. When I am close enough, I hail her.

"Nimue!"

She smiles widely and raises her hand in a wave. I pull my snorting horse to a prancing stop in front of her. I swing down, throw my reins over the neck of my horse, and pull Nimue off hers. She shrieks with surprise but can't say anything else when I cover her mouth with a kiss. She squeezes me tightly back.

I don't release her until trotting hoofbeats thud on the muddy track near us. I pull away with reluctance but can't keep a smile off my face. Nimue's cheeks are pink and she laughs breathlessly.

"Merlin?" says Arthur. "Is this who I think it is?"

He dismounts and helps Guinevere off her horse. Both are smiling.

"Arthur, Guinevere, this is Nimue, Lady of the Lake." I take her hand. My heart hammers from Nimue's unexpected presence and the strangeness of introducing her to my oldest friends. I have been visiting Nimue in her secluded lakeside dwelling for over a year, but she has never come to my home, and I have never taken Arthur to see her. She is one of four women who dwell there to worship the goddess in this land. They were chosen as children for their abilities to influence the elements, and Nimue has an affinity with water.

"We are very pleased to meet you," says Guinevere. "We have heard much about you."

"Not enough, though," says Arthur. "Merlin is very

secretive. It's wonderful that you have finally come to visit."

"Why have you come?" I turn to Nimue, worried. "Is something wrong?"

"No, no," she says and looks up at me with a shy smile. "I missed you."

My heart bursts open, and it's all I can do to not embrace her once again. Arthur nudges Guinevere with a grin, but I ignore him.

"I missed you too."

"Come," says Guinevere. "You must be tired after your journey. Let us ride back to the villa."

I help Nimue mount her horse, swing myself up in the saddle once more, and we turn for home. I keep sneaking glances at Nimue, and often she looks back at me with a sweet smile. I want nothing more than to hold her in my arms once again. It's been too long since I've visited.

Within the villa's palisades are two unknown horses, their lauvan flowing with the slow wriggle of relief after a long ride. Arthur frowns.

"Who visits so soon after the storms? Everyone wants to ride today, it seems."

Servants move to take the horses to the stables, and others feed the pigs nearby. Two dogs sleep in a doorway to our left. Nimue looks around the yard with interest.

"This is your home, Merlin? I like it. It's much busier than mine."

"That's not difficult," I say with a smile. "It's only the four of you, after all."

"True. The village isn't far, but it's sleepy also." She holds out her arms when I offer to help her dismount, and I hold her far longer than strictly necessary.

"I want to give you a proper greeting," I whisper in her ear. She blushes and looks up at me from under her eyelids.

"Merlin," Arthur calls out. "They say Morgan is here. Come, let's see what she wants."

I curse under my breath, then take Nimue's hand and lead her to the main hall. Arthur holds the door for Guinevere and waits for us to enter. It's dim inside after the brilliant sun of our beautiful day, and I blink while my eyes adjust.

Morgan sits before the low fire with a cup of wine by her side. Her long dress of deep red matches her ruby lauvan so well, it's a wonder she can't see them. A fur mantle covers her shoulders. Her delicate face is composed, and her lauvan are stiff with determination over her black hair. She has come for a purpose, which is no surprise—she and Arthur do not have much to say to each other these days.

A figure sits quietly beside Morgan on the bench, and I sigh inwardly. Of course, Vivienne accompanies Morgan. She is her most trusted servant and confidante. Vivienne's dark hair is pulled back in braids beside her bright eyes, and her dress of soft green hugs her body well. It always does, although her breasts are heavier since the birth of her child by Morgan's servant Mordred, five years ago now. Vivienne glances at my face, then down at my hand, entwined with Nimue's. She raises an eyebrow when her eyes reach mine again and gives me a wicked smile.

Morgan and Vivienne both here together? I question my wisdom at bringing Nimue with me into the hall. I have too much history with these two.

Then Vivienne's eyes drift to Nimue's and she gives a start. Nimue's hand tightens in my own. Do they know each other?

"Brother," says Morgan when we enter. She rises smoothly and walks over to embrace Arthur. I distrust her immediately. She and Arthur haven't been on good terms for years, and now she acts the loving older sister? Morgan wants something.

Arthur is certainly able to give. He is well respected among the lords in Gwent and is renowned for his successes on the battlefield as well as for his diplomacy. Most consider him wise and silver-tongued.

Morgan, since her husband died, has continued to espouse his view of the Saxons—namely, that they should all leave our lands immediately. Guinevere's presence as Arthur's wife has always rankled Morgan, since she is the daughter of a Saxon chief and embodies the diplomacy that Morgan so despises. Now, she gives Guinevere a cursory nod, and a brief curtsey to me.

"Please, sit." Arthur waves at benches before the fire. "Tell me, Morgan, what brings you to the villa so early in the year? The roads are still muddy."

"Almost impassible in places," Morgan says. "But I have come before the campaign season to plead with you one last time. I have gained the support of many local lords, and my forces are not inconsiderable. With the help of your troops and whoever may follow you, I believe we now have enough men to push the Saxons out of Gwent for good. Indeed, we may be able to force them to the river Severn if the battles go well. I know you are interested in making peace with some of them." Her eyes flicker to Guinevere. "But too many more will never accept a truce and want only our lands for themselves. It is time to rid ourselves of this scourge once and for all, and we have never been better positioned to do so than we are this year."

Arthur gathers his thoughts for a moment.

"Morgan," he says gently. "It pains me to be at odds with you, truly it does, but you must know that I have no intention of backing out of the treaties I have made. Do you expect me to send Guinevere back to her father? No, I'm afraid the peaceful Saxons are here to stay, with my blessing. But the raiding tribes have no interest in peace, and I will gladly fight by the side of your men to push them back this summer."

Morgan smiles tightly.

"I had hoped that time would make you more reasonable, but it is not to be. We will fight our battles separately. I and my supporters are not interested in joining forces with a Saxon-lover."

"Morgan, we fight for the same thing," Arthur says in exasperation. Morgan shakes her head.

"No, Arthur, we do not. You fight for peace at any cost. I wish to preserve our homeland and our fellow countrymen from invaders who have no right to be here. But that is enough talk of war. Tell me, what is new since last I saw you? How fared you this winter?"

Arthur leans back and shrugs, seemingly happy to put talk of fighting aside.

"It was a good harvest, so we were comfortable. Yourself?"

"Well enough." Morgan nods to Nimue. "And who is this?"

"Ah," says Arthur with a smile. "We just met her ourselves."

"This is Nimue," says Vivienne. My jaw drops. They do know each other. "The Lady of the Lake."

"Oh, yes," says Morgan. "I recall."

"Do you know her?" I ask Nimue. She nods tightly.

"Vivienne used to be the Lady of the Hearth, until she deserted her role and we had to find a replacement."

"And now you have deserted your place to be with Merlin?" Vivienne tsks. "Dear me, perhaps now isn't the time to cast judgement. Not that I don't understand the allure." She throws me a knowing smile and I wince. I don't really need Nimue to know I slept with Vivienne years ago. Not now that they know each other.

"I'm only visiting," Nimue says in defense. "I have not deserted."

"Nimue, my dear," Morgan says. "You must have some

affinity with water. Will you tell me more? I am curious, ever since I heard of Vivienne's talents." Morgan's eyes flicker toward me, and I know she's thinking about my own abilities.

"I can sense when it will rain," Nimue says in a quiet voice. "And the water can tell me who enters it, if I ask."

"Fascinating. And where do these abilities come from, do you know?"

"Usually passed down in the family," Vivienne says, and Nimue nods.

"My aunt was also the Lady of the Lake, in her day."

I wonder at Morgan's interest, only because her fascination with my abilities often borders on the obsessive. I know she would give anything to have powers of her own. Unfortunately for her, the three people here with powers were born with them.

Morgan stands.

"The day is young, and we'd best be on our way."

"Leaving so soon?" Arthur looks confused. "You will stay for a meal, surely."

"Thank you, brother, but it's a long ride back, and Vivienne will be wanting to see her child, I'm sure." Morgan kisses Arthur on the cheek, nods to the rest of us, and sweeps out. Vivienne curtsies and follows her mistress. Arthur, Guinevere, Nimue, and I are left staring at each other in bewilderment.

"Did Morgan really think she would sway your opinion, Arthur? After all this time?" I ask.

"Perhaps she wanted to give me one more chance," Arthur says slowly. "Hope is not easily vanquished, and we are family, after all."

"Let us put the visit from our minds," says Guinevere firmly. "Come, Nimue, have some wine. Tell me all about yourself. Merlin has said so little. I want to know everything."

CHAPTER XII

Jen tosses me placemats from a drawer in the kitchen of her basement suite. Her roommate's door is open, and the room mercifully empty. It's much more freeing to talk with Jen without extra ears listening in. We are here for an early morning breakfast before Jen goes to work, so that she can hear about my visit to Potestas headquarters.

"I really don't like you at Potestas," she says. She pulls out a bag of bread from the cupboard and frowns at it as if she wants the bread to conform to her will. "The more you go there, the more likely you'll be caught."

I spread the placemats on the table and Alejandro lays down knives and forks at each setting.

"I wish you wouldn't worry, Jen. I am an excellent liar." Jen looks at me sharply but says nothing. Alejandro coughs and I ignore him. "Besides, I won't get an opportunity like this again. They invited me in. I'm gaining information I need to thwart their plans. How can I stop now? And really, what will they do to me?"

"The last person from Potestas shot you and tried to throw you off a mountain," Alejandro points out. Jen gestures to Alejandro with an exasperated look at me.

"Exactly. You shouldn't be flippant about these people."

"March has assured me that Drew was a rogue, a loose cannon, and that she has her people under wraps now."

"And you trust her?" Alejandro asks.

"No, not really," I admit. "I have a sneaking suspicion that she was behind Drew, and only invited me to headquarters to find out what my powers are. But still," I say loudly to cut off Jen's objections. "Since I'm on my guard, I can use Potestas how I want, and stay alert for danger."

Jen is silent, but she cracks eggs into a hot frying pan savagely, as if trying to knock sense into each one. Alejandro shakes his head and pulls plates out of a cupboard. I lean back and stare at the eggs sizzling in their butter.

Jen and Alejandro aren't entirely wrong. I'm not gaining that much information from my Potestas visits, possibly not enough to balance out the potential danger if they find me out. My purpose at Potestas has changed, although I haven't told Jen and Alejandro that. Perhaps they can sense it. I'm not done with Potestas yet—I need to know more about the spirits from that library.

The knowledge that I'm collecting about their connections to the spirit world is invaluable, to me at least. There are answers about the spirit world to questions I've never known I should be asking. I can't give up this chance to learn more.

March is an enigma. I don't know what her motivation is, not truly. Why does she want to connect with the spirit world? I don't trust that her tales of innocence are true concerning Drew's actions, and I'm left wondering about the volcano in the spring. If she is ruthless enough to condone an eruption that threatened lives, what is she willing to do next? Set off a tsunami, that's what.

"Eggs are ready," says Jen. I take a stack of toast to the table and Jen follows with the hot pan. She sets it down on a folded tea towel then says, "I still don't like you going."

"Then you haven't heard the worst of it," I say.

Alejandro sits down and glances at me while he butters a slice of toast.

"Which is…" Jen says with exaggerated patience.

"I've volunteered to collect an artifact for Potestas. March and I will dive off the coast to retrieve it from a shipwreck." I slice some egg and pop it in my mouth.

"What?" Jen yelps. Alejandro stares open-mouthed. "There

are so many things wrong with that, I don't know where to start. Do you even know how to scuba dive?"

I laugh.

"Oh, Jen, you know better than that. I've told you, I know how to do everything." She glares at me, and I amend, "It's been a while, but I'll manage."

"So, you'll be alone on a boat, in the middle of the ocean, with a woman who might be able to call up spirits to take you down if she suspects anything? A woman who may have already given orders for your death last month?"

"When you put it like that, it does sound dire," I say. "But I'm not entirely defenseless, I will remind you. And she has no real reason to suspect me."

"Why did you volunteer?" Alejandro asks.

"That's a better question. I didn't do it to be reckless. No, March mentioned—casually, I might add—that removing the artifact may set off a tsunami that will flood the coastline from Prince Rupert to Portland. I volunteered to come in the hope that I might be able to stop this disaster, or at least mitigate it. Possibly knock March on the head when she's not looking, if necessary."

Alejandro looks wind-blown, but slightly mollified. Jen's eyes are wide with horror.

"A tsunami? Seriously? We need to tell the authorities about this."

"Come on, Jen. What are you going to say? A diving trip will cause a massive, destructive rising of sea levels? I think not. No, it's up to me, I'm afraid."

Jen stares at her plate of untouched egg on toast. I reach over and lift her chin. Her fearful eyes look into mine.

"Cheer up, Jen. I've fixed worse and survived worse." She smiles weakly and I release her chin. "Besides, I have a feeling the artifact might be connected to earth lauvan. If I can be on the spot, I can disentangle the lauvan and stop anything from happening."

Alejandro nods with understanding. Jen sighs.

"Fine. I still don't like it."

"I know," I say.

"We need to know more about Potestas and March Feynman," says Alejandro. "Jen and I will keep digging."

"Yes, we will," Jen says with determination. "March's dirt will not stay hidden for long."

I smile. I'm lucky to have these two.

"Be careful, will you? Don't do anything I would do."

"Isn't that the truth," Jen grumbles.

We pass the rest of breakfast in lighter conversation about Jen's next job and Alejandro's plans to visit a nearby hiking trail. I depart with a full stomach and a contented mind, and the drive to work in my yellow Prius doesn't bother me as much as usual.

My phone pings, and I glance down at the passenger seat. It's from an unknown number, but the message makes my lips open in a wide smile.

Test inconclusive. Requesting larger sample size to draw appropriate conclusions.

It's Minnie, I'm certain. I move to answer, but Jen's wagging finger in my mind stops me—she would kill me if she saw me texting while driving. At the red light, I answer Minnie.

Further experimentation Monday, 7pm.

I lean back and press the accelerator with gusto. I haven't felt this eager about an upcoming date in ages. Minnie and I clicked the other night, really clicked, and more time spent with her will enliven my days.

It's not love, certainly not. I hardly know the woman, despite our meetings to date. She knows more about me than I her. And there's no way I'm traveling down that road right now. I can't let myself love again—I don't think I could survive the loss once more. But she could be the best sort of diversion. Yes, Monday night can't come soon enough.

CHAPTER XIII

I'm in a benevolent mood after Minnie's text, and the faces of my undergraduate class appear fresh-faced and eager to my eyes. They're here for summer classes to learn about Anglo-Saxon literature, something I am intimately familiar with, and today I'm happy to oblige.

I touch briefly on Beowulf and a lesser known poem called the Husband's Message. The first time I heard the latter was sitting around a fire while a traveling bard recited poetry for his supper. It was summer, the sky was darkening, and the camaraderie was comfortable. The words of the poem are almost unrecognizable after so many years and translations, but the essence has been retained.

Once we've looked for enough allegories and kennings for my taste, I introduce the Seafarer, a poem about an old sailor who reflects on his life at sea. It ends as an allegory to finding a path to the Christian god, which I can't recall from earlier versions, but no matter.

"Before we discuss the poem in more detail—and I'm assuming everyone has read it already—I'll recite a few lines out loud so you can get a feel for the tone of the poem. 'Not for him is the sound of the harp, nor the giving of rings, nor pleasure in woman, nor worldly glory—nor anything at all unless the tossing of the waves; but he always has a longing, he who strives on the waves.'"

A young man in the back row knocks over his water bottle. Liquid sloshes over the floor, and he drops to his knees to catch his errant bottle.

"No need for reenactments, I assure you," I say to him. "We can imagine the waves in our minds."

The class titters, but underneath the sound grows a chorus

of voices. Oh, no. Not now.

"I'll continue. 'And now my spirit twists out of my breast, my spirit out in the waterways.'" The voices grow louder, buzzing in my ears. "'Over the whale's path it soars widely through all the corners of the world.'" They call out to me, a few voices rising above the rest. I strain to hear what they say, even as I try to block them from my mind. "'It comes back to me eager and unsated.'"

I must look pained, because a student in the front raises her hand.

"Are you okay, Dr. Lytton?"

I wave away her question.

"Fine, fine. Thank you. Please form groups and discuss the role of the sea in the poem."

The students break into chattering groups and I perch on the edge of the desk. I want to cover my ears with my hands but refrain to avoid strange looks. The voices practically shout at me, warring with the noise of busy students chattering.

What is happening? Am I descending into madness? It's happened before, but not for centuries. Shattered memories of myself thrashing in the woods after Nimue's death threaten to claw their way to the forefront of my mind, and I push them down with force. And if it is madness, I no longer have a psychologist to help me through—Minnie saw to that.

The chattering slows, and I know I need to continue my lecture, but the clock says I have five minutes left. The Seafarer's ocean will have to wait until next class.

"Jot down your notes, and we'll continue our discussion next time," I say loudly over the voices. Scraping chairs and noisy talking only add to the cacophony, and I sweep out of the room with haste. Mercifully, the voices are quiet outside the door, and I breathe deeply with relief.

My reprieve is short-lived. When I turn a corner, the voices begin again, loud and insistent. I stop and hold the wall to steady myself against the onslaught. A janitor with a mop and a water bucket on wheels looks at me with concern, but I don't meet his gaze. It's all I can do to stand upright.

For the first time, two voices rise above the rest with clear words.

"Is it him? Is this his son?"

"Does he know?"

What is this? Do they speak of me? What do the voices know of my father? I close my eyes to hear better, all thoughts of resisting the voices forgotten. Is this a fragment of my fevered imagination, or are these voices external to my mind? What can I find out? Do they have answers to questions about my father that I've had for centuries? Questions such as why I have these abilities, was my father like me, and are there others?

The outside world falls away, and the only sense is hearing. It's overworked by the endless shouting of voices. Although I strain to distinguish one voice from another, no clear words rise above the din. Time loses meaning, and I don't know how long I remain in the deafening void.

A hand grabs my arm and firmly shakes. My eyelids fly open. Wayne stands in front of me, alarm etched on his face.

"Merry! Are you okay? What's going on?"

"Wayne." I shake my head to clear it. The voices grow fainter. The janitor throws me a suspicious glance as he pulls his mop bucket around the next corner.

"You were tranced out, in the middle of the hallway. You should have seen your face. I thought someone had stabbed you by your expression." Wayne releases my arm and searches my face.

I take a deep breath. What am I supposed to say to him? That I'm hearing voices?

97

"Thanks, Wayne. I felt a bit off for a moment. Nothing to worry about." I pat him on the shoulder and move away. "See you later."

Wayne stares after me, his expression bewildered, but I need to get home. Theories are swirling in my mind, theories about what the voices are. I need to corral my notions and come up with a plan. I'm made too vulnerable by the voices. It must stop.

I drive home as fast as traffic and my rented yellow taxi will allow and burst into my apartment. Alejandro is not here, for which I am grateful. I don't want to wrap him up in this talk of voices, especially since I'm still not convinced they aren't in my head. I grab a piece of paper and a pen from my satchel and let my thoughts flow onto the paper.

What are these voices? Are they hallucinations from an unstable mind, or are they external? If I assume they are external, it would make me feel both better and worse. Better, because my mind is still sharp, and worse, because then I have an unknown foe.

I can rule out human-produced sounds, since only I can hear them. That leaves the spirit realm, which feels far more likely now that I've seen a little of what Potestas does.

But where do they come from? Are spirits roaming freely in the world, somehow? Are there many secrets at Potestas that I am not privy to? If the voices are elementals, then they must be one of the four types. I can rule out air and earth, since attacks have been sporadic, and both these elements are present everywhere I go. I haven't been near fire lately. That leaves water.

Have I been near water at every episode? I think back to each occasion. On my hike in the woods, there was a creek when I heard the voices. Today, in class, a student spilled his water on the floor, and in the hallway, the janitor had a full mop bucket. What about at Wayne's lunchtime fight club? Ah, yes, there was a water fountain in heavy use.

I lean back and stare at the paper covered in my untidy scrawl. I am being contacted by water spirits.

But why are they here? It was my impression, from what I've learned from Potestas and Anna, that the spirits exist on another plane and cannot contact the physical world, except through special amulets. That appears to be the whole point of Potestas, after all—bridging the gap between worlds. How are the voices talking to me? And they spoke to Fiona at headquarters, also, about a father and son. Is Potestas meddling in experiments that I don't yet have the clearance to know about? I need to talk to March at the next meeting. I have half a mind to tell her directly that I can hear the spirits. Perhaps with that revelation she will allow me into the upper echelon of Potestas. Then I can finally understand how to stop them, these people who think nothing of erupting a volcano or unleashing a tsunami.

Unless—perhaps the spirits have answers for me. Does Potestas know what the spirits say? Do they know something about my father? Am I the only one in the dark? I assume he is the reason I do not age, the reason I can manipulate lauvan. Can Potestas give me the answers to questions about my father that I've asked for fifteen centuries?

In the meantime, I must figure out how to protect myself from falling into another trance. I reach over and pull Braulio's notebook off my bookshelf. The pages fall open, and my fingers leaf through them until I reach the water elementals section. There are a few incantations he discovered from various sources, ones that will repel spirits like water off a rock in a stream.

But if I block the voices, how can I hear if they have more to say? Perhaps I can find my own answers through listening to the elementals.

The front door clicks open, and Alejandro strides in.

"Hello, Merlo," he greets me. His eyes fall on Braulio's notebook. "What are you researching today? Can I help?"

"I'm simply perusing your grandfather's research. It's such fascinating work." I snap the book shut and slide it back on the shelf.

My attempt at deflection leaves Alejandro's face covered in frowns. He looks hurt, as if he senses that I'm being less than truthful.

"Where have you been?" I ask, and Alejandro's lauvan wriggle in discomfort.

"Here and there," he says, and I wonder if I'm not the only one with secrets. "Oh, I have news."

"Yes?"

"Jen and I found something on March Feynman."

I sit up straight. I like to have some ammunition in my back pocket when dealing with an enemy. Leverage is almost always useful.

"She has a younger sister," he says. "Her name is August Tremblay. She's a cook at a fancy restaurant downtown, so she doesn't seem to be part of the Feynman empire."

I shake my head in amazement.

"You've been working hard. But what shall we do with this information? I'm not certain taking a hostage is advisable at this point."

"A hostage?" Alejandro's eyes widen. "No! We want to talk to her, find out more about March. That's all. Honestly, Merlo, come live in the twenty-first century with the rest of us."

"You want to strike up a conversation with her at random?"

"That is the plan."

"Well, I don't have any better. Name the day."

"Tomorrow, if we can find her home address."

CHAPTER XIV

Minnie suggested a sushi restaurant near her house, so I stroll down Fourth Avenue on Monday night with pep in my step. There are busy knots of people outside every restaurant, coming or going or waiting for friends. The evening air is warm enough for shirt sleeves, but cool enough to be pleasant. The smell of cooking food wafts past my nose, and my stomach asserts itself.

Minnie waits outside the restaurant. Her strappy sandals match her yellow sundress perfectly, and she holds a small white purse close to her side. She appears relaxed, but her lauvan are tightly coiled in anticipation. I quicken my steps.

"Evening, sunshine," I say when she spots me. She looks confused and slightly offended until I wave at her dress. Her face brightens in a laugh.

"Cheeky. Come on, we'd better get in line. This place is more popular than I thought."

"Don't fret." I hold the door open for her and we sidle past waiting groups to the hostess desk.

"Hi. For two? Do you have a reservation?" the girl behind the desk says brightly.

"Lytton, for seven o'clock."

She scans her book.

"Lytton? Hmm, I don't see it."

There is no reservation. I put my arm on the desk as if to help her search her book and hold one of her floating lauvan between my finger and thumb. I rub it gently and concentrate.

"That's right, Lytton. I think it's right there." I point at a random line, and her face brightens.

"There it is. Right this way, please."

We weave between crowded tables until we reach a corner

spot by a window. I hold the chair for Minnie, and she sits with a bemused smile, as if she is rarely helped to her seat. I'm not surprised—it's rather out of fashion these days. It never fails to please, though, so I won't give up on tradition quite yet.

"Good day?" I ask once we're both seated.

"Yes. Mostly work, but I got out at lunch for a paddle. Paddle boarding," she says when she notices my quizzical look. "My office is right near the beach. I love being on the water."

"Sounds relaxing. I tend toward the mountains, myself, but I can understand the allure. It's too nice to be cooped up inside. I try to work as little as possible in the summer."

She laughs and lifts her water glass.

"Amen to that."

We chat a little in this vein while we decide upon drinks and food choices. It's not until our platters of sushi arrive that I bring up Minnie's dreams.

"You suggested this date, so I suppose your dreams can't be too terrifying after the wedding." I pour soy sauce into little dishes for both of us.

"They definitely showed up, but like you said, I should take it scientifically. One instance is not enough to draw conclusions from." She smiles at me and pops a sushi roll in her mouth. The tip of her pink tongue whisks across her lips.

"Can you describe one for me? I'm curious." I would love to know what Minnie thinks of me in her sleep. I dip some tempura in its sauce while I wait. She answers slowly, a little diffident, perhaps.

"They're all really strange. Not dream-strange, but they happen in strange times and places. Let's see, last night I dreamed that we were in a noisy market, hung with blue and gold banners. I was holding a chicken, of all things, and it was thrashing around and squawking. You were standing beside a

103

whole barrel of silver fish. Everyone was dressed as if it were a historical reenactment."

A shiver crosses my shoulders. I know the scene she describes.

"What did I do then?"

"You hadn't seen me yet, and you plunged your hands into the fish. Then you saw me, and the look on your face was hilarious." Minnie shrugs, then looks at me with a question in her eyes. "What are you thinking?"

I have no idea what is happening here. She described exactly my first encounter with Isabella, my sixth wife whom I met in Muslim Spain at the turn of the last millennium. Is it possible that our lauvan connection is somehow feeding my memories into Minnie's mind?

"I don't know what to think." I try for a smile, although it feels false to me. "You have a vivid imagination."

"There's no denying that." Minnie shakes her head and picks up a sushi roll with delicate chopsticks. She pops it in her mouth, chews, then says, "What about you? Do you ever dream about me?"

Her smile is teasing, and I grin.

"You're not my shrink anymore. I don't have to tell you everything." She laughs. I ask, "What about your condition?"

Her eyes grow momentarily concerned and flicker around my head before settling on the nearly empty sushi platter.

"We can talk about that another time. I'm handling it."

The few remaining lauvan over her eyes twitch and shift. Lauvan covering the eyes often indicates self-deception. What is she hiding from herself? Is it about the severity of this condition she won't talk about? My toes curl in their shoes, and I realize I am anxious for Minnie.

I switch to lighter topics, and we finish our meal in pleasant conversation. As I ask the server for the bill, Minnie looks over

104

my shoulder. Her eyes widen in recognition.

"Ella! Hi, nice to see you here."

I turn to see a short brunette in a jean skirt towing a gangly man in artfully ripped trousers.

"Minnie, hi! I was craving sushi tonight, so we stopped by here for takeout." Ella notices me for the first time. "Oh! Sorry, are we barging in on a date?"

"It's okay," Minnie says. "This is Merry. Merry, meet Ella and Jonathan. Ella and I went to university together."

"Pleased to make your acquaintance," I say, standing up and shaking their hands. They look taken aback at my formality, but I find showing more politeness tends to leave one in the driver's seat of many interactions.

I take my seat again, but not before Ella's intake of breath sounds quietly through the din of the restaurant. Her head whips toward Minnie, and Minnie looks abashed.

"Well, don't let us get in your way. Nice to meet you, Merry. Minnie, I really think we need to do coffee. Tomorrow?"

"I'll text you when I'm free," Minnie says quietly. Ella and Jonathan leave, and Minnie plays with her napkin on the table. Her lauvan droop in dejection.

I know what this is about. Ella knows that I used to be Minnie's client, and Minnie will get an earful tomorrow. By the looks of it, Minnie thinks she shouldn't be here.

I'm tempted to tweak Ella's lauvan out of annoyance for her throwing a sour note on our evening, but she is too far away, and it wouldn't satisfy anything except my pique. I glance at Minnie's fidgeting lauvan and sigh quietly.

"Can I give you a ride home?"

I go to bed early, disappointed with the bitter ending of our agreeable date. Will Ella convince Minnie to never see me again? I'm astonished by how much that possibility distresses me.

I'm thirsty after our sushi, so I fill a water glass and gulp half of it before placing it on my bedside table.

I almost welcome my inevitable dreams tonight. Perhaps memories of my past can distract me from the turmoil in my present. I fade into sleep soon after I lie down. The quiet sounds of Alejandro watching the television lull me into slumber.

But dreams do not overtake me immediately, as they usually do. Instead, restless fragments of memory fall on top of each other, sounds and words drowned out by a chorus of excited voices that wavers in and out like a badly tuned radio. I see Celeste, the Eiffel Tower, a green alpine lake, a crowd of people bowing in a vaulted chamber, a rearing horse, a woman under the flow of a waterfall, a bonfire...

The images race one after another, accompanied by nothing but the voices. I shout to interrupt the incessant, wordless chorus that rings in my ears. I don't know how to make it stop, and images flicker faster and faster in my mind's eye.

Hands grab my shoulders. My mind, already frayed by the relentless voices, orders retaliation. My arms rise before I can even open my eyes and my fingers grasp for any lauvan that I can reach. I grip and pull, hard. Someone cries out, and I don't know if it is me or my assailant. I wrench the lauvan in my hands tighter, and a scream of pain finally forces my eyes open.

The room is dark, but enough light filters in from the city's glow to illuminate my attacker. It's Alejandro, his face contorted in pain. He cradles his right hand in his other arm.

I sit up, aghast. What have I done? What kind of dream could have disabled my senses enough to attack my friend?

"Alejandro," I gasp. "I'm so sorry."

Alejandro is in too much pain to answer. I reach out and he flinches. My heart stutters at the sight.

"I can help. I promise, I'm awake now."

Alejandro nods, his grimace unchanged. He holds out his injured wrist with hesitation. It hangs at an odd angle, and the lauvan surrounding it are snarled and knotted. It's a simple break, severe yet easily fixed.

"It will take a few minutes, all right? Then you'll be fine. Hold on."

I work with deft fingers to untangle the knots. Alejandro doesn't watch but stares at the opposite wall and takes deep, measured breaths.

"One final jolt, then it will be over."

"Like when you healed Jen's back?" Alejandro's voice is raspy with pain and apprehension. When I healed Jen's broken back a few weeks ago, the realignment was unimaginably painful. The memory must have left an impression on Alejandro.

"Nothing so painful, I promise. One, two, three."

On the last count I pull the final knot free. Alejandro's hand swings back into its correct orientation and he yelps.

"Merlo!"

"I did warn you. How does it feel?"

Alejandro rolls his wrist experimentally.

"Fine. Like new."

I sigh and flop back on my pillow.

"I'm so sorry, Alejandro. I don't know what happened. I was having a disturbing dream, and your hand on my shoulder—I was confused."

Alejandro smiles weakly.

"I know not to wake you from your sleep in the future. You were thrashing around and shouting—I thought you would want to be woken from a bad dream."

"I would, I would. Only—for your own sake, perhaps leave me be."

Alejandro stares at me for a moment.

"What was the dream about? Sometimes it helps to talk about it."

"Just—flashes, images, so different from—" I shake my head. "It was nothing. Don't worry about it."

Alejandro stares at me with a hint of disappointment then gets up unsteadily from his perch on the bed.

"I think I'll get some sleep. Goodnight, Merlo."

He walks to the living room and shuts my bedroom door gently on the way out. I rub my face with frustrated vigor. How do I rid myself of these voices, these water spirits that are everywhere? Why do they disturb me at odd times? I need to control them—I can't hurt my friends from my hallucinations.

I eye the half-full water glass beside my bed with distrust. Are the voices coming from it? Does any exposed water harbor unwanted one-sided conversations? I drain the glass, then close my eyes and fall gratefully into true memory-dreams.

CHAPTER XV

Dreaming

I run through the streets of Corinth, the darkness almost complete. Only light from a thin sliver of moon appears between buildings, and then only enough to confuse my eyes with shadows. I leap over a sleeping beggar whose legs protrude from a shadowy doorway, then around a cart left in the road. The street is narrow, winding, with buildings placed in a haphazard fashion and so close together that the second stories almost touch. My long cloak flows behind me with my speed, and I am grateful that my short tunic doesn't hamper my escape. I hear no following footsteps anymore but don't dare slow my pace until I find a place to hide. With the Byzantine Empire ruling in Corinth, the laws are clear about fraternizing with a married woman without her husband's consent.

For once, I was doing nothing untoward. But who would believe me? Certainly not her husband, who failed to notice that we were both fully clothed and pouring over sheets of paper instead of bedsheets.

My blood pounds in my ears, and I gasp for breath. Where should I hide? I'm too rattled to change my appearance. Better to lie low for a while, transform myself with a disguise, and leave town. It's the easiest thing to do. I could leave forever, but I have friends here. I'd like to stay for a while. Perhaps a few weeks will let the husband forget about me.

I'm on a familiar street now. It's wide and as straight as these city streets ever get. This is a richer part of town, and the inhabitants enjoy the extra space. The house I'm currently working on is close. I can hide there for the night and be at work earlier than anyone. It's perfect.

I turn at an arched doorway and slip through the door, unlocked since no one is yet living here. The owner John Doukenos, my patron, is a wealthy man who works as an overseer in an imperial silk-weaving factory. It's the only place in Corinth that produces the costly fabric in its delicate, colorful patterns, since the manufacture of silk has been under a monopoly by imperial decree for centuries.

It's the trend these days to decorate buildings with as much art as possible—there is so much wealth from trade with the Venetians who bring goods from Egypt, the West, and the Crusader Kingdoms of Outremer that a veritable revival of art has exploded in Corinth. I've reinvented myself as a mosaic designer, and my mosaics are pretty good, if I say so myself. They're certainly good enough for John Doukenos, who has money but is not from the upper echelons, who have their own prized artists.

The house is dusty from renovations, although all is quiet and dark this late at night. I sigh deeply, safe for the moment. The husband has three retainers with him, and while I might have been able to fight them all, it was far more prudent to run. I haven't survived this long by being reckless. I sit on an unfinished windowsill that looks out into the inner courtyard and lean against the wall in relief. It's hours still until daybreak. I should find somewhere to curl up for the night, but right now I'm content to calm my racing heart.

The door rattles, and my breath stops. Have they found me already? Should I run? There is one back door, but if they've tracked me this far, I might not be safe anywhere. It's time to fight. I have the advantage of the entrance, at least—they will only be able to enter one at a time, which gives me a great advantage. I am an uncommonly good fighter, after all.

The door creaks open. I position myself in the shadows

110

beside the door frame and wait, both hands up at the ready. The green lauvan of the newcomer glows faintly. I don't hesitate.

My fingers dig in deep, and the cool smoothness of the strands flows against the webbing of my fingers. I pull hard. At the same time, I kick the man's feet out from under him. He falls with a pained groan, and I look out the door for my next assailant.

The street is empty. Where are the others? The horrible truth slowly dawns on me. The husband's lauvan are maroon. The man on the floor has green lauvan, the same green as…

"Alexios?" I whisper. "Is that you?"

Alexios stirs and moans. Named after the emperor, as so many are, Alexios is a carpenter, employed by our patron to build furniture for the upstairs bedchambers. He's greatly skilled and is a good friend of mine. Even in the darkness of the hall, the green strands surrounding his right shoulder glow with many knots. I've broken his shoulder, by the look of it. If I don't heal him, he will never work again. He has a wife and three small children who depend on him. I swallow. I must heal him. I've never told him about my abilities, but I suppose it has to happen sometime. I hope he can forgive me for hurting him.

"Hold still," I say to him and bend down. I swiftly unpick knots and massage twisted strands. I even take out a knot between his shoulders that must be bothering him. He finally stirs and lifts himself off the ground. His hair is mussed, and his black beard shows up starkly against bloodless skin, even in the faint moonlight.

"Merlenos?" he says in a rough voice. "What are you doing here? Why did you attack me?" He rolls his arm around. "I thought it was broken. How is it healed?"

I almost relish the dark. This way, I don't have to see the look on his face.

111

"I have been teaching Lady Theodora logic and harmonics. That's all, I swear. Her husband found out tonight and chased me away. I hid here, heard you come in, and assumed you were he. When I realized my mistake, I—healed you." I swallow, but Alexios says nothing, so I continue. "I have special abilities, that I can use for healing, among other things."

"Are you a witch?" Alexios' voice is calm, measured. I shake my head, then remember he cannot see me in the dark.

"What is a witch? I don't worship any devil, if that's what you're worried about. I was born like this."

Now I wait. What will he say?

"All right. You need a place to hide for the night? Come to my house. It's small, but you are welcome all the same."

"Truly? What about the healing? You don't mind?"

"It sounds like a useful ability to have around. Don't worry, I won't say anything. Come, it's late. I hope you don't mind waking early—little Nikos is always up at dawn."

I shake my head and allow Alexios to pull me to my feet. Not only did he forgive me for attacking him, he brushed off my abilities and invited me into his home when I'm on the run. I am lucky to find friends like Alexios.

CHAPTER XVI

Alejandro isn't in the apartment when I awake, so I busy myself making coffee and toast until the front door clicks.

"Good morning, Merlo," Alejandro says in a chipper voice. "I have your mail."

"Thanks. Here's coffee." I hand him a mug, and he slurps it in appreciation. "How's your wrist?"

Alejandro waves the appendage in question.

"Never better. Don't stress, Merlo. It was an accident."

Perhaps, but it still shouldn't have happened. If I can't understand the spirit voices, then I must ignore them, information about my father be damned. I can't let a bodiless hallucination control me. I sip my coffee in reply.

"I met up with your neighbor, Gary," says Alejandro. "He's a nice old guy. We spoke for twenty minutes, at least."

"He can talk your ear off, that's for sure."

"No, it was interesting. He used to be in the air force. And he was a skydiving trainer after that."

"I didn't know." Alejandro has a knack for ingratiating himself with new people. He's close with Jen, Wayne is now a friend, he found an acquaintance named Liam, and now Gary. "You're good with people."

"If you're interested in what people have to say, they will say a lot," Alejandro says. "They sense real interest."

"Ah, there's my problem."

Alejandro laughs, but stops when there is a knock at the door.

"Who's that?" he asks.

"Either Gary, come to finish his train of thought, or Jen, for some unknown reason. Come in," I shout toward the door.

Jen walks into the kitchen a moment later. She is dressed in a sensible yet stylish pencil skirt and flowing chemise. Alejandro gulps the rest of his coffee.

"Good morning, you two," she says, and looks at Alejandro. "Did you tell him yet?"

"Not yet," Alejandro replies.

"Tell me what?"

"We found something out about March Feynman," Jen says. I give her an exasperated look.

"I hope you're being careful. These people are dangerous, and I don't want you two involved. I'm a mole in the organization—isn't that enough?"

"It's not just about you," Jen shoots back. "Drew pushed me off a cliff, remember? If I hadn't known you with your lauvan thing, I'd be in a wheelchair right now. I don't buy it that he was rogue, not at all, which makes Potestas both dangerous and in need of being taken down. I might not be able to spy like you, but I can dig for info. Now, do you want to hear what I found or not?"

I sigh in defeat.

"Of course. Spill it."

"Good. March Feynman is one of the biggest, most silent investors in Vancouver. She has her fingers in so many pies, she's starting to dip her toes in, too. She got a settlement from a divorce, some high-roller with bags of money, and used the cash to invest. She obviously knows what is worthy, because her net worth has grown like crazy over the past twenty years."

"That's how she supports Potestas," says Alejandro. "It's all her own cash. Potestas is her hobby."

"Sounds about right. Interesting."

"That's not all," Jen says. "We know where March's younger sister lives, August Tremblay. Through some miraculous digging, we found out that she lives on a boat that is moored on Granville Island. So, I hope you're free after work, because we're going to visit her."

"And ask what?" I'm impressed by what they have found out, but I'm not sure about the August angle.

"Just chat. Find out a little more about her and her older sister. See if we can smell anything fishy."

"Besides the fish market," Alejandro adds. Jen grins at him. I put up my hands in surrender.

"All right, we'll do it. Since you two have worked so hard on figuring it out. I'll go in disguise, though—I don't want word getting back to March that I'm a spy."

"Good," says Jen. "We'll meet on the bridge at six o'clock. I'll text Wayne, too." She pauses, then says in a different voice, "There's something I need to ask you, Merry."

I rinse my mug in the sink. The voices clamor in my head, trying to pull me into a trance, but I shut the tap off quickly and face Jen.

"Yes?"

"You know that poster I bought you in Paris, the one that had your clone in it?"

"Yes."

"I thought the woman with your double looked familiar, but I couldn't remember why. Then it occurred to me, she looks just like a woman in your sketchbook." Jen has the decency to look slightly abashed. "I didn't try to look, I swear, but I couldn't help seeing her when I photocopied the book for you. And—" She swallows. "I've been doing more research. If I enter your name into the genealogical database, there are a few matches from different eras. But if I change the spelling of Merry Lytton, or of Merlo Nuanez, a lot more comes up. I even found a picture."

Jen extracts a folded piece of paper and flattens it on the counter. It's a printout of a scanned daguerreotype from the eighteen fifties. Eighteen fifty-one, to be precise. My face is strained as I pull a rope with two other men in bright sunlight. I recognize the place—I was dismantling the Great Exhibition in London. This must be from a newspaper of the time.

"Not to mention those photos in the back of your sketchbook," Jen continues. "I know you said you would tell me soon, but I think soon should be now. I've waited long enough." She bites her lips and awaits my response.

I don't answer right away. I gaze at her, wondering how this day came so soon. I'm never ready to reveal. Every time has the potential for disaster.

Alejandro shuffles his feet back and forth in his agitation. I glare at him.

"I need to shower," he announces and slides out of the kitchen in haste. Jen looks open-mouthed at me.

"Does Alejandro know? Before *me*?"

"Not by choice," I say and sigh. "His uncle spilled the beans without my knowledge. Come on, I have something for you."

I walk to the bookshelf in the living room where a book awaits Jen, left there for this very moment. It's a copy of T.H. White's *Merlin*. Although there are plenty of stories I could choose from, White's whimsical retelling is amusing. I slide it off the shelf and present it to Jen.

"What's this?" she asks.

"Read this. If you keep an open mind, it will enlighten you."

"Do you have a secret code in here I should decipher? What's the deal?" Jen shakes the book upside down, perhaps hoping for loose sheets to emerge. I chuckle.

"Nothing like that. Read it and come back. We'll talk then."

Jen sighs in exasperation.

"Really, Merry? You're putting this conversation off again?"

"Just read it."

116

"Okay, fine. Whatever. You're running out of chances, though." She tucks the book into her purse.

"I know."

My phone pings with a text. I move swiftly to view it and see Minnie's message.

"Who's that?" Jen asks with interest.

I deliberate on what to tell her then decide on the truth.

"Minnie Dilleck. We went out for dinner last night. It ended on a sour note, so I didn't know if I'd be hearing from her again."

"What did she say?" Jen tries to peer over my shoulder at my phone, but I hold it out of reach.

"She says that my friend is very nosy," I say. Jen punches my arm. "No, she said, *Thanks for dinner. I also like Mexican.*" A smile crosses my face before I can master myself. Jen laughs.

"I guess you did something right."

At ten to six, I pull into a free parking spot on a steep hill facing Granville Island. The slope is extreme enough that the sidewalk has ridges built into the concrete, and I yank at the rental car's handbrake with misgiving. I would have parked on the island itself, but the parking is so tight that even my little tricks don't help. It's not far, and it's a beautiful evening for a stroll. From my vantage point, the water is calm and glitters in the evening sun.

The bridge to the island is busy with foot and vehicle traffic, on their way to dinner or to the market. I pause midway and lean over the railing. The fish market is on a dock nearby, and the boats are doing a lively trade in the dinner rush. A light breeze wafts the smell of salt and fish my way, and I close my eyes. A memory surfaces, of my time at sea in the seventeenth century, entering the port of Batavia after a long voyage. The smell of the docks, fish and tar, squawking chickens being loaded onto ships, sacks and barrels of spices scenting the tropical air, cries of joyous sailors finally making land…

The voices start again, and I groan. I keep my eyes closed and begin to chant an incantation under my breath, one from Braulio's notebook. The voices waver in intensity, like a badly tuned radio. I chant a little louder. A voice rises above the rest.

"Does he know? It's him…"

My chanting falters. I don't want to be tranced, I can't afford the vulnerability, but I need to know what the voices say. They grow louder immediately, as if they sense my reluctance to repel them. I am swept into a trance. The voices don't say anything else of interest, but still I can't escape. My tight fingers grip the railing, but I can't shake the spell.

A hand squeezes my shoulder. I gasp and surface from the trance. Alejandro's concerned face peers into mine.

"Merlo. Are you okay?"

"Fine," I say quickly, trying to regain my composure. "I was simply—thinking."

"It looked painful," says Wayne from my other side. "I wouldn't recommend it."

I grin weakly. Jen points down at our feet.

"Look. Two crabs. They're a long way up."

Two Dungeness crabs scuttle over the edge and drop with flailing legs into the water below with a splash. I shake my head.

"Strange. Well, shall we meet this August of yours?"

We turn toward the island and walk forward, but my feet are immobile. My torso swings in a remorseless arc toward the wooden boardwalk. I catch my fall with my hands, but my body jars with the impact.

Jen shrieks and Wayne laughs, but Alejandro gives me his hand.

"It's not like you to be clumsy, Merlo," he says with a frown. He attempts to haul me up, but my feet are stuck fast to the ground, and it's an awkward rise.

"Are you okay, Merry?" Jen tilts her head at me. "That was weird."

"I'm stuck." I bend down and examine my feet. Blue lauvan the color of the northern sea in a storm are entwined with my own brown strands and lash my feet firmly to the wood. "There are water lauvan attached to me. How did that happen?"

Jen looks around wildly.

"Do you think they're watching us right now? How did they get to you?"

"The crabs," says Alejandro slowly. "I bet they did it. Just like the seagulls in your apartment a few weeks ago, Merlo. Remember?"

I do remember. Air spirits controlled birds to wreak havoc in my apartment, back when Drew was trying to attack me. It seems likely that the crabs are under similar compulsion.

"But why? Why now, I mean?" I work quickly to undo the knots in my lauvan. "Am I being tested?" Or are the water spirits not being controlled anymore? The voices I hear everywhere seem to indicate that they have been at least partially released. I don't speak this theory out loud. "There." I release the final lauvan and rise. "Now we can go."

CHAPTER XVII

We stroll along the busy sidewalk on the island, past colorful store fronts selling art, inching cars on the narrow road, and tourists licking ice creams. A playground crawls with happy children, and there's a line-up outside a restaurant that overlooks the water. Jen bumps Alejandro's arm more often than strictly necessary, and Alejandro's lauvan respond with a wriggle each time.

The dock lies on the far end of the tiny island, and it's a walk of no more than three minutes to reach the relative quiet of a parking lot at the water's edge. I turn into a narrow opening between buildings and reach for my lauvan.

"What are you doing?" Jen asks.

"Creating my disguise," I say absently. I won't change too much—same gender and age, same height—but I need enough difference that August could never identify me.

"What did you bring for a disguise?" Wayne asks with a look of skepticism. I grin and pull the final lauvan in reply.

I am rewarded with a shriek from Jen and gasps from the other two. I touch my head to feel the shaggy blond hair now on top, then rub my chin on the overgrown bristles there.

"That's insane," Wayne breathes. "You're completely different."

"That's the idea," I say. Jen looks me over.

"I'm getting surfer vibes from you. You even have the board shorts." She touches my head gingerly. "Is your hair crusty from salt?"

"The devil's in the details. Shall we proceed?" I gesture toward the ramp. Alejandro grins and leads the way. Wayne pauses at the top.

"Maybe I should stay here, watch for suspicious people. I

don't want you three to be cornered with nowhere to go."

"Who are we expecting?" I ask in bemusement.

"That's a great idea, Wayne." Jen smiles at Wayne then glares at me. "When will you start taking Potestas seriously, Merry? You said yourself that you don't trust March, and the Drew incident…"

"It can't hurt to take precautions," I say to placate her. "Shout if there's a problem, Wayne."

"Will do." Wayne melts into shadows behind the building, and we continue down the swaying ramp to the dock.

It's a small jetty with room for only a few boats. I wonder how much it costs to moor here. Perhaps August is wealthy also. It's possible, although living on a boat is an eccentric choice if so. It's more likely she receives funding from her big sister.

I amble down the rocking platform, doing my best impression of a relaxed surfer-type. Jen giggles behind me, and Alejandro shushes her with a smile in his voice. I look around with unfocused interest until a low sailboat appears, perhaps thirty feet long, with gleaming wood decking and bright brass fixtures. The sail is furled into a clean white roll on the boom.

A woman sits on the aft deck on a folding chair, her feet on the bulwark and a glass of wine in her hand. A large book lies on her lap, and at a glance it looks like a cookbook. The woman's undyed graying hair is pulled into a loose ponytail at the nape of her neck, and she wears a tee shirt with frayed neckline and comfortable-looking shorts that have seen better days. Her square face is unadorned by makeup and is currently in an expression of contented repose. Swirling around her torso are lauvan the color of a tropical lagoon, but around her head the lauvan are the hue of a blustery northern sea. Why is August's head surrounded by water lauvan?

"Hey," I say in my best surfer impression. "Sweet ride.

121

You're living the dream."

The woman looks up, her face resigned at the interruption. I gather it's not an uncommon occurrence.

"That I am," she agrees.

"I'm Chad," I say with practiced spontaneity. I reach out my hand, and the woman leans forward with a small sigh and shakes it. She sets her book down and I flop onto the edge of the dock, kick off my shoes, and dangle my toes in the cool water.

"I'm August," she says.

"Rad name. Did you pick it, or are your parents just awesome?"

"Unoriginal, I expect. I was born in August."

"Hey, guys, come meet August," I call over my shoulder to Jen and Alejandro, who have been pretending to look at a motorboat moored three spaces down. "August, these are my good buddies Jane and Alex. There's nothing like being near the water with an awesome sunset going down with friends."

"It looks like it will be a beautiful evening," August agrees.

"You off for the night from your day grind?" I say.

"Ha, no. I'm a pastry chef for Shimmer, a restaurant in Yaletown. I have to be at work in an hour." She stretches back in her chair. "But I can soak up the rays first."

"Hey, wait," I say slowly and turn to Jen. "You said that March chick's sister works at Shimmer." Jen's eyes are wide with uncertainty, but I don't need her to do anything. I look at August. "Do you know August?"

August replies with caution.

"That's me. Do you know March?"

"Yeah. Jane here got in with March's group a while ago. Super-secret and all that. Weird shit going down."

August sighs again.

"Yes, weird shit indeed. March believes some crazy stuff

122

and has roped a lot of people into her brand of crazy." August sips her wine, but I watch her lauvan. They twist uncomfortably, and I can tell August doesn't mean what she says. She believes in the spirits but is afraid of what March is up to. Her eyes narrow. "Why do you know anything about me?"

"Came up in conversation." I flip my toes through the water to send a glittering arc dancing through the sunset. "She gets pretty cozy if you're having troubles. Jane's sister was going through a rough patch, she told March. March must have wanted to relate and mentioned you."

August swirls the wine in her glass. She doesn't look comfortable that March speaks of her.

"And she let you tell your friends about the org?" This is directed at Jen. Jen glances at me briefly and nods in reply.

"I can see things," I say to rescue Jen. "They wanted to talk when they found out. But I don't know, man, organized group meetings aren't my scene."

"I understand completely." August gestures to her boat. "I prefer my own company, for the most part."

"There's a weird aura over your head," I say with studied nonchalance. "Do you want it there?"

Alejandro glances at me in question, and August touches her hair. Her eyes narrow in suspicion, and she sits up straight.

"What do you mean? What are you talking about?"

I raise my hands in defense.

"Whoa, whoa, I was just wondering. I told you I can see stuff. I thought your sister must have done something."

"No. I mean, I don't know." She waves her hand over her head and it passes through the strands without ruffling them. "Why is it there?"

I shrug.

"Who knows. Like I said, that group is doing weird shit.

123

Maybe doing it to you, when you're not looking. It's totally not on the level, what they're planning. I mean, usually I say live and let live, you know? But sometimes you gotta take a stand."

"What has she done?" August mutters to herself, still fruitlessly waving her hand over her head. Then she stares at me. "Take a stand? What are you planning?"

I shrug again and kick my feet in the water lazily.

"We've got ideas. Don't want you running to big sis, though."

"I don't believe in anything March is up to, and she's heading down the wrong path," August says with heat. "If you have a plan to put a stop to this nonsense, I want to help."

Bingo. I glance at Jen and Alejandro in triumph, then turn to August.

"You're not gonna let sisterly love get in the way?"

"We aren't close," says August. "March has always had secrets, and way more ambition than I've ever understood. And her followers, well, it's almost cultish, isn't it? And I don't like what they're doing. Not that I believe a word of it." Her lauvan twist with the lie. "But she shouldn't be exploiting vulnerable people. Normally, I don't like getting involved, but…"

"There is something going on with your aura. I could probably help, but if you don't believe it's real…" I shrug.

August stares at me for a while. She worries her lips.

"Okay, maybe there's something to it," she bursts out. "Can you really fix it? Whatever is going on around my head?"

I nod slowly.

"Yeah, I bet so."

"Then, please. I will help you stop March, if you fix this." She waves at her head. I give her a toothy grin.

"Awesome."

124

Our negotiations are interrupted by shouting from Wayne, followed by a crashing noise. I leap up and run barefoot down the dock. It sways underfoot, and Alejandro's footsteps pound behind me.

At the top of the ramp, Wayne grapples with a large man dressed in casual slacks and a polo shirt. Two similarly dressed men wait for an opening to pin Wayne to the ground. They tussle in the shelter of the boathouse, so the few people who venture to this non-commercial part of the island won't see them.

I don't hesitate, and to his credit, neither does Alejandro. We fly toward the two waiting opponents, who barely have time to turn around before we are on them. My opponent wears a forest green polo shirt with a company logo, and his muddy gray lauvan beckon. I accept the invitation and bury my fingers deep. He yells in pain and clutches his side but recovers quickly and barrels into me. We fall to the ground and roll until my arm releases to throw a punch. His jaw snaps sideways, then our continued roll brings his own fist smashing into my gut.

The blow forces breath out of my lungs and I wheeze, but I've been in enough fisticuffs that being winded doesn't pause my attack. I pull a handful of hair and lauvan and jolt his head backward. His yell turns into a scream of pain as I twist the lauvan in my grip. His rigid body slackens as he falls unconscious.

I push my body off the ground and survey the scene. Wayne still grapples with his opponent, with the occasional fist or leg flying. They look evenly matched, and Wayne holds his own. Alejandro is still up, but his opponent is a trained professional and Alejandro is losing ground. A fist connects with Alejandro's cheekbone with a sickening crack and I leap in. Handfuls of yellow lauvan fill my hands and I wrench them downward. The man's head jerks back and his torso follows. Alejandro jumps out of the way of the man's feet, which fling around in an arc. The man lies, stunned, on the pavement.

Wayne's fist streaks out and cracks against his opponent's head. It lolls sideways, and the man falls to his knees and then to the ground. Wayne puts his hands on his own knees and breathes heavily. He looks up at us.

"I didn't know I was training for everyday life. You are always interesting company, Merry."

Alejandro laughs, a little wildly. I grin.

"I keep you on your toes. Come on, let's drag these deadweights out of sight."

Alejandro grabs an arm of one of the unconscious men, then peers at the polo shirt logo more closely. It's an insignia of a stylized mountain, wave, cloud, and flame in a circle.

"I recognize this. It came up during our research into March Feynman. It's a security company, bodyguards for hire. March owns it, of course."

"Here for August, I presume," I say. "March is not to be trifled with. Here, I'll take his other arm."

With the final security guard groaning incoherently next to his fellows in the shadow of the dumpster, I wipe my forehead with the back of my hand.

"We'd better wrap up our talk with August. There will be more where these came from."

Wayne stares at me and shakes his head slowly.

"You don't know how weird it is to see Merry Lytton speaking through this random guy's mouth."

I chuckle.

"Come on, let's collect Jen and get out of here."

Jen waits for us at the bottom of the ramp, my shoes in her hand. When she notices Alejandro's bleeding forehead, she runs to him.

126

"Alejandro, are you okay? I can't believe you guys were fighting up there! Who the hell were they? What's going on?"

"Security detail," I say. "Looks like March keeps a close eye on her little sister. Overprotective, I call it."

"I wonder if August knows?" Alejandro asks.

"Let's find out."

I stride down the dock with the other three following. August stands on the dock with an uncertain air.

"What's going on?" she calls out while we walk toward her boat.

"Did you know about your security detail?" I ask. "They tried to beat the crap out of us just now. Not cool."

"What?" August is clearly horrified. "I have no such thing."

"Then dear sis likes to keep tabs on you."

"Damn it, March," August cries out. "Will she never just leave me alone? It must be her, no one else has the money or interest to do that. I had no idea. She has no right. I'm going to call her right now."

"Don't do that," Alejandro says. "You don't want March to know you know about the guards, in case she tries something different. Act normally with your sister."

"I guess you're right." August's shoulders slump, then she waves to Alejandro. "Can I get you some bandages?"

"No time," I say. "There'll be others. We gotta go."

"What about the aura?" August clutches one hand to her head.

"I can't now. Can we meet soon? Somewhere else?" I pull out my wallet and remove a piece of paper. I don't dare give her a business card with my name on it, but my phone number will be fine. I wiggle my fingers at Jen. "Pen?"

She thrusts her hand into her purse and extracts a pen from the depths. I scrawl my number and push it toward August, who takes it with shaking fingers.

"Text me with a time and place to meet, and we'll talk more," I say. "And deal with that aura. Let's do it in the next day or two, there's not much time."

August nods tightly and smooths her hair again. Jen tugs my sleeve and we walk quickly down the dock. I can feel August's eyes boring into my back.

Once a large motorboat is between us and August, I reach out a hand to stop Jen. Alejandro halts as if tied to Jen with string, and Wayne pauses behind us.

"They didn't see you, Jen, so you can stay the same. Stay still, Alejandro."

I reach for Alejandro's lauvan and deftly twist and pull. Alejandro's face melts and is replaced by a thin-faced, pale young man with floppy brown hair. Wayne whistles.

"Don't worry, you're next," I tell him. "I don't want our attackers recognizing your face, either."

Wayne looks apprehensive but stays still while I manipulate his lauvan. He emerges as a tanned thirty-something with dreadlocks and a tee shirt that says "Freshly Baked" under a picture of a cannabis leaf. Jen starts to laugh, and Wayne feels his face and hair.

"What the hell, Merry?" But his face opens in a grin. "I need a mirror."

I reform my own lauvan so that I'm different again—same face but with a buzz cut. I walk forward, but Jen tugs at my sleeve again.

"I should have a disguise, too, just in case they see me later," she says. When I open my mouth to protest that our attackers never saw her, she leans forward and whispers in my ear. "I always thought it would be fun to be blond for a day."

I grin and reach toward her head. One twist and her black locks shiver into blond. Jen picks up a handful and studies it.

"Nice, Merry."

"They'll be looking for three men," I say. "So, Wayne and Alejandro go first, then Jen and I will follow. Meet at the bridge."

Wayne nods and strides forward, his dreadlocks swinging on his back. Alejandro's thin face looks back with worry at Jen, but he follows Wayne without a word. Jen and I wait for three long minutes, then emerge at the base of the ramp.

At the top, two of the men we felled earlier stand in the shadows. One is developing an impressive black eye. Jen's lauvan spasms with jagged fear, although outwardly she is calm. I put a casual arm around her shoulder and she leans in gratefully. Her body trembles slightly.

We pass the men without incident and walk as quickly as we can to the bridge without arousing suspicion. Wayne and Alejandro wait for us there, Alejandro dancing with impatience.

"We're here, we're here," I say. "Did that conversation with August go as well as you hoped?"

"Better," says Alejandro. "She's willing to help us, and we're meeting again soon. That was great, Merlo."

"Let's not forget you guys were attacked," says Jen, but she looks satisfied now that the danger is behind us. "And Merry, your surfer dude impression was perfect. I didn't know you were such a great actor."

"Oh, Jen," I say. "Don't you know by now—"

"You know how to do everything," Jen finishes with a laugh. "I know."

CHAPTER XVIII

Dreaming

I've been south for the winter. The memory of last year's storms that shut us in for days still haunted me by autumn, and when the first cold snap closed in on us, I bade farewell to newlyweds Arthur and Guinevere and rode south. A merchant ship from a settlement on the coast offered to take me and my horse across the channel, after some persuasion. We rode until the north wind no longer cut through my cloak like a knife.

But when spring arrives, I itch to return to my friends and my home, and my trusty steed and I make our way north. We pass through the lands of the Franks and sail on another merchant vessel across the channel. Days after landing, I pass through the more familiar forests of Gwent.

By midday I am famished. In my saddlebag are provisions for journeying, not the solid meal I crave. The thought of halting my journey to hunt and make a fire rankles, so close to my destination, and I console myself with the thought of Guinevere's table.

The track I follow forks. One way leads to Arthur's villa. The other, I now recall, winds into a dell in which Arthur's sister Morgan lives with her husband Idris. Her dwelling is only moments away.

I am torn. I have no desire to trespass on Morgan's hospitality, mainly because I wronged her in the past and have avoided her ever since. Arthur and I did visit in the autumn, and she was nothing but hospitable to me then, but Arthur and Idris were both present. Would she turn me away from the door? What would I say to her? It is unlike me to waffle so, but I've never felt right about how Morgan left Uther's house, and the role I played.

However, there is a promise of food if all goes well. Arthur's villa is still a half-day's journey away, and my stomach is unwilling to wait that long. I tug my horse's reins toward Morgan's home.

A longhouse sits in a clearing in the woods. Its fresh thatching glistens from a recent rainfall. A few outbuildings surround it, but all is quiet except the clucking of contented hens in the dirt between buildings.

Morgan emerges from behind the longhouse when I approach. She wears a kerchief to hold back her hair, and her dress is tucked up into her belt to keep it out of the spring mud. When she sees me, her eyes widen.

"Merlin," she greets me. Her lauvan spark with surprise, but without embarrassment at her lack of formal dress in my presence. I take that as a good sign and dismount.

"Morgan. It's a pleasure to see you."

She doesn't respond directly to this, for which I don't blame her.

"I presume you have a message from my brother?"

"No." I pat my horse's neck. "I have been away for the winter, in the south. I am on my way to Arthur now, but hoped to break my journey here before my last push through Gwent."

"That explains your dark skin," she says. "Come in, then. I expect you're looking for a meal. Fortunately for you, I was about to dine myself."

She whistles loudly, and a boy bolts out of a nearby shed with straw in his hair. Morgan tsks but doesn't comment on the boy's sleepy demeanor.

"Feed and water Lord Merlin's horse. Don't unsaddle the beast—he'll be leaving soon."

The boy nods and leads my horse to the shed. I follow Morgan to the house, looking to be fed and watered myself.

131

"Where are your servants?" I ask when we enter the empty hall. "Vivienne, Mordred, the others?"

"It's planting time. I've sent all the able bodies to work the fields for a few weeks." She shrugs and waves me toward another door, which leads to a kitchen. "It happens every year. There is often a shortage of field hands, and the crops must be sown. I admit, I don't mind the solitude. I can manage well enough on my own for a while."

"And Idris?" Morgan's husband is unpleasantly loud, and I'm surprised not to have heard him yet. Morgan grimaces.

"He's been ill since the solstice. His sickness comes and goes, but this time it seems determined to stay. He's too ill to leave his chambers." Morgan bustles around the kitchen. She collects bread, cheese, and a few onions for our repast and places them on the heavy wood table in the center of the room.

"And it's only you to nurse him?" That feels like a heavy charge for one person, even though I'm sure Morgan is capable enough.

"It's not difficult," she says, waving her hand in dismissal. "My cousin Morgause is here to help as well. She's out for a walk now. Idris doesn't need much. I do my duty, no more and no less."

"Not a lot of love lost between you, I can see." I speak with a calm voice, but Morgan's lauvan bristle.

"Should there be? I was given to him without my consent, and I am not the meek, obedient sort of wife that he wanted. He's not an easy man to live with." She reaches for a flask of ale, and dark bruises in the shape of fingerprints appear from under her sleeve. She sees me stare and twitches the sleeve down.

"I can see that," I say softly.

"I don't want your compassion, Merlin. It's a little late for that." She sets the flask on the table with more force than necessary. "Come, we will eat here. No need to stand on ceremony. It's only us."

I'm happy enough to sit and fill my mouth without another word, but Morgan's bruises leave me feeling more wretched than ever. Not only did I betray her innocent trust in our relationship, but I let her marry brutal Idris without a word of protest. True, Uther would have dismissed my meddling, or would have thrown me out if he'd thought I was making love to his daughter, but I could have tried. My bread doesn't taste as good with my loss of appetite, but I try to force it down to give me strength for the afternoon journey.

"It's good to see you, Merlin," Morgan says. I glance up with surprise. Morgan's expression is open, and her lauvan flow freely with no hidden emotions. "You're a cad, but a familiar, friendly one. The people here are mostly dull and sullen. I'm the mistress of the house, and they never treat me as anything else. I suppose I should be grateful that I can keep control over the household without much fuss, but I miss the conversation of intelligent equals. Vivienne is the only one who comes close, and I miss her when she's gone." She bites into her cheese.

"Your cousin, Morgause? I don't remember ever meeting her. Is she good company?"

Morgan laughs in derision.

"Morgause? She's simple. Only good for giving directions to. She's a sweet enough soul, but certainly not a thinker. She had a fever as a child and was never the same since. She visits sometimes, and I take her under my wing, but she is no equal." Morgan sighs. "I feel sometimes that I expect too much out of life. Is there supposed to be something more, or is this my lot and I should accept it?" She laughs without humor. "Never mind me, Merlin. I've been in my own thoughts for too long with everyone gone. Soon enough the hall will fill, Idris will

133

recover and shake sense into me, and all will be forgotten."
She stares into her ale cup.

I am spared from answering by the arrival of a young woman. Her round face wears a smile unencumbered by cares of the world, and her eyes wander over the two of us with a dreamy vagueness.

"Morgause," Morgan greets her. "Now that you're in, could you take Idris his meal? Here is the tray."

Morgause takes a moment to answer.

"Yes, Morgan." She nods slowly as though she has deciphered the answer to a complex riddle and picks up the tray. She exits without acknowledging my presence, and I wonder if she even noticed me. Morgan rolls her eyes.

"There's Morgause. At least I can send her to Idris sometimes. And she's strong enough to carry the water in every morning."

"Morgan," I say suddenly. "What of Idris' campaign plans this year? Last year he pushed Heolstor's tribe past the White Hills. If he's too ill to leave his bed, what will happen?"

"There will be no changes," says Morgan with firm resolve. "I will provide direction to the men, and Idris has capable advisors who will instruct me. Idris and I may differ on many points, but we are united in our goal to rid Gwent of the Saxons."

"You're still following Idris on this?" I glance at Morgan's wrists, and her eyes harden.

"Idris has nothing to do with my resolve. My mother was murdered by a Saxon horde, cut down far before her time. They are all alike, the Saxons, desirous of our land and willing to do anything to get it."

"Do you remember anything I taught you?" I say quietly. "About my travels among the Saxons? About the similarity in every people?"

134

"I've been disinclined to believe your teachings since I left my father's house. Your lack of honorable action discredited much of what you said, frankly. I don't have patience to sort through your hypocritical lessons."

Chastened, I'm not sure what to say in my defense.

"Just—consider that everyone you meet has a story, a family they love, a desire to live in safety, a need for food and a home. That's all."

Morgan shrugs.

"You won't change my mind over supper, so let's not rehash this topic. Since we are alone, I did want to ask you something. I met an old wise woman in the autumn. She came here looking for a place by the hearth for a night. Idris might have minded, but he was too indisposed to care. We spoke long into the night—the poor woman probably wanted to sleep, but she knew so much that I couldn't help myself. She told me herblore that not even you taught me, and she had much to say about the world beyond this one."

"What do you mean? Was she a Christian convert?"

"Not at all. In her youth, she was a handmaid to a priestess of the old ways who had been trained in Eire. The old ways speak of a world of elementals, spirits that control the shape of the physical world. That's why the druids always gather in sacred groves, to better communicate with the spirits there." Morgan leans forward, her eyes wide. "Have you ever seen such spirits? Surely, the lauvan you see are connected somehow."

I shake my head.

"This isn't the first I've heard of spirits, but I've never seen anything to convince me they are real. Sorry, Morgan. Why do they interest you so?"

"The old woman spoke of how the priestesses used to harness the power of the spirits to perform great feats. The

135

stories she told! It was mesmerizing. How I longed to enter her tale, gather the power of spirits for myself, escape this dreary life and soar with the wind." Morgan's eyes have a faraway look, and her face holds such hope and peace that I almost wish that such a thing were possible for her.

"I've never seen such feats. Do be careful should you ever encounter them. People get hurt when they meddle with things larger than they can comprehend."

Morgan's eyes focus on me with immediate intensity, and her ruby lauvan grow jagged.

"You're as bad as Idris. Are you trying to put me in my place, stupid woman that I am? Trust me, I have enough men controlling my life without you barging in with your unwanted advice. I thought you might understand, but apparently not."

"I only wanted to warn you to be safe."

"I'm sure." Morgan folds her arms. "Your horse is likely ready, when you're done eating. Don't let me keep you from your important manly business, traveling when and where you please. I'll just sit here with my spinning."

Morgan's lauvan make her appear as prickly as a hedgehog, and I wonder how I keep misjudging her. I don't know whether the tales this wise woman told were truth, but I stand by my advice. My own explorations with lauvan have taught me caution. But Morgan has heard enough from me. I shudder inwardly at the thought of being trapped in this dwelling forevermore, with people I dislike, unable to leave at a whim as I always do, and my heart breaks for Morgan. But she has heard enough advice and pity from me, and I have nothing else to offer that she wants.

"Goodbye, Morgan." I stand. "Thank you for the meal and the conversation. Should you ever need assistance," I glance at her wrists again. "Please send for me."

"Farewell, Merlin," she says without rising. Her lauvan

remain prickly. "Give Arthur my love."

CHAPTER XIX

The meeting is in the afternoon, but the cupcake shop is closed Wednesdays, so I enter the store unimpeded. I'm late due to an animated conversation with Alejandro about the nature of belief and lauvan gathering. There won't be a chance to mingle and chat with the other members, nor an opportunity to look at the notebooks in the library.

People are filing into the central meeting room when I open the door to the common area. I move toward a straggler. The young woman smiles at me warmly.

"Afternoon," I greet her. "I'm a little late. Can you tell me what this meeting is about today?"

"We're preparing an amulet," she says. "We do it quite often—it takes a number of sessions to make even the weakest amulet—but everyone is here today to finish up this one. It's a biggie."

"How does one prepare an amulet? What's the process?" What am I getting myself into?

"March will lead us in a session to give the amulet more spiritual presence." She pats my arm. "Don't worry, it's easy, and March gives full instructions. You'll be fine."

She leaves me with this inadequate explanation and walks toward the meeting room. We are the last to enter, so I follow her and find a seat near the back. As with so many things in life, I'll have to find out through experience.

Everyone is seated in rows, hushed and looking forward in expectation. March stands in front, her face as calm as her lauvan. She gazes over the pedestal, on which lies a silver ring. It is liberally covered with multicolored lauvan, but not so thickly that I can't see a large blue sapphire nestled in the silver band.

When we are all seated and hushed, one member closes the doors with a soft thump. March smiles at us all.

"Good evening, my friends. Thank you for coming. This is an important, even momentous event. It is the penultimate step to the beginning of a new world. Everything we have done so far has been in preparation for this event. Tonight, we will prepare the final amulet to bring the spirits to the physical plane. Once this amulet is prepared and we have collected the grail from the shipwreck, we will have everything we need to perform the final ceremony. The spirits will join us, our senses will be opened, and powers beyond imagining will be ours."

There it is, laid bare. This evening brings Potestas one step closer to channeling an elemental spirit into each human host who sits in this meeting room with me. Each person here, innocent or unscrupulous, generous or greedy, pure or evil-hearted, will have the power to control the elements, just as Drew did when he tried to murder me.

I think back to Wallerton, when Anna communicated with the spirits on the mountain. I watched while the spirits siphoned away Anna's lauvan, and Anna grew weaker until she fell unconscious. As much as March thinks she knows, Potestas is playing with forces that they don't understand.

Not only is the rest of the world in danger from this group of power-hungry egomaniacs, they in turn are in danger from the spirits. This must stop. I must stop it. Suddenly my plan to wrest away the grail from March seems laughably inadequate, and I hope August has some ideas.

"Please," says March. "Close your eyes, and I will lead us in our ceremony."

Everyone obediently closes their eyes. I keep mine half-open to watch the proceedings. March places one hand on either side of the ring and closes her own eyes.

"Take deep, slow breaths. One." She breathes in. "Two.

139

Feel yourself descend into a place of deep calm, where your most fervent desires, hopes, and dreams dwell. Be in that place in this moment, feel them fill your heart."

I raise an eyebrow. I didn't expect a meditation session, and nothing is happening yet. I wonder how long this ceremony will take.

"Once you are in that place of peace and intent, send those hopes, dreams, and desires out into the room. Let them join with the hopes of all the others. Channel them onto this ring before me. Believe, believe with all your being, that this ring will grow in power and strength with your faith, that it will bring us one step closer to the sprit connection we all crave. Believe with all your strength."

One by one, lauvan detach themselves from the audience and float slowly toward the ring. Reds, blues, greens of all descriptions, golds and silvers and grays, the deepest velvet purple and the palest ivory, all twist in coiling spirals to the front. They descend like softly drifting feathers onto the ring and wrap around it tightly. After a few minutes of this, I can no longer see the ring. March continues to speak about hopes and spirits in an even, chanting tone, which must act as a mantra to help the audience stay in a meditative state.

I stare, openmouthed, at the spectacle. I have seen it before, of course. Any religious worship has a similar scene. Generally, the lauvan drift aimlessly into the air but sometimes attach to a nearby cross or relic. I didn't expect it here, though. Not in a room full of such varied people, not led by a businesswoman behind a cupcake shop. I close my mouth with grim certainty. March and her followers know what they are doing.

March stops her chanting, and one by one the audience members slow their lauvan shedding and open their eyes. March floats her hands above the ring, which now pulses with multicolored lauvan. She closes her eyes.

A writhing mass of blue lauvan rises from under her shirt where a necklace of power must hide. The strands slide down each arm and converge on the lauvan surrounding the ring. Within seconds, there is a huge ball of blue lauvan that covers the ring and March's hands until neither can be seen. It pulses once, twice, thrice.

Then the blue lauvan slither back up March's arms and dive under her shirt. Left behind are the lauvan of the ring, but they are multicolored no longer. Instead, they are the same blue of the lauvan from March's amulet. March's wine-red lauvan shudder from excitement, one of the few emotions I've seen from March. She opens her eyes and lifts her arms with a triumphant smile.

"It is done!"

The audience cheers and claps. I shake my head in wonder until I remember my place here and clap alongside my fellow Potestas members. What happened here? How did the blue lauvan, presumably water lauvan from an elemental, change the color of the ring's strands? Or did they take the multicolored threads in tribute and replace them with their own? And how can I find out?

CHAPTER XX

March ends the ceremony with a few parting congratulations, and the audience stands and mills about in a disorderly shuffle toward the exit. The faces that surround me are excited, hopeful, eager. I stand slowly, willing to let the majority leave rather than fight dozens of people flowing toward the door. Before I reach the aisle, March materializes beside me. The gap between her followers closes behind her.

"Merry. A word, please," she says once in hearing distance.

"Of course."

Onlookers eye me curiously as they pass. March gestures for us to sit down once more.

"Thank you for volunteering your time and energy on this mission," she says.

"One might even say a quest," I say. She laughs heartily.

"For the grail? Just so. I appreciate your volunteering, since it will make the journey much safer. We're lucky to have you—diving certification isn't widespread."

"When do we go?" I want to stop the thanks, unnecessary since I will subvert her plans at sea.

"That's why I'm here. The boat is ready and waiting. Ideally, we would leave tomorrow, but it is really up to you."

My eyebrows rise. March is eager to retrieve the grail.

"I'll have to find a substitute for my classes that day, but it shouldn't be a problem."

"Excellent. Pack an overnight bag—the journey will take the better part of a day each way. We should arrive home midday on Friday, all going well. Come to the Fraserside Marina at noon tomorrow and look for the *Spirit of the Sea*." She stands. "Thank you again, Merry. I look forward to completing our quest together." She smiles at the word.

"May our journey prove fruitful." For me.

It's another hour until I pick up Minnie, so at home I jump in the shower to freshen up. Women in this era have much higher hygiene standards than those in previous centuries, and I always aim to please.

It isn't until soap is lathered over my body that the voices start. I curse and scrub faster. This is ridiculous, and I don't know how to stop it. Perhaps I can be quick, and they won't bother me for long.

Are the spirit lauvan in the water affecting mine? I examine my lauvan hastily, but the strands in the water flow smoothly over my body with no entanglement. My own cloud of loose strands wraps as tightly as they can around my body for protection.

The voices grow louder, more insistent. Individual shouts rise above the rest, with cries of "*Listen!*" and "*Hear us now!*" and "*The son!*" I grip my head in frustration and fear.

My vision tunnels, in and out again, and I rub my hands through my hair to rid it of lather. I must get away from the water before I fall into a trance I can't escape. My vision narrows once more, but I slam the tap off.

The last of the water circles down the drain and carries the fading voices with it. I lean my forehead against the cool tile of my shower. My breath comes in a heavy pant, accelerated by my close call.

This is insane. I can't even clean myself without peril. It occurs to me that tomorrow I will be on a boat in the middle of the ocean. This can't go on. I must figure out how to control the voices, even if their untold messages are tantalizing.

I grab my towel and dry off in a rush then throw on pants and head to the living room. My half-hearted attempts to research blocking strategies in Braulio's notebook didn't turn up much, but I'm certain there is more to find.

I feverishly flip through pages, scanning Braulio's notes to find mention of blocking, defense, or water. There are pages after pages of notes, reams of material, but I don't find something of interest until halfway through.

This is another instance of using one element to impel or counteract the action of another element, in this case using fire for protection against water. The author of this book indicated its use by those in peril from flooding, common in his region. Water will be repelled, and the user strengthened and bolstered by the spell. It involves lighting a candle and repeating the following prayer...

I read through the litany then jump to the kitchen for a candle, paper, flint, and pocketknife. It's a matter of moments for my practiced hands to create a spark that lights the paper and then the dry wick—matches are too fallible, so I've never bothered relinquishing my flint—and the candle's flame flickers at the ready. I hold it before me and chant the short prayer, which is an invocation to a god of fire.

The first time through, nothing happens. The second time, the ephemeral lauvan of the flame solidify and reach orange tendrils toward my own waving cloud. The third time, they gain enough momentum to touch mine and intertwine with the brown strands.

I keep chanting, delighted that something is happening. Good old Braulio. More orange lauvan stream from the little flame and weave throughout my own. A wave of nausea passes over me, and I swallow. Then my knees weaken and wobble, and it's all I can do to stay upright. I allow myself to kneel on the ground to avoid dropping the candle. My eyes widen. I'm supposed to be strengthened, according to Braulio. What is happening?

Vertigo spins the room around me. I can't continue this test. Something is not right. Perhaps Braulio wrote down the inscription wrongly. I blow out the candle, but the orange strands remain trapped in my lauvan. I pick each one out, and as they slither away from my lauvan, they melt away into nothing.

When all trace of orange is gone, my head stops spinning and my stomach settles. Clearly, something was mistranslated. Perhaps water needed to be present to counteract the fire lauvan within my own. I'm tempted to try it again in the shower, but my stomach recoils from the memory of nausea, and I flip through the book again to find a different spell.

Braulio lists another incantation, this one also short but without the need for a candle. It doesn't sound quite as effective, but I memorize it just in case.

I pause my search to dress for my date with Minnie. Alejandro walks in the door as I exit the bedroom.

"So?" he says immediately. "How was the meeting? What happened?"

"Right, yes, Potestas."

The incident in the shower drove the ceremony from my mind, but at Alejandro's words it comes flooding back. I wonder what to tell him and decide on a pared-down version. He and Jen are already too worked up about Potestas, and I am handling the situation. There is no need for Alejandro to be more involved than he already is. I will figure out how to hush the voices before my ocean voyage and then stop a tsunami and take the grail away from March. It will be fine.

"There was a lot of chanting and closed eyes," I say. "They attempted to transfer their lauvan onto an amulet, to strengthen the connection to the spirit world. Once there was enough, March used her own amulet to turn the lauvan to elemental strands." I omit the part about this amulet being the last piece of the puzzle before the grail arrives. "Oh, and I'll be gone tomorrow at noon, overnight. We're fetching the grail. As always, you're welcome to anything that's in the fridge while I'm gone."

"Tomorrow?" Alejandro blows air past his lips. "Should we be finding higher ground?"

"Have a little faith. I'm sure it will be a piece of cake to dismantle." I'm not sure at all, but Alejandro's worried face needs reassurance. To my surprise, he looks an odd mixture of hurt and disappointed.

"I can help you if you need it, Merry. You know that, right?"

I pause, undecided. The obstacles are piling up. The tsunami, my subterfuge within Potestas, the voices I still haven't controlled—but I don't want to involve anyone else further. And I've sorted out worse on my own. I can handle it.

"Thanks, Alejandro. I know."

Alejandro nods tightly.

"I'm going to the pub with Liam. I guess you don't want to join us."

"I have a date with Minnie."

Alejandro grins.

"I understand."

146

I ring the buzzer of Minnie's three-level apartment building, its window frames freshly painted white. She answers quickly with a crackle of static.

"Hi, Merry. I'll be right down."

Minnie appears in another fetching sundress, the blue of a hot summer's sky. Her lauvan squirm happily when she sees me, and mine wave back. Her hair drapes over her shoulders in loose waves.

"Fancy a walk before dinner?" I ask. "It's a beautiful evening."

"That sounds great. I love the sea breezes on the coast— when I moved here, I found the closest place to the ocean I could afford, and I haven't moved since. The apartment has seen better days, but the location is worth it."

"Where did you move from?"

"I was born and raised in Calgary, did my degree there too. But a few years ago, something called me out here." She shrugs with a smile. "I can't explain it. I only knew a few people. Most assume I came for the weather or the sea, but it felt like more than that. It felt like I belonged here. Have you ever felt that?"

I consider the endless locations I have lived in my long life.

"Never for a place. People make me feel that way."

Minnie nods in understanding.

"I get that. Maybe that's why I don't feel ties to Calgary anymore, since my parents passed away."

"I'm sorry," I say with heartfelt sympathy. Minnie's lauvan swirl slowly, tightly, with the sorrow she still carries.

"Thanks," she says. "I know you know how it feels."

We walk in companionable silence for a few moments.

"I must admit, I was surprised to see your text," I say. "I felt sure that you had reconsidered your stance on dating a former client after last time."

147

"I did think about it," she says. "Ella tried her best to dissuade me. I'm not certain why I texted—I shouldn't have, really—except that I really like you, and it felt worth the risk."

The only answer I'm capable of giving is a returning smile to her shy one. We walk a little further with my lauvan dancing from Minnie's proclamation. Chatting people pass us, cars trundle by, but I'm only aware of the swish of Minnie's blue dress and the warmth of her body near mine.

A car honks loudly right beside us. Minnie shrieks and grabs my hand. Her warm fingers slide into mine as if they belong there. She laughs in relief when she realizes the noise was only a car horn.

"That scared me!" She notices her hand in mine and blushes. "Sorry."

"Don't be." I squeeze her hand lightly before she can pull away. In return, she laces her fingers through mine, and we continue along the road, hand in hand. After a silence alive with warmth and a soft palm, I speak.

"Any more dreams? What do you think about when I'm not there?"

Minnie squeezes my hand with a laugh, but her lauvan tighten. Is it from fear or embarrassment? It's difficult to tell.

"A few. Last night we were on an old sailing ship. You had long hair, big floppy boots, and those silly short pants that they used to wear before the French Revolution. The waves were huge, but you held onto the ropes and laughed then pulled me closer, so I could lean out over the edge to see dolphins playing in the bow wave. Then, another night, we were in a large room lit by a roaring fire and torches on the walls, and you were playing a harp and singing to a crowd of people. I held a feather and a thick piece of paper in my hand, except it was soft and pliable, not like paper at all." Minnie exhales. "Bizarre, isn't it? What is wrong with my brain?"

"It is bizarre," I say slowly. I recall the first scene as if it were yesterday. I amassed a sizeable fortune in Venice in the late seventeenth century and used it to indulge in a life of frivolity. Then I met Zanetta, and she brought me down to earth in the best way possible. That first spring we met, I took her to sea in my ship, and we sailed for Sicily. We stayed in my summer manse on the eastern shore and made love until the sun broke over the horizon of the glittering Ionian Sea. I wonder if Minnie dreamed about that.

The second dream could have been from many different eras, except for the detail about Minnie holding a quill and parchment. The most likely scenario is of my time in Breton in the late twelfth century. My wife Marie was a poet and would often transcribe my rough *chansons* into far more polished poetry.

Either way, these dreams of Minnie's are too close to my truth for comfort. What is going on? Why are my memories playing in her dreams? I don't know how I feel about having my past reviewed for someone's nightly entertainment.

Minnie turns us around a corner, and the ocean appears between buildings, glittering in the evening sun, a bronze sheen making it look like molten metal. It's busy with picnickers, people playing volleyball, and children splashing in the shallows. Past the din of the happy crowd another sound emerges.

The voices. Damn it, not now. My footsteps slow, but I try to ignore the voices as they grow louder.

I must miss something that Minnie says, because she looks at me oddly.

"Are you all right?"

"Fine, thanks." My voice sounds strained, despite my best efforts to control it. "Almost ready for dinner?"

"Sure. Let's walk along the beach for a few blocks. We'll

149

be really close to the restaurant then."

I grit my teeth but give a semblance of a smile.

"Sounds good." I can ignore the voices for a few minutes, surely.

The voices grow louder, more insistent. The beach sounds fade until all I hear is shouting. My vision starts to tunnel. I let go of Minnie's hand and cling to a nearby lamppost. Feverishly, I recall the words of one of Braulio's incantations, and start to mutter it under my breath.

This incantation isn't as showy as the fire one, but the voices immediately flicker and fade. My vision stabilizes. Although I can't reduce the voices to less than a dull roar, at least I can see again. Minnie's hand is on my back, and I can finally hear her.

"Merry! Talk to me. What's going on? Are you okay?"

She rubs in comforting circles, and even through my preoccupation her touch is balm. I shake my head in a vain attempt to rid my ears of the roar.

"I—I, uh…" I'm too shaken to lie. Clammy sweat beads on my forehead. "I started hearing voices, and I can't figure out how to make them stop."

Minnie's hand stops on my back. She takes my arm in a firm grip and leads me to a nearby bench. The couple occupying it take one glance at my pale face and leap up to give us space.

"When did this start?" she asks in her professional voice, calm and collected.

"I don't know, a week ago, perhaps." I take deep breaths to calm myself.

"And these voices, what do they say?"

I start to laugh at the absurdity of this. Minnie must think I'm having a psychotic episode. I know quite well that the voices are spirits, but there's no way I can tell her that.

"If you needed another reason not to date a former client, there it is."

"I'm not thinking that at all." A hint of exasperation colors her voice, then it softens. "I'm more worried about you. Hearing voices is often symptomatic of—well, I strongly suggest you have a proper evaluation. Don't try to handle this by yourself. There are things we can do to help."

"I doubt that," I mutter. Minnie shakes my forearm gently.

"Please don't say that. I want you to be well, Merry. Please let me help. I'll set up an appointment for you, shall I?"

"Fine." I look at her concerned face and relent. "Sure, thank you." I have no intention of going to any "evaluation," but I don't want Minnie to worry about me, and this seems to be the quickest way to lessen her fears. I sigh past the din of the voices. "I don't know that I'm up for dinner anymore."

"Of course, of course," she says quickly. "Whatever you need. Do you want me to drive you home?"

"No need, I can manage. Let's walk back to your house. I left my car there."

Once we turn the corner away from the beach, it's a quiet walk, both in my head and between Minnie and me. I don't know what to say and am already mourning the loss of our burgeoning relationship. If she wasn't concerned about dating me before, she certainly will be now. I picture her friend Ella, with a smug "I told you so" written all over her face.

In front of her building, we stop. I look at Minnie, a few strands of her navy blue lauvan swirling over each eye.

"I'm sorry," I say. I wave my hand in a vague circle. "For this. Not working out, I mean. I really wanted it to."

"I'm not going anywhere," she says, suddenly fierce. "Stop taking on the world by yourself, Merry Lytton. You'll go home, have a good night's sleep, set up that appointment, and call me the minute—the *minute*—things go south. Do you hear

151

me?"

I can't look at her intense face any longer, and gaze instead across the road while I control my emotions. I nod. She puts her soft hand on my cheek to turn my head around, then lays her lips against mine. It's a brief kiss, but so sweet that it leaves me with eyes closed and mouth wanting more.

"Good night, Merry," she whispers, then walks to her door without another word.

CHAPTER XXI

By the time I pull the rental car into its underground parking space, I have convinced myself that Minnie's care and concern at the end of our truncated date were a result of her psychologist training and her desire to help people. Almost certainly, she will have no interest pursuing a romantic relationship with me in the future.

Despite that kiss.

I don't want to go to my apartment yet, only to pace the living room like a caged animal. My apartment complex has landscaped grounds, so I walk outside and stride along the meandering paths.

Minnie won't date me anymore. I've certainly ruined any chance I had of that. Damn spirits. It doesn't really matter, since we wouldn't have been together for long in any event. But then I think of her sweet smile and the blush that rises to her cheeks at the slightest teasing, and I groan in frustration. How could I let these damn spirits destroy what I have with her? Not that it was much. Not that I could ever let it become anything.

I kick a rock on the ground and it skitters away in the dusky gloom to clang against a metal pole. I look up. I'm at the outdoor swimming pool on the opposite side of the building from my balcony.

A pool. Full of water.

As if they were waiting for me to notice, the voices scream all at once. They hammer me with a barrage of sound, and I am completely unprepared. My vision tunnels and I can see nothing, hear nothing except for the roar of shouting voices. My feet stumble forward, my hands claw at the gate to the pool, and there is nothing I can do to stop moving. The voices have complete control.

I shuffle forward, hardly aware of doing so. My next step lands on nothing, and I pitch into the void. Cool water envelops me. Water lauvan touch my own strands, caress them, and some of the voices change from a shout to a song. Individual voices become clear and sharp.

Water fills my mouth, covers my sightless eyes. I try to recall Braulio's incantations, but even if I could remember the words, my mouth won't move. I concentrate on speaking the words in my head, but nothing happens.

"Listen, son of he. Listen."

"It is time."

"Will you hear us now?"

My shoulder nudges the rough bottom of the pool. I wrack my brain to find some way out of this, but nothing comes to me. For fifteen hundred years I've managed to emerge victorious from every predicament, but when I encounter spirits, I am left bewildered and out of my depth. Is this it? This is how I will finally meet my demise, at the bottom of an eight-foot swimming pool?

Strong hands grasp my shoulders and haul me roughly up. I am powerless to assist, sightless and immobile as I still am. Someone pushes me onto the deck of the pool, and the voices shout angrily behind us. Then I am dragged by my arms away, through the gate, and over closely trimmed grass. The voices fade, and I cough water from my lungs.

Once the coughing fit subsides, I open my streaming eyes to see the face of my savior. Alejandro gazes at me with worry and frustration in his eyes.

"Thank you," I gasp and flop onto my back, spent. "You saved me."

"I didn't know if you wanted to be saved. Are you going to tell me why you jumped into a swimming pool to drown?"

Alejandro thought I was trying to kill myself? I suppose it must have looked that way.

"Yes. Let's go upstairs where it's dry. I have things to tell you."

"It's been going on for about a week," I say to Alejandro once we have dried off and put on clean clothes. I found him waiting for me on the balcony with a beer at the ready. "At first I didn't understand what was happening—all I could hear was indiscriminate shouting on occasion—and it wasn't until I realized I could only hear them when water was nearby that I concluded they were water spirits."

"And you're sure? What do they say?"

"I'm fairly certain. They keep mentioning something about a son and father, wondering if I know something. It's all rather vague. I haven't been able to hear more because I fall into a trance if I let them take over."

"Have you tried anything to stop them?"

"There were a few incantations in your grandfather's notebook, but they were ineffectual. One was a clever little spell that wove fire lauvan in with my own as a barrier for the water lauvan, but it made me feel terribly nauseous, so I stopped. It was supposed to strengthen, so something must have been lost in translation."

Alejandro takes a slow drink from his bottled beer.

"Unless you're different," he says, his tone contemplative. "It's a spell to protect against elemental lauvan, and you were affected by it. It reminds me of when you made that lauvan barrier over your front door, and you couldn't pass through, even though Jen and I could."

155

That was when Drew and his air spirit were attacking me, and I tried to make my apartment spirit-proof.

"What are you saying?"

Alejandro shrugs.

"I don't know. You don't have any idea why you have your powers, do you? Or why you never die? I wonder what the connection is between that and how you react to elemental barriers."

I purse my lips and blow through them in thought, then take a deep draft of my beer. I don't know what to think about that. I suppose it makes sense that my ability to see lauvan is related to the elemental lauvan that surround us all, but how? Are there strands wrapped up with mine, like those entangled with August's? I dismiss that thought almost instantly, but then recall the thin brown threads among my thicker lauvan. I assumed they were mine, simply thinning from centuries of existence, but what if they are not? A yawning void of frightening new possibilities opens before me, and I long to experiment with the thin threads.

"You said the spirits were talking about a son and a father. Do you know who?" Alejandro looks up at stars appearing in the dusky sky.

"My impression was that they were talking about me. As if I'm the son." I shiver. "I've wondered about my father my entire life, written off the mystery too many years ago to count. You understand how I am intrigued."

"Then who is your father, and how do the spirits know?" Alejandro releases a long breath. "Let's focus on the immediate threat. I know you want to know about your father, but how about you don't drown first?"

I nod reluctantly, but Alejandro is right. Knowing who my father is, whatever the spirits know, won't matter much if I'm dead.

"I've read the notebook thoroughly, but your grandfather's research is unfortunately coming up short."

Alejandro taps his fingers on the glass of his bottle in thought. Then he sits up straight and looks at me with a gleam in his eye.

"Is the Potestas library still open?"

CHAPTER XXII

It is fully dark now, but the door to Sweet Thing is still unlocked. Inside the dim store interior, I touch Alejandro's shoulder.

"Wait. We can't enter as ourselves. March stops me when I enter the library, and you aren't a member."

"Are you going to change our looks again?" Alejandro asks with an eager tone. "Because I have a few suggestions."

I chuckle.

"We'll need to look like members, so your form is predetermined, I'm afraid."

I reach for Alejandro's lauvan, and he closes his eyes with an air of patience. He is very accepting of all this. I suppose his grandfather Braulio introduced my strangeness to him years ago. It takes a few moments of fiddling and knotting, but eventually Ben stands before me, the young man from the other night. I can't recall the exact details of his visage, but it will hopefully be close enough to remain unnoticed.

While Alejandro runs his hands over his new face and peers into the reflective window of a refrigerated display case, my fingers touch my own lauvan. The only members I can recall in detail are Anna and Esme. I dismiss Anna from consideration, as she is too important within Potestas to escape notice. As well, she is likely to be here tonight, given her involvement. Esme, however, is an excellent candidate. I tweak the necessary lauvan, pulling threads here, twisting others there, until I am confident that Esme's form will emerge at the final pull.

My body transforms through a breathless nothingness to a shorter vantage. I adjust my stance to accommodate the heavy breasts and female hips of middle-aged Esme. It always feels more foreign to be a woman than to be an animal, perhaps because I expect to change drastically within an animal form, and not so for another human. Alejandro whistles.

"I can't decide what is more amazing, turning into an eagle, or being able to spy using someone else's body."

I grin.

"Stick around, and it's always an adventure, right?"

"Exactly."

I walk to the door marked "plumbing," but pause with my hand on the knob.

"Let me look in first, make sure neither of us are already in there."

Alejandro's face wrinkles as he processes my wording. I open the door a crack and peer in.

There are only three people in the common area. A young woman lies on a couch with her eyes closed and ear buds firmly plugged into her ears. An older man reads a book on an armchair nearby, and a middle-aged woman looks in the fridge in the kitchen.

"All clear," I whisper to Alejandro. "Let's go together, no one's looking."

I pull the door open wide and stride in with Alejandro on my heels. The young woman listening to music doesn't stir, and the man reading the book glances briefly at us with disinterest before returning to his reading. The woman in the kitchen closes the fridge door and looks over at us.

"Evening, Ben. Esme, dear, I love what you've done with your hair. A new color was just what you needed for summer. It's so natural, where did you have it done?"

Damn it, I forgot Esme had dyed black hair. I gave myself naturally dark locks, not much different from my own.

"A little place on Commercial," I say with a wave of my hand. "I can't recall off the top of my head. A lovely couple

159

run it. I'll dig up the name for you later, shall I?"

"Thanks, I'd love that." She frowns. "What are you doing here so late?"

"Ben wanted to check something in the library. I thought I'd lend a hand. It's not as if I sleep much these days. Darn insomnia."

"Well, best of luck. I won't keep you." She puts a jar of jam on the counter and rustles in a cupboard for some bread. I bump Alejandro's shoulder with mine and jerk my head toward the library. He follows close at my heels.

Once the library door closes behind us, Alejandro breathes a sigh of relief.

"I don't know if I'm cut out to be a spy." He flops into an armchair. "That was stressful. I'm sweating."

I laugh and sit in another chair.

"It gets easier with practice. Although, I'm annoyed that I forgot about Esme's hair color. It's all about the details." I grab the two notebooks from a side table and toss Alejandro the one marked "Trevor" in black marker on the cover. "Here, these notebooks are a compilation of research from the books in this library. The notes are not organized in any way, and are on every topic imaginable, so our work is cut out for us."

"We're looking for any mention of protection against water spirits, right?" Alejandro peels open the cover of his notebook.

"Correct. And good luck."

The only sound for the next half hour is of flipping pages, and the occasional interjection from Alejandro, which always subsides with a quiet, "Never mind." My notebook is disappointingly lacking in defensive methods, possibly because Potestas is more interested in contacting the spirits than driving them away. I wonder if we'll have to read the source material and despair when I glance at the multitude of volumes that line the bookshelves.

"Merlo," Alejandro says, his voice strained with suppressed excitement. "I think I have something." He offers me his notebook, and I grab it. "At the bottom of the page."

Trevor's writing is a crabbed scrawl after Gail's looping script. The final entry on the second page is written in black ballpoint pen.

It's a suspect source, but the diary of Anton Lapierre from his travels in Haiti has a spell that protects against the ocean lwa, the lwa being spirits of the unseen world. Lapierre describes a ceremony in which seawater, dirt, a burning branch, and the breath of a child are joined together to create a totem of protection when the practitioner hums at a certain frequency. The knowledge of the exact pitch is passed down from elders. When the protection is complete, the practitioner claps three times to finish the spell.

"Yes," I breathe. "This could work."

"And it uses an object instead of yourself," says Alejandro. "So hopefully your lauvan don't get tangled up with it."

I shove my hand in my pocket and extract my flint and pocketknife, still there from my trials earlier. A ripped page from the notebook provides fuel for a fire.

"There are plenty of earth and air lauvan floating around here, and I have fire," I say. "Now I need water."

"Will a glass from the kitchen do?" Alejandro pushes himself off his chair and stands expectantly.

"Perfectly. Grab an empty glass while you're there, will you?"

Once Alejandro bounds out of the room, I fish in my pocket for my car keys. They will do as an object on which to affix this spell. I lay them on the side table next to my flint and the paper just as Alejandro bursts back into the room. He places a full glass of water next to the keys and an empty glass beside it then stands back, his lauvan jiggling with anticipation.

Voices call me from the glass of water, but I ignore them. Hopefully, it won't be long before they stop, if this incantation works.

I read through the incantation once again to commit it to memory. I won't have long once the fire starts burning, so I must be as efficient as possible. The voices grow louder. I strike my flint with the pocketknife until the paper sparks and catches fire, then I drop the burning paper into the empty glass and start to hum. I raise my voice against the shouting from the water glass and vary the pitch of my hum, watching the objects for any sign of an effect.

At a high-pitched hum, tiny, ephemeral orange fire lauvan flash up from the burning glass toward the keys. I hold the frequency and take only sips of air in between my hums. Dancing silver air lauvan float down from the drafts in the room. Long blue threads coil sinuously out of the water glass and over the keys, and earth-brown strands rise from long lines on the ground to the top of the table. All four types of elemental lauvan wrap around the keys in a glowing mass of color, swirling in and through each other, beautiful to behold.

My face must reflect my wonder, because Alejandro says, "Is it working?"

I nod while continuing to hum. I can hardly hear my own sounds over the shouts. Are there enough lauvan now? I bring my hands up and clap once, twice, thrice.

My brows contract. Something is happening to the lauvan around the keys. No new strands join the swirling ball, but the ones that are there pulse. Their light brightens and dims, brightens again. A shiver passes over them, and as one they change color.

Now they are all a uniform brown, the same chocolate color of my own strands. My eyes widen in surprise.

"What is it?" Alejandro says, his voice urgent and low.

162

"Tell me!"

"They changed," I say. I pick up the keys in wonder. "Now they look like my lauvan, not elemental ones."

"It worked."

Only the faintest whisper emerges from the water glass. My face breaks open in a wide smile.

"Yes, it did."

Alejandro punches the air, and I lean back in my chair with relief. I have something, something that truly works in my fight against the voices. It's the most hope I've had in days. And tomorrow, on the water, I hopefully won't be overtaken by the spirits.

CHAPTER XXIII

March wants to meet at noon at the marina, so Alejandro arranged to meet with August at ten. I packed my satchel with a few essentials for our overnight trip, including a surprise for March that I've been playing with all morning, and am dropping it at the door when there is a knock.

"Jen," I say when I swing the door open. "You're early."

"I need to talk to you." Her face is grim, and her golden lauvan are jagged and taut.

"Come in." I wave her to the living room and she marches to the couch. She perches on the edge and waits for me to join her. Her body almost buzzes with nervousness.

"What are you trying to tell me with this?" Jen brandishes a book at me, my copy of T. H. White's *Merlin* I gave her a few days ago.

Here we go. I've been waiting for this moment ever since I gave the book to Jen. Ever since she came to me with her research into my past, in truth. I lean into the couch and place my feet on the coffee table, feigning a nonchalance I don't really feel. Jen will find out the truth today, one way or another. If Jen could see my lauvan, she'd be shocked at the contrast. They are almost entirely still and tense. Waiting.

"What do you think I'm trying to tell you?" I ask Jen back.

"Don't play teacher, Merry," she says in exasperation. "Seriously. What are you getting at?"

I put my hands behind my head and lean back until I'm staring at the ceiling.

"If you can't even guess, then you're not ready to know," I say to a crack in the ceiling above my head.

The couch moves, and I turn my head to look at Jen. She stares at me, frustration and wariness on her face. She's silent.

"Okay, look at your facts," I say, assuming my teaching voice. Jen must hear it, because her lauvan relax at the familiar tone. I continue, "I have strange invisible abilities. I was born in Wales, but you can't find any records. I have no living family. I used to go by a different name only a few years ago, and you've found traces of that name far longer ago than should be possible. You've found multiple photographs and paintings of men who look astonishingly like me, throughout time, all with similar names. And now I've handed you a book of Arthurian legends, which I've said connects everything. What is the logical conclusion?"

Jen shakes her head in hopeless denial. Her lauvan quiver. She closes her eyes when she speaks.

"Merry, are you trying to tell me that you're Merlin?"

I bring my hands down to my knees as I close my own eyes.

"Say it again. Please."

"What, Merlin?"

"Yes." I sigh deeply. "It's been so long since anyone has called me by my true name."

The apartment is silent for a long time. I don't dare open my eyes. Jen's gaze is practically searing a hole in my cheek, but I can't face whatever emotion might be lurking there. Bewilderment? Fear? Revulsion? I've seen it all. I wait until the silence is so loud it rings in my ears. Then I turn my head and look at her.

She stares into my eyes, her face unreadable. Something in my expression must answer her unspoken question, for after a few moments, her face melts into something I didn't expect.

Pity. And sorrow.

"Oh Merry," she gasps. "Has it just been you? For all those years?" When I nod, she cries out, "How can you bear to be so alone?"

I turn my head back to the ceiling and squeeze my eyes

shut, overcome. Her answer cuts deep, right to the center of me. And yet with its very perceptiveness, it gives me hope that I will not remain alone, for the foreseeable future. I will have friends, and that means more than I can express.

"Do you believe me?" I say.

Jen seeks out my hand with tentative fingers. When I respond with a ferociously tight grip, she places the other hand on top.

"I don't know how, but yes, I do. Every crazy word."

I look at her again, and her eyes are moist with unshed tears. Then she releases my hand and slumps into the couch with an exhalation of breath. She looks sharply at me.

"This is for real, right? This isn't your idea of a terrible joke?"

I shake my head.

"Afraid not."

"I don't even know where to start. I have so many questions." She makes a frustrated noise, as if the questions stick in her throat. "The book you made me read. Fact or fiction?"

"Jen. You know my abilities. That hasn't changed. I can see and manipulate lauvan, and I am immortal."

"Immortal, as in you would come back to life if I stabbed you?"

"I hope you aren't planning to. I've never tested my limits. If I am gravely injured, I can always heal myself with lauvan, and with my experience, my reflexes and skills are good enough to avoid injury in the first place, for the most part." I look down at my hands. "I've considered killing myself from time to time, but I've never followed through."

"What?" Jen looks a bit panicky, as if I am planning suicide right now. I tsk.

"Don't look at me like that. If you had lived for fifteen

166

hundred years with no long-term company and no end in sight, you'd consider it too."

"Why didn't you? Not that I'm advocating it, I just wondered, what made you stop?"

"Fear," I say. "Fear of unfulfilled promises, fear of what comes next—is there an afterlife? Would I be a part of it, being as different as I am? Is this my one chance? My sense of self-preservation is as well-honed as it has ever been."

"Fifteen hundred years," Jen says in wonder. "Tell me about back then. Holy cow, you are a walking, talking history lesson." She leaps to the edge of her seat. "You know what happened back then! You have answers to history's greatest questions! Oh my gosh, what historical figures did you actually know? Was Arthur real?"

She's almost hyperventilating. I start to laugh.

"Calm down, Jen. You'll pass out from excitement." I check my watch. "And there's no time. We need to meet up with August, then March is expecting me on the boat. I have to stop a tsunami, remember?"

"Ahh!" Jen lets out an inarticulate growl. "You're leaving me hanging now?" She grips her head in frustration, then sighs. "Fine. But we are going to sit down for about three years and you are going to answer every single question I have. Oh, that's why you know so many languages. And play the harp. And—"

"I promise we will talk later. I look forward to it." I stand and reach out a hand to pull her up. "It always seems unfair how sometimes I have too much time, and other times there isn't enough." Jen pulls herself up and grabs her purse. I touch her elbow. "Jen?"

"Yes?"

"I don't know how to say how much your acceptance, your belief, means to me. I can't count the number of times I've

167

been slapped, run through with a sword, chased out of town as a witch, or had to leave because a close friend couldn't handle my truth."

Jen hugs me around the middle, and I rest my head against her hair briefly.

"I'm glad you finally worked up the guts to tell me." She pushes back and looks at me with a pained expression. "But please stop taunting me with words like 'sword' and 'witch' when you have no time for storytelling. It's unbearable."

I laugh loudly then steer her to the door.

"All in good time."

Jen's lauvan are vibrating, but she doesn't unleash her questions until we reach my yellow rental car to drive to our rendezvous with Alejandro. When the car doors close, she starts.

"What year were you born?"

I press the ignition button and pull out of my parking space.

"Four hundred and fifty, or thereabouts. The reckoning of years was not as important nor as precise back then."

"Of course, of course. And where?"

"What is now northern Wales, in a cluster of houses too small to be called a village. Perhaps there were ten families? I lived with my mother, and my uncle and his family. I never knew my father—I was conceived at the Beltane fires, and he was a stranger to my mother."

Jen stares at me with her mouth wide. When I glance at her with a raised eyebrow, she snaps it shut.

"Sorry," she says. "I was overcome by the fact that this is real. Beltane. Holy cow." She shakes her head, then resumes

168

her questions in a brisk voice. "What then? When did you meet King Arthur? Assuming he was real."

"Oh, yes, he was real." I pause for a moment of recollection. Arthur's face swims before me with its curly brown hair and dancing spring-green lauvan. "My mother died when I was fourteen, and my uncle kicked me out. Frightened of my abilities, you see. I may have occasionally terrorized my cousin, but it was always richly deserved." Jen snorts, and I continue. "It was rough for a while, but I was eventually taken under the wing of an old harper. He taught me his trade, took me around with him to beg for bread in exchange for a night of song. He spoke often of the druids in Eire—Ireland—where he was trained for a time. When the harper died, I traveled there and joined the brotherhood."

"Stop, Merry." Jen puts a hand on her heart. "I might explode from excitement." When I stay silent, she cries out, "I was just joking! Keep talking."

"This will be a long tale if you want my whole life's history."

"This is literally the most I have ever heard you say about yourself. Keep going."

"All right, let's see. I was in Eire for a while, but I didn't have the patience for training, nor the desire to submit to authority."

Jen laughs.

"No change there, then."

"Show me a sixteen-year-old who has. That's where I got these, by the way." I expose the small, green oak leaves tattooed on my inner wrists. "Full initiates eventually earn the whole design—remember I drew it for you a while ago?—but I left well before then. I traveled far and wide, earning my bread through song and by my sword, once I had picked up some skill from the Gepids, a band of Germanic people with whom I spent a winter.

"Eventually, when I reached the age of twenty-three, or thereabouts, a ten-year-old boy approached me while I was fishing for my supper and invited me to his home. His father, Uther, asked me to stay and tutor his son for the winter once he heard I had been schooled by the druids." Jen's breath sucks in at Uther's name. "I remained Arthur's tutor until he was old enough to need an advisor, then a friend. And then a digger of his grave."

Jen puts a hand on my shoulder.

"I'm sorry, Merry." Her voice is sorrowful and a little guilty. "We can stop if you like."

"It was long ago."

"But do you ever really forget the love you have for people who are gone?"

"Never," I whisper. There is a pause, then I clear my throat. "Next question? We're almost there."

"Guinevere. Was she real? And if so, was she the cruel adulteress that the stories say?"

"Real, yes. Did she have an affair? Yes. Cruel? No. And the affair was as much Arthur's doing as hers. They moved past it and grew to love each other very much. Oh, look, we're here."

I chuckle at the frustrated noise that comes from Jen.

"Storytime later, Jen. Now, we try to save the world."

CHAPTER XXIV

Alejandro stands at the end of the parking lot, but he's not alone. Another young man chats with him. He's of average height, with light brown hair and features that are not striking, but the overall effect is quietly pleasant.

"Who is that?" I ask. "Doesn't Alejandro remember why we're here? It's not for a party."

"That's Liam," Jen says. "I met him the other night, Alejandro invited me out for drinks." At my raised eyebrow, Jen swats my arm. "It was just drinks with friends. Anyway, he's a good guy. Alejandro probably brought him along for back-up, since Wayne is working today."

"And what does he know, may I ask?"

"I don't know what Alejandro told him, but presumably nothing weird." She waves her hand over me. "You know."

"I should hope not. Let's meet this infamous Liam."

We get out of the car and walk the short distance to the others. Alejandro waves when he sees us, and both his and Jen's lauvan wiggle at each other happily. I suppress a smile.

"Hi Jen. Merlo, meet Liam. I hope you don't mind I asked him along."

I shrug and offer my hand to Liam, who takes it with a firm grip. His bearing is confident and calm. He looks ready for anything. I don't know why Alejandro invited him along, but he looks up for the job.

"Good to meet you, Liam."

"You too."

"Where did you two meet, anyway?" I ask. Alejandro has been strangely vague about this, but Liam readily answers.

"We're both teaching at a school downtown, for English-as-a-second-language students."

"Oh?" I look expressively at Alejandro, who flushes.

"I didn't tell you because I wanted to make sure it was working out. I'm applying for a visa to stay here."

Jen maintains a straight face, but her lauvan twitch with eagerness at Alejandro's pronouncement. I'm no less interested in his news—it has been a relief to have someone else around who knows me. I'm glad he will stay for a while longer.

"Good news. Unfortunately, we have no time to celebrate. Is there a reason you decided to bring Liam along?"

"I wouldn't take no for an answer," Liam says. His lauvan wave at me, cheerful and brazen. "He let a few things slip, and I love a good scrap. Count me in."

"I hope it won't come to that," I say. "But it might. Liam, I'm not sure what you know, but I'm meeting someone here in secret. I hope she will have information to help me prevent a calamity. She may be followed by a security detail, so it's your job to alert me if they get in the way. You and Alejandro will walk the periphery, and Jen and I will head down into the gardens for our meeting. Shout if you have a problem. It's not a large place, and the acoustics are probably good, since the gardens are built in an old quarry. Any questions?"

"Let's do it." Liam rolls up his sleeves. I glance at Alejandro, who nods sheepishly. Liam is an interesting character—I'll have to get to know him better after this.

It's an overcast day, a cool summer's weekday morning, and few people are at the park as a result. A driveway leads to paths that meander to a large glass conservatory on the crest of the hill. Even though the main flush of flowers is over, the gardeners in charge of the botanical gardens have planted enough blooms to weather the transition from summer to autumn.

Before we cross a bridge to the main lookout, I hold up a hand. Everyone stops.

"Alejandro, go this way." I point over the bridge. "Circle around and watch for suspicious figures. Yell if you find trouble. Liam, take that path and do the same."

Alejandro and Liam both nod and peel off down their respective paths. Jen and I carry on into the sunken garden. I brush past a blooming salvia, and the scent from a nearby lemon verbena drifts over me. The garden is tranquil, a hidden oasis in the city. Cars and city noises are muted in the green bowl, and only the occasional conversation from passing visitors disturbs the peace. I stop for a moment and pull at my lauvan to change into the surfer man that August met before. Jen wiggles with impatience beside me until I walk again.

We turn a corner around a wide buddleia, its conical purple flower clusters waving with our passage. A large man in a pastel blue polo shirt and tan trousers waits beyond. He eyes us, then stands in the center of the path.

"There's a private function here today," he says in a deep voice. "No entry to the rest of the gardens."

"Oh? What's the function?" I eye the man's maroon lauvan, which appear as unyielding and solid as his physical form. "It's a cool day for a wedding."

"But perfect for photos," Jen pipes up. She slips an arm through mine. "Can we sneak a peek? I love looking at wedding dresses. We promise to be quiet."

"Sorry, no entry." The man's expression is unchanging.

It was a good attempt on Jen's part, and I squeeze her arm to tell her so. Then I pull out all the stops.

"Is the function for August Tremblay?"

That provokes a response. The man starts forward, his posture menacing and his lauvan extended toward us.

"You need to leave, now. No entry to the gardens."

"But we just got here," I say. I gently maneuver Jen behind me. The man presses his finger to an earpiece.

"Engaged with two hostiles, a man and a woman. Requesting back-up."

"Now, now, no one is being hostile here except you," I say. "No need for that. We'll be on our way. Forward."

"Back away, now," he barks then approaches me with hands outstretched.

"You asked for it," I mutter then leap forward. I slam into his waiting chest, and while his arms encircle me in what he believes will be an easy grab, I thrust my hands into the lauvan at his side and pull hard.

He drops like a stone, face contorted with pain and wheezing for breath. I hold out a hand to Jen.

"Come on, we don't have long."

Jen stares with wide eyes at the incapacitated guard as she runs past. We jog down the hill.

"That's not your first fight, is it?" she says. I laugh.

"Certainly not. And I suspect it won't be my last, if there are more guards on the way."

Pounding feet behind us turn my prophecy into reality. We pause beside a bucket of tools left by a forgetful gardener, and I am struck by inspiration. I stop and select a trowel and a small garden fork.

"What are you doing?" Jen hisses in panic. "They're coming!"

"Stopping them, of course." I plant my feet firmly on the ground, test the heft of the tools in my hand, and wait for the guard to appear around the bush.

A grim face above a green polo shirt materializes around a

174

rhododendron. I don't hesitate and throw the fork end over end toward my target. It plants itself squarely in the man's leg, and he gasps in pain. The trowel swiftly follows and knocks him unconscious.

"Seriously? Garden tools?" Jen looks incredulous. "That seems a little—underhanded, or something."

"I haven't survived this long by always fighting fair."

Jen opens her mouth to reply, but a man in a purple polo shirt leaps out of nowhere. He wraps burly arms around Jen and pins hers to her sides. She lets out a stifled squeak of alarm, then her face scrunches in determination, and she struggles fiercely. He holds her with ease.

I don't hesitate for a moment. In a flash, my arm reaches up and my fingers grasp some lauvan around the man's head. He grunts in surprise and pain and loosens his grip on Jen long enough for her to wriggle free.

He responds swiftly with a punch to my face that I didn't anticipate. I duck with a hair's width of room to spare. He follows up with a punch to the gut that catches me off guard and forces the air out of my lungs. I double over.

There is a hissing noise, as from air escaping a pressurized container. Almost immediately, the man cries out in pain. My mind races through the possibilities and settles on the most likely. I back away with my eyes shut until I am a safe distance away.

"How long have you been carrying pepper spray?" I ask Jen in a conversational tone. She watches the man writhe on his knees with a queasy interest.

"Ever since Potestas kidnapped Alejandro."

"Good. Although you're one to talk about fighting fair."

"There is nothing fair about three hundred pounds of male muscle attacking a woman who only goes to the gym when she remembers."

"True enough. I never said I didn't approve." I take her hand. "Come on. Let's meet August and get out of here."

There are no more guards between us and our rendezvous point, which is a bench in an alcove enclosed by shrubbery near the pond. August waits for us there, her hands and lauvan both twisting with anxiety. Only the blue water strands entwined around her head flow calmly.

"Hey, August," I say in my best surfer voice. "We don't have long. Your guards are everywhere."

"What?" August's lauvan shoot out in her agitation. "Damn March. I'm moving after this. I wonder if Nova Scotia is far enough away. I am done with her interference in my life."

"Yeah. So, how do we take her down?" I ask. We need to get to the point. March's security will be on us within minutes.

"Right, right. I have some ideas." August waves at her head where the water lauvan twist. "Could you do something about this while we talk? I don't want you to leave here without fixing it."

"Yeah, sure." I put one knee on the bench to steady myself while I examine the water threads entangled with her own. There aren't many, so it shouldn't take long.

"Great," she says with feeling. "I can't stand another minute knowing it's there. Okay, as for March, I know she's planning something big, really soon."

"Yes, we know that," says Jen. She glances around her nervously. "She's going to—"

August holds up her hand.

"I don't really want to know what she's doing, honestly. Now, March keeps things close to her chest. Only her closest confidantes know anything, and even they don't know everything, I'll bet. She has charisma, but truly connecting with people is not something that comes naturally to her. Trust me, I know." She winces as I tug at one of her lauvan by

176

mistake. "How's it going up there?"

"It's coming," I say. "Keep talking." The blue threads slither out one by one and drop to the ground, where they dissolve into transparency.

"She has a safe at her house," August continues. "Who knows what she keeps in there. The key is one of the charms on her bracelet. Good luck getting it, but as a last resort, I imagine she has some pretty interesting stuff in there." The second-to-last water strand falls out at my gentle pull. "And if you really want to get her…" August's voice trails off. I pull out the last water lauvan.

"It's done," I say.

"Yes?" Jen prompts. 'What were you saying, August?"

August looks at Jen with complete blankness. Fear flickers on the edges.

"Who are you?" she whispers. "Who am I?"

Jen looks at me in bewilderment then back at August.

"You're August Tremblay. What do you mean?"

"I don't—I don't—" August looks at us in panic. "Where are we? What's going on? I don't understand." Her lauvan flare up with true terror.

"It's okay, August," says Jen in a soothing voice. "You're in Queen Elizabeth Park. Did you—eat something funny?" Jen moves forward and places a hand on August's shoulder to reassure her. August shrinks from Jen's hand and Jen snatches it back, then looks at me. "Is she tricking us?"

I gaze at August and her tightly woven lauvan, then look down at the fading water strands on the ground with a frown.

"She's not tricking us. If I had to guess, the water lauvan that I took out were affecting her somehow. It looks like she now has severe amnesia." I squat down to look into August's terrified face. "What do you remember, August?"

Tears run down her face, and she sniffles.

177

"Nothing. Nothing! What is happening to me?" Her voice rises in hysteria. "Get away from me, both of you! I don't know you!"

"Can you fix it?" Jen asks me with urgency.

"No, I have no idea what was done, and the water lauvan have faded away." I glance around, but no one is in sight yet. "Come on, we need to go. We're not getting anything else out of her in this state."

"We can't just leave her here!" Jen looks scandalized.

"The guards will find her and take her to March, I have no doubt. We need to leave before they find us again. Come on." I grab her hand and she doesn't resist. We flee the heart-wrenching sobs behind us and run to the stairs. I glance back when we're halfway up and see two polo-shirted men converge on the hedge-lined bench.

At the top of the stairs, two men grapple under a drooping cedar tree. One is the man with the green polo shirt, looking distinctly ruffled. The other is Liam, who bleeds from a gash above the eye. Before Jen and I can say a word, Liam twists with an unexpected motion and wraps his arm around the other man's neck in a stranglehold. The man's eyes bulge, and he pulls at Liam's arm.

I release my lauvan disguise and revert to my true form. Before the man can break free, I run forward and yank at the lauvan around his head. He goes limp and Liam lowers him to the ground. He looks up at me with surprise and interest.

"Nice trick. Care to spill the beans, Copperfield?"

"Oh, probably, later." At Jen's unbelieving look, I say, "Come on, everyone else knows my badly-kept secret, why not this random guy that Alejandro met at work? I grow tired of disseminating. But enough chatter—let's find Alejandro and get out of here."

We jog around the top of the garden's bowl and back over

the bridge without meeting another polo shirt. Alejandro appears from an adjoining path with a large bruise ripening around his eye. He holds his side as if it pains him, and the knots in his forest-green lauvan are clear from here. Jen runs up to him.

"Did you get hurt? Here, let me help." Jen lifts Alejandro's arm and lays it over her shoulders. Their lauvan wrap around one another.

"I'm wounded in a fight, too," says Liam to me. He points at his bleeding forehead with a grin. "Did you bring along another helpful girl for me?"

I laugh, and we continue down the path to the parking lot.

"You're on your own for that. Thanks for coming, though. We needed the extra hands."

Liam's face turns serious.

"Did you get what you came for?"

"Not entirely," I say. Alejandro glances back at me with worry in his eyes. "There were complications."

"What will you do?" says Alejandro, then he winces at the effort of talking. Jen holds him up with more determination.

"I'll have to wing it," I say with a shrug. It's a blow to not have more ammunition against March, but I'm no worse off than before, at least. We reach the yellow Prius and Liam looks at it with a barely suppressed smile.

"Is this yours?"

"It's a rental," I snap. Jen giggles, and I narrow my eyes at her. "I have to meet March at the boat now, I'm already late. Let me fix you two up quickly, and I'll be off."

"Right here?" Jen glances at Liam. I sigh.

"Liam was in too deep the moment Alejandro let him come today." Alejandro looks abashed. "But if Alejandro trusts him, that's good enough for me. I'll let you two do the heavy lifting of explanation, though."

Liam's wound is superficial, and it's the work of a moment to flick the lauvan out of their snarl. Liam flinches at my sudden hand movement, then his face clears.

"My headache is gone."

I don't answer, only turn to Alejandro and work on his deeper hurts.

"I'll do more when I return," I say to Alejandro. "I don't have time to make you feel perfect, so take it easy for a while." I massage a knot and comb through a few others on his side, and he breathes in deeply.

"That's better. Gracias, Merlo."

"That will have to do." I stand straight and fish my keys and wallet from my pocket. "I have to run. You three have some talking to do, so drinks are on me." I pass Jen a few bills. She hugs me briefly.

"Be careful, okay?"

I smile at her in reassurance.

"I'll see you soon."

CHAPTER XXV

I take the highway south, toward the marina where March's boat is moored. Scenarios run through my mind, ways to take the grail from March, each plan as full of holes as the next. Assuming we find the grail, assuming I can disentangle the lauvan to prevent a tsunami, assuming March keeps the grail in an accessible place... I tap my fingers on the steering wheel but come up with no foolproof plan. As I told Alejandro, I'll have to wing it.

I exit the highway and zoom along a side road, past farmland on one side and shipping yards on the other filled with machinery and new cars lined in rows after their sea voyage. The marina is on the Fraser River, the wide body of water that created the flat delta surrounding it. Where there are no shipping yards, deciduous trees flank the river's edge.

I park in a sparsely populated parking lot and take my satchel from the passenger seat before slamming the door closed. It's a simple marina, with only one administrative building next to a chain-link gate that leads to the docks. I key in the passcode that March provided, and the gate swings open.

The dock shifts beneath my feet when I walk down the rows. I pass huge motorized yachts, long sailing boats, and tiny dinghies. When I walk down the second to last row, March appears on the deck of a large yacht.

Business must be good. This is no cramped motorboat. March has a luxury yacht that probably sleeps eight or ten. It gleams a sparkling white and looks ferociously fast.

When March sees me approach, she waves.

"Merry! Glad you could make it. Welcome aboard the *Spirit of the Sea.*"

I come alongside and step onto the stern, where a platform

is low enough for boarding—and diving. I climb up two steps onto the spacious aft deck. The polished wood floor gleams underfoot, and March shakes my hand.

"I hope you have all the equipment we need," I say. "I only brought my personal effects."

"We're fully equipped, not to worry," she says. A middle-aged man walks out of the cabin, wiping his hands on a rag. March turns. "Ah, this is Captain Brown. Captain, this is Merry Lytton. He'll be joining us for our trip."

"Welcome aboard," the captain says in a gruff but friendly voice. "Ever been at sea?"

"Oh, yes," I say. I assume a two-year voyage on a three-masted sailing ship counts.

"Good, good," he says, then turns to March. "Are we ready?"

"Whenever you are, captain." She nods, and a bright gleam fills her eye. She looks at me and winks. "Let us commence with our quest."

March brings me inside the cabin, and I suppress a whistle. We're in an airy seating area with couches and a big-screen TV, which leads into a dining room with a bar that separates it from the galley. Behind the galley wall, the console of the bridge peeks out. I follow March down stairs that descend on the left side to the lower cabin. There are four doors from the landing, and March stops at the forward-most one.

"Here is your cabin," she says. A door opens to a roomy apartment with a full bed and long, shallow windows that run along either side of the bow.

"This will do nicely. I've certainly slept in worse at sea." Lashed to an open rowing ship in the stormy North Sea was the worst.

"It's only for a night, but I hope you'll be comfortable. Once you're settled, you're welcome to join us on the bridge."

March exits, and I place my satchel in a drawer. Just then, the voices start through the open window. I dig my keys out of my pocket and stare at them, but the elemental lauvan that had surrounded them after the spell are now wispy, tenuous things. There is a lifespan on the spell, apparently. I'd better do it again. I open the drawer and extract a water bottle, a piece of paper, my flint, and a gold chain from my satchel. Quickly, trying to drown out the building torrent of voices shouting for my attention, I light the paper and place the open bottle on a ledge. I can't hear the engine start over the shouting, but the ledge begins to vibrate the water in my bottle. I hum.

Fire, air, water, and earth lauvan from my flint weave together. I direct them to the gold chain with my incantation and a nudge from my finger. They twist sinuously together around the chain. Little by little, the voices grow muffled. After I clap my hands and the spell is complete, I place the chain over my head and tuck it into my shirt. The voices are still present, but they are merely annoying instead of deafening, and I feel in no danger of falling into a trance.

I breathe a sigh of relief. That's one hurdle conquered. Grails haven't been retrieved, nor have tsunamis been diverted, but I can travel on a boat without falling into the water against my will.

I climb the stairs and pass through the galley to the bridge, where the captain stands at the wheel and March pours over charts. The boat powers downstream, out toward the open strait.

"Merry, would you like to see where we've located the *Minerva Louise*?" March taps her finger on the chart and I dutifully join her. It's on the far side of Vancouver Island, near where the island emerges from the protection of the cup of mainland which surrounds it into the vast Pacific Ocean.

"Looks like it will be a bumpy ride," I say. "Having no land

183

buffer."

"Fair weather ahead," says the captain. "But expect swells of four meters."

"We're expecting to arrive at the shipwreck early this evening. Slack tide is at seven o'clock. Since it's still light out at that time, I'd like to dive when we arrive to retrieve the artifact."

I glance at the captain, who stares out the window with a casual disinterest that is reflected in his lauvan. March whispers in my ear.

"He thinks we're treasure hunters, knows nothing about Potestas. I pay him enough to not ask too many questions." She raises her voice slightly. "We'll spend the night in a nearby cove, and power back at first light, unless we need to dive again, in which case the next slack is mid-morning."

"So, we have a long trip ahead of us," I say. The voices, although not debilitating, are wearing on me already.

"Yes, so I hope you brought a book or something to do."

"I'll probably have a nap. It was a late night." I gaze out the window and watch a small sailboat gamely cross the mouth of the river.

March's phone chimes, and she checks her texts. Her happy calm devolves into slump-shouldered worry, and her lauvan droop in dejection.

"What's wrong?" I ask. I'm curious to know what could affect her like that. Did a Potestas amulet break?

"It's my sister," she says. "She's had a set-back. She had a terrible car accident a few years ago and lost her memory, permanently. She was living under constant care, couldn't look after herself, not fully, anyway. A few months ago, I brought her into Potestas and tried healing her with the power of the spirits. And wouldn't you know, it worked." She gave a sad smile. "August had her life back. For a while, at least. I knew it couldn't be permanent, not until I complete the full ceremonies, but I had hoped it would last for longer than this. And if it stopped now, for no reason, maybe it won't work in the future either. I don't know. I wanted to give her a real life again. The amnesia devastated her."

"I'm sorry," I say with real feeling. March nods in acknowledgement. I'm sorrier than she knows, since it was me who broke the healing lauvan. Now I'm left wondering about March's true motives. I've pigeon-holed her as simply power-hungry, but she might be coming from a good place. I sigh. It's always the way—evil exists, but so few humans are truly so. I remind myself that March's motives may be good, but the means to her ends are not. Erupting volcanoes, attempted murder, and potential tsunami are hard to justify.

"I'll take that nap," I say after a long pause.

"Sleep well," March says, her gaze turned inward as she stares out at the rolling waters.

CHAPTER XXVI

Dreaming

The long robe of crimson wool of the figure before me sweeps dead leaves along its path. The wearer, a druid named Orin who has seen at least sixty winters, walks with a carved staff for support, although his steps are strong and sure. His thin hair is wispy on top, and flutters in the light breeze that reaches us even in the protection of the trees. His feet tread with little sound, unlike the steady clomping of the two boys behind me. My own feet are noiseless, but then I have had much practice hunting my dinner since I left my uncle's home. Loud feet do not eat, after all.

I am fed well enough at the village where the druid acolytes are housed with village families who are honored to contribute to the training of the order. But despite the ample food provided by my host family—a kind-hearted man, his rosy-cheeked wife, and their two small children—my sixteen-year-old body is always hungry. Never mind. I have suffered worse. I try to breathe deeply and open my mind to all the sensations of the forest.

Rare sunlight passes through the leafy canopy of trees and falls in a speckled pattern on the brown dirt below our feet. Birds twitter above, and the wind rustles leaves with a whisper of sound. The drying soil releases an earthy scent that mingles with the green freshness of plants surrounding us. I open my fingers wide to touch stray lauvan that float past, and they slide over my hands with a cool tingle that makes me smile.

At a tall elderberry bush, Orin stops and turns. His face is stern, but his eyes are soft and reveal his true nature. I'm lucky to have Orin as my master, and I do my best to keep my insolent tongue under control. I don't always succeed, but Orin has more patience than I probably deserve.

"Observe the elderberry," Orin says. The other two boys shuffle around so that we form a semicircle around Orin. Pert is a loud, scrawny boy with feet he despairs of ever growing into and a shock of auburn hair that flies in every direction. Annun is dark-haired, quiet, but with a humorous streak that comes out during our moments of freedom from our studies. We are an unlikely trio but have bonded through our shared experiences under the tutelage of Orin.

"The properties of the elderberry are manifold," Orin continues. He murmurs a blessing, then snaps off a gray twig covered with elongated green leaves. "It can be applied as a fresh paste to reduce scars, the flowers can be dried and steeped as a tea for a cold, and its berries can be juiced to alleviate fever."

"Aren't you going to mention berry cakes? It's their most important purpose, after all," I say before I can stop myself. Pert snorts, and Annun sighs quietly.

"I attempt to teach you what you don't already know," says Orin in a calm voice. I look down, chastened, and he continues his lecture. "There are many purposes for elderberry. Indeed, dried elderberry flowers were even strewn on summoning fires when the spirits were still heard."

The other boys and I glance at each other in bewilderment.

"Spirits, master?" Pert ventures.

"Yes, those which inhabit everything in this world of ours, every rock, tree, river, and storm."

"Do you mean the elementals?" Annun says. "I didn't think they were actual beings."

"That's correct. When they still spoke to us, we called them spirits. They taught us much."

"Why have we never heard of this?" I ask.

187

"There is much to teach, and much to learn," is the calm reply. "You are hearing of it now. The spirits speak to us no longer, so the information is of little pertinence. But the leaves of the elderberry have excellent focusing properties and could allow even the most mundane acolytes to hear the spirits with ease."

"Why did they stop speaking?" asks Pert. We are all fascinated by this unexpected segue. So far, our training has focused on herblore and healing. This is the first hint of any deviation.

"No one knows. The last ceremony at which there was contact that we are aware of was twelve years ago. Since then, nothing."

The elementals, or spirits as Orin has taken to calling them, are a made-up construct, as far as I'm concerned. I can see the secrets of the elements through the lauvan, and I have never seen anything that hinted of sentience. Since I can see what others cannot, I'm confident that I am right. There is no such thing as spirits.

My skepticism must show on my face, because Orin turns to me with a smile.

"I see you do not believe, Merlin. That's all right. Know that there are mysteries in the world, and no one can comprehend everything. Indeed, although I will teach you many things during your training here, and your knowledge will become vast and deep, that is the most important lesson of all."

The sky is overcast, and a fine rain soaks my cloak. I stand outside with Arthur and the fighters of his house to attend the funeral of Morgan's husband Idris. He finally succumbed to his wasting illness and left Morgan a widow. I can't say I have any tears to shed for the man, noisy, brutal, enflaming bastard that he was. Morgan is dry-eyed and performs her duties with composure and enough gravitas to avoid censure. I'm sure that, in her heart, she rejoices at her freedom. Under Roman law, which is followed more by custom than by force, all her possessions would revert to her nearest male relative, in this case Arthur. Arthur will not hear of it, though. He and Morgan will follow the older customs, where a widow has many rights. Arthur has a good heart, but I also suspect he doesn't want to endure the wrath of his older sister, who would never forgive him if he swooped in and took over.

Morgan is flanked by Vivienne and Mordred while she watches her servants lower Idris' body into the prepared grave lined with stones. The body is wrapped in a finely woven linen cloth, dyed a soft blue using woad. A man in a long robe of undyed wool and a tonsure intones in Latin. Morgan has paid a local monk to chant over Idris' body, as it was his wish. Officially, the Romans were Christian, but it never fully took root here in the outposts of the Roman Empire. Now that the Romans are gone, the old ways are followed. But the occasional wandering monk passes through these lands, and there are some who listen. Most of the funeral-goers rustle with boredom while the monk drones on, but they maintain expression of solemnity. The servants, meanwhile, shovel dirt on top of the body, and it is soon lost from view.

We file inside Morgan's longhouse for the funeral feast. Inside, the atmosphere is lighter, as if we have left brooding Idris in his grave and his influence is no longer felt in the house. Morgan is already inside, giving directions to servants and ushering guests to seats by the fire. The smiles that flit across her face as she speaks with her guests are so genuine, it

189

makes me realize how little I've seen her smile since she left Uther's house. I want to go back outside and spit on Idris' grave, but it is likely not the best action for continued diplomacy among the warlords.

I sit between Arthur and Gawaine on a long bench before a trestle table. Guinevere is not with us, as there is no love lost between her and Morgan, and Guinevere didn't want to distress Morgan during her husband's funeral. Servants bring out large platters of cut meat and thick slices of wheat bread, along with delicacies such as pigeon pie and sturgeon stew. With the arrival of mulled wine, the atmosphere changes from subdued lightness to cheerful joviality. Goblets clunk together and greetings are called out between tables. Morgan moves around the room, speaking with guests and thanking them for coming.

When she reaches Arthur, we all squeeze together to make room for her on the bench. She sits between me and Arthur with a sigh and accepts a goblet of wine from a passing servant.

"Plenty of well-wishers here today," Arthur says. Morgan laughs without humor.

"Because Idris was so well-loved." She takes a sip of her wine. "Never mind, it's good to see my neighbors gathered together. It's not often that I visit with them. Perhaps it will be more often now that I have no invalid to tie me here."

Arthur's lips thin at Morgan's bitter tone, but he doesn't dwell on the subject.

"Morgan, what do you plan to do with the fighters of your household, and those who have gathered under Idris' banner? Spring is almost upon us."

"And with it, battle-season." Morgan nods thoughtfully. "You may direct them, for now, based upon one question. What are your campaign plans? How will you use my forces?"

"To battle Saxons, of course," Arthur says with a lopsided

grin. "What else?"

"Good," says Morgan. "That was the right answer. Don't forget, our mother was killed by one. None of them are welcome in our lands."

Morgan beckons to a serving girl. When the girl bends to hear her mistress' will, Morgan whispers an instruction and the girl hurries off. Moments later, she appears with two objects in her hands and passes them to Morgan with a curtsy.

"Here, Merlin." Morgan passes me one of the objects. It's a wooden crucifix of the Christians, carved with an image of their dying god spread out on a cross.

"What do you want with this, Morgan?" I ask with curiosity. "Did Idris convert your house?"

"No, although he considered it near the end. No, I was given it by a wandering monk. I wanted to know, what do you see when you look at it?"

"A wooden crucifix?" I'm puzzled by her question. She looks at me meaningfully.

"No, what do *you* see?"

Ah, she means the lauvan. I lower my voice.

"Hundreds of lauvan of all colors, so thick I can scarcely see the cross underneath."

"More than another object, then."

"Yes."

Morgan sits back with a satisfied smile, then she puts the other object in my hand.

"And this?"

It's a bowl of beaten copper the size of my two cupped palms. It, too, swirls with a thick layer of multicolored strands.

"The same," I say. Morgan nods.

"I thought so. I can almost sense it, the power in them, that there is something more to them than other objects."

I doubt she can sense anything, but what do I know?

Perhaps she can. She would be the first I've ever met, though. I'd love to hold out two crucifixes before her, one with lauvan and one without, to see if she could tell the difference, but finding one without strands from worship might be tricky.

"Perhaps there are other ways to sense—otherness," Morgan says quietly. "Not only your way."

"Perhaps," I say, trying to keep the doubt from my voice. She looks so earnest.

"I will keep searching," she says. "You were schooled in Eire. Could you tell me where? I may send Mordred there to speak to the druids about this."

"Take care, Morgan. You may spend a lot of time searching for answers that aren't there."

Morgan's lauvan bristle, but she tries for a nonchalant response.

"These days, I have only the running of this estate—no children to manage, no invalid to care for—and I find myself with more time than I've ever had. Why not spend it on something that I truly wish to explore?"

I shrug. She deserves a little happiness. If that is what she wishes to do, why not, indeed?

"I will give you directions to the druids. I hope you find what you search for."

CHAPTER XXVII

The last of my dreams are fragmented, filled with nameless shouting that doesn't cease when I open my eyes. My berth rolls from side to side with the motion of the moving boat, and my window reveals small mountains of ocean with green land far in the distance. The sun is shining, however, so I escape my room and join March on the aft deck, where she sits on a deck chair, writing in a notebook.

"Afternoon, Merry," she says with a smile over the roar of the motors. "Sleep well?"

"The movement of the boat is very soothing." If I didn't have someone shouting in my ears, it would be.

"Yes, I always find I sleep better at sea. There must be something instinctual about it—swaying hammocks, rocking babies to sleep—it seems to be a common pleasure."

I nod absently. Are the voices a little louder than they were when I fell asleep? The noise is still manageable, but I find it difficult to think. And thinking is something I need to do right now, since August's promised information didn't materialize. The only plan I have is to somehow lift the grail off March while she's sleeping. It's a plan fraught with difficulties, but it is all I have. And it's all I am likely to come up with, if this noise doesn't cease. I rub my head with weary fingers.

"I see you were interested in the library at the org," March says in a chatty tone. I pull myself together and concentrate on her words.

"Yes, fascinating stuff. Are you finding much of use?"

"Oh, yes, if you read it with the right mindset, looking for connections." She puts her notebook down and leans back. "Trevor and Gail are really quite adept at picking out relevant information from the books they read. Once you look for it, the similarities are everywhere between different religions and belief systems, especially if you view through a lens of knowing the spirit world is behind it all. I've been interested in this for years, but it's only recently that I've figured out how best to reach the spirits."

"And how is that?"

"I used to strive so hard to reach them, but Gail and Trevor have found time and again that reaching the other plane is more about letting go and relinquishing control. You must let the spirits come to you and connect with you, let those connections form organically. It's about nurturing the connection, not forcing it." She laughs. "It's been a learning curve for me, I can tell you. I'm not good at giving up control, not these days. There's too much of that in my past to readily submit to something else. But it's necessary, and the benefits are many."

"Doesn't the tsunami concern you?" I ask in a casual manner. March looks at me sharply.

"Of course it does, of course. It's a terrible risk, and if it does occur, disastrous for some. I just can't see another way forward without the grail. Sacrifices are never easy."

Sacrificing others is easier than giving something up yourself, however. March's lauvan indicate she is sincere in her concern, which is almost more unnerving than if she didn't care. She really thinks her goal is worth lives.

"There are a lot of people at the org, all wanting to connect with the spirits for their own reasons." I lean my back against the railing. "Can I ask, why do you want it?"

"Can you imagine the power?" March spreads her arms wide, and for once her lauvan are as enthusiastic as her body language is. "What good I could do? With the power of fire and air, imagine the revolution in energy. Or water, relieving droughts in impoverished countries, or the homes that could be built for those in need, overnight. And those are only the ideas

194

at the top of my head! Once we have these powers, I'm sure the possibilities will become much clearer."

"You're a wealthy woman, March," I say in a quelling tone. "Surely you can help those in need already."

"But not enough, not nearly enough. Yes, I sponsor a women's crisis support service, and a few other charities in the area. But think of how many more I could help escape terrible situations. The lives I could improve, the justice I could mete out."

I gaze at her in consideration.

"Justice—does this mission strike a personal note for you?"

March's lauvan wiggle with her affirmative, but she doesn't answer my question aloud.

"There is so much good I can do in the world, if given a chance."

I nod. It's harder and harder to concentrate on March's words. The voices are growing louder, and it's all I can do to hold onto the thread of conversation. I grip the railing with whitened knuckles and sway far more than the motion of the boat warrants. I'm too dizzy to let go of the railing and examine my chain. My vision darkens, and the last thing I see is the sky above.

March's surprisingly strong hands grab my shoulders and throw me onto the deck. My vision is still dark, but I manage to bring my hands to my throat. My fingers fumble with the lauvan around my chain, and somehow twist them enough to soften the voices by a margin. My eyes clear, and I'm left panting on the deck.

"Merry, are you all right?" March's concerned face peers into mine. I take a deep breath and release it in a sigh.

"Yes. Bad vertigo for a moment. I don't know what happened, that's not usual for me."

March pats my arm.

"Are you sure you're up for this mission? We can turn back now if you're not absolutely certain."

"No, no. I'll be fine." I try for a weak smile and push myself to my feet.

"Well, perhaps you should rest a little more," she says. "Help yourself to food in the galley."

"Thank you, I will."

I escape the aft deck before March can ask any penetrating questions. My incantation must be reapplied every few hours. Now, I know.

The boat corners the end of the island and motors up the far side. The waves are larger, rolling in from the vast expanse of the Pacific, but the large yacht cuts through them.

Once in my cabin, I take off the gold chain around my neck and lay it on a non-slip mat, along with my flint, pocketknife, paper, and glass of water. I light the paper and quickly say the incantation. The lauvan weave together, with a little help from nudges of my finger. When it is done, I hesitate, then light another paper and say the words again. Another layer of lauvan forms, thinner and weaker than the last. Apparently, this is a spell of diminishing returns. I'll have to reapply it before we jump into the water, but it will do for now.

I slip the chain over my head and then rummage in the drawer for Braulio's notebook tucked in my satchel. I need all the ammunition I can get for this dive. Who knows what I might encounter in the depths? I will be enveloped in water, after all.

There are a few incantations, some ideas for weaving together lauvan from air and earth that I memorize. There isn't

196

a lot of air down there, but I will have bubbles escaping from my regulator. And when we are near the bottom of the seafloor, there will be earth lauvan. The notebook occupies me until my stomach rumbles. A quick glance out of the window reveals a pile of dark clouds mounting on the horizon. I frown. The captain said the weather would hold. Where did those clouds come from? I stir myself and venture up to the common area.

March is in the galley preparing dinner.

"What can I do to help?" I say.

"Ah, Merry. Chop up these carrots, will you? And be extremely careful—the motion of the boat can throw you off your cutting."

"Not to worry, I've been at sea before." Deftly I slice the carrots into sticks for eating raw. March stirs a pot on the stove.

"It's a simple spaghetti tonight, nothing fancy. I didn't cook too much, because we'll be diving soon. We can eat more after our ascent."

"It smells delicious." I take cutlery out of a cupboard and place it on non-skid placemats on the dining room table. March follows with two plates of pasta and we sit.

"Thanks, March," I say.

"Bon appetit," she says. "It will do until we get back. I didn't want to bring more people than was strictly necessary on this trip, so I'm cook and adventurer both."

We begin to eat. I'm surprised by how hungry I am, but breakfast was a long time ago, and there wasn't time for lunch after meeting August. After a few bites, March speaks again.

"We'll be at the site shortly, so after dinner we can set up our gear. The weather is a little dicey, but hopefully it will hold off until we complete our dive. My plan is to drop anchor a few dozen feet from the wreck—we can see it on our sonar—send down a guideline for us, then follow that down to the bottom and use a compass from there. The wreck is on an underwater cliff, but itself is only sixty feet below the surface, so we should have plenty of time to search before our air runs low. Slack tide is for a solid twenty minutes with minimal current for ten minutes on either side, so our window is sufficient, but there is no time for loitering. The *Minerva Louise* is miraculously intact for such an old vessel. There may or may not be overhead environments to worry about. But you're certified for that, so we can explore. Tell me when you reach seven hundred psi on your air gauge, and we'll head back to the guideline and ascend to fifteen feet for our three-minute safety stop. Did I miss anything? Any questions?"

It's been about twenty years since I went scuba diving, and if I hadn't read up about the new standards online yesterday I would be lost. Luckily, my brain is freshly minted with new information, so I smile.

"Sounds like a good plan. And if we don't find anything tonight?"

"Then we try tomorrow morning at the next slack."

I nod and return to my spaghetti. We lapse into silence. It's only now that I notice the movement of the boat over the ocean swells increasing. The sauce on my plate slides back and forth.

"Rough seas ahead," I say. March frowns.

"As long as you're comfortable, I'd like to dive even if it's rough. Once we're under the water, we won't notice."

I shrug and continue to eat. My mind runs over incantations and ways to keep myself safe from trances. After a few minutes, March clears her throat.

"You seem preoccupied, Merry. Is everything all right?"

I can't tell her the truth—that the water lauvan are attacking me, and I'm trying to steal the grail from her—so I take refuge in generalities.

"This is an important expedition we're on. I was considering what might change after this. Plenty, I presume."

"Oh, everything." March's voice grows animated. "We certainly are on a momentous adventure. Once we have the grail, and then perform the ceremony, everything will change." She pauses, then says, "I've spoken at length about what I want to do, but what about you? What do you hope to accomplish with your new-found powers?"

I stare at the spaghetti on my fork.

"I'm not sure I even want any," I say. It's true—I have enough powers of my own, and I'm nervous about how much the humans involved will give up being the hosts of spirits lodged in their bodies. "I'm new to all this. I don't know enough yet."

March laughs gently.

"Give it a little time, I'm sure you will come around. Tonight, you can dream of the possibilities. I find sometimes the hardest part is expanding my mind to think outside my own sphere of knowledge."

I make a noise of acknowledgement, but don't answer. The captain calls out from the bridge.

"Ms. Feynman? We're ten minutes from the site, twenty from slack tide. Better suit up."

"Thank you, captain." She turns to me. "We'll have to continue our dinner later. Pop your plate in the fridge and meet me on the aft deck in three minutes."

"Aye aye," I say, which garners a smile from March. I take my plate to the galley then hurry to my cabin. I slip my surprise for March under my shirt to hide it. One more incantation, one more layer of lauvan on my chain, and I'll be as prepared as I can be. I hope it's enough.

199

Out on the aft deck, I hold onto the railing and take a moment to breathe deeply. The land is close and covered with a dense layer of coniferous trees that extend to the edge of the rocky shore. The trees are dark and forbidding from the ominous clouds that loom overhead. A few drops of rain drizzle on my hair. The sea is much rougher than I expected, and a storm is brewing. A flash in the distance draws my eye. Was that lightning? The noise of the motors is too loud to hear the crashing waves that are evident from white foam spraying the land's edge. A bald eagle surveys us with an impassive glare from a nearby branch.

March emerges and moves to a cabinet against the wall, which opens to reveal two sets of diving gear. She pulls out a large black bag and tosses it to me.

"Here's your dry suit. I've already prepared the other gear, so we'll simply have to check it over and go. There isn't a lot of time to spare."

I nod and unzip the bag. When March turns to open her own, I open the pocket of the larger vest attached to a tank in the cabinet and place the surprise inside. The pocket is zipped up and I'm rummaging through the dry suit bag by the time March turns around.

Thank goodness for the Internet, because I've only ever donned a wetsuit before. I manage to slither into the fleece lining and dry suit without mishap despite the heaving deck, and even pull the neck seal over my head with some semblance of ease.

"Here, I'll zip you up," March says from behind me. There's a rough tugging at the back of my suit, then the sound of a zipper pulling. "Zip me too, please?"

I turn and yank at March's stiff zipper to seal her into her suit. She sticks her fingers into her neck seal and squats. At my perplexed look, she grins.

"Don't forget to let the air out of your suit, otherwise you'll bob around like a balloon."

I follow her lead and trapped air hisses past my chin.

"I've mainly dived with wetsuits in the past," I say by way of explanation. March waves my comment away.

"There's always so much to remember. That's why it's best to dive in pairs, as you reminded me. Your boots, hood, and gloves should be in the bag as well."

"Approaching the site," crackles a nearby intercom. "I'll drop anchor in a minute. You're sure you want to dive in this weather?"

March presses a button on the wall.

"Yes, thank you, captain. We're almost ready. We'll wait for your go-ahead."

March presses a button, which lowers the platform on the stern until it is nearly level with the sloshing water. She sits on a ledge in front of the cabinet and puts her arms through the vest holding her tank. She stands with a grunt.

"I always forget how heavy these things are. Thirty pounds of lead weight as well as the tank—I'm glad I go to the gym regularly."

I sit on the ledge and emulate March's motions. When I stand, my legs working hard to keep my balance on the angling deck under the extra weight, she moves toward me.

"Let me help you adjust your BCD." She plays with the straps of my vest until she is satisfied. While she works, I examine her BCD—short for buoyancy compensation device, I now recall, although when I learned, there was no such thing—and the many hoses and straps dangling from it. I try to remember what I read yesterday.

"All right, time for buddy checks," March says. "I'll do yours first. Weights are in, check." She tugs gently on two toggles on my vest. "The weights are integrated in this BCD, so you'll have to pull these forward if you want to release them."

"Of course." I vaguely remember seeing a diagram.

"Air checks." March pushes a button on a tube attached to my BCD, and the vest inflates. She puts a regulator to my mouth. "Breathe." I oblige, and she repeats with a second emergency regulator before tucking it into a hanging strap. March checks my gauges, looks me over, and declares herself satisfied.

"Now it's your turn," she says.

I repeat all her motions. I'm sweating from a combination of nerves and wearing a sealed suit and fleeces. When I'm finished, she hands me a mask.

"Adjust this to fit your head, put on your gloves, then we're ready to go."

When we've donned our final gear, March presses the intercom button.

"We're ready anytime you are, captain."

"Send down the dive flag," says the captain through the speaker. "Then jump in. I'll come and watch."

March takes a red and white striped buoy attached to a weight and rope and heaves the weight overboard. It splashes and sinks without fuss until all that's left is the bobbing buoy.

"We'll do a backward entry off the boat's platform." says March. "Ready to make history, Merry?"

"Absolutely," I say with more confidence than I feel. We pull on our fins, waddle onto the platform with difficulty due to the swell and hold our masks and regulators against our faces. March counts to three, then we tip over backward and fall into the sea.

The cold water is a shock against the exposed skin on my head, although on the rest of my covered body it's only a mildly cool sensation. I bob up to the surface with wide eyes and take my bearings. I can scarcely see March through the rolling seas, and when she is in a trough she disappears. A flash of lightning illuminates the boat against the backdrop of menacing trees, and I swim quickly to the buoy. There is a mild current despite the slack tide, and I can imagine we don't want to be caught at full flow.

At the buoy, we take a moment to clear our masks and prepare ourselves, a difficult task in the swell. Another flash of lightning brightens the sea. March makes the hand signal to ask if I'm okay, and I respond in the affirmative, although I'm feeling very far from okay. I take out my regulator for one final breath of fresh air then clamp my teeth onto the mouthpiece and let the air out of my BCD to follow March into the depths.

CHAPTER XXVIII

It's a relief to be below the frantic waves and in the quiet of the ocean. For quite some time, as I follow March down the guideline, all I can see are the rope and greenish murk around me. My ears fill with water, and the main sound is the hiss of air into my regulator when I breathe in, and the gurgle of bubbles when I breathe out. The voices are still present and possibly even clearer, but they are faint enough with the application of my charm that I can ignore them for now. There are thousands of tiny plankton floating in front of my mask. The larger ones are even discernable, like the ctenophore that floats by, ridges along its clear, grape-shaped body fluttering in a refracted rainbow of colors.

And everywhere, all around me, are streaming veils of water lauvan. They flow and float past my eyes, twirl lazily in tiny eddies, drift in the mild current. They glow with a faint glittering light that reminds me of bioluminescence. It's quite dazzling.

Before long, the seafloor looms darkly below. March waits for me on the rough rocky ground, hovering expertly a foot above the floor to avoid damaging the plumose anemones attached there. I am not so graceful and bounce a few times before I sort out the correct amount of air in my BCD to float without sinking or racing to the surface. March waits patiently and consults her compass. Once I gain control, she flicks on her flashlight and indicates for me to do the same. Then, she signs for me to follow her and swims away.

I follow, glad for the flashlight to dispel the gloom. Colors other than green and black appear in the small circle of my light's beam, purples and reds and yellows of encrusting growth and small, slug-like creatures. It's quite fascinating, and I'm almost tempted to go diving once I'm back in Vancouver.

My left fin encounters resistance. Did I catch some seaweed? I look back, an ungainly procedure that involves twisting in my cumbersome vest and readjusting air in my suit. There is no seaweed. Instead, some of the water lauvan that dance around me have looped around my ankle.

My heart drops. This isn't usual. It must be connected to the voices. More lauvan wrap around my right foot. I shake it, a slow movement under water, but the strands don't budge. As if emboldened by the success of the first lauvan, more threads join them until my feet are scarcely visible. I kick and kick to no avail.

My mind races through Braulio's notes. Will one of his ideas work? I concentrate on thinking one of the incantations, but since I can't say the words out loud, there is no effect.

I let some air out of my BCD to drop to the sea floor, where my tank clangs on the rock. I gather as many earth lauvan as I can from the surface of the seafloor and pull them tight between my hands. Water lauvan continue to collect on my body, and my lower legs are fully encased by blue strands. My tank scrapes along the bottom, and I realize with horror that the lauvan are slowly, relentlessly pulling me along. I yank the earth lauvan taut and use them to scour my legs to dislodge the water threads.

Little by little, the water lauvan float off. I rub as fast as I can underwater. When I have removed half of the strands, the rest lift off and drift away, glittering with an innocent light.

I suck back air from the effort but try to calm my breathing, partly because it uses air from my tank faster than it should, and partly because the harder I breathe, the more difficult it is to breathe through the regulator, which only increases my anxiety. I kick back to the beam of March's flashlight.

205

A fish passes me, possibly a perch of some sort, and then another. A black shape looms out of the darkness, and the wreck of the *Minerva Louise* emerges. By my estimation, it's an iron-hulled schooner, perhaps sixty feet long. Its two masts collapsed decades ago, but the hull is remarkably intact, although riddled with holes where iron-eating bacteria have nibbled through. March's shadowy figure floats over the top of the gunwale, then down into the belly of the ship. She glances back to make sure I'm still behind her, then her flashlight winks out from view.

My legs jerk down. I look back with my heart in my stomach, and sure enough, the water lauvan are back. Even through the barrier of the chain, the voices shout, too quiet and too many to hear distinctly. The lauvan pull me backward, far faster than I can swim. I scream but there is no one to hear me underwater. My fingers scrabble at the rock passing below, and my gloves scrape over the rough surface before gaining purchase.

I hold on with all my might. I consider pulling out my diving knife to bang my tank—the only noise that will carry far enough for March to hear—but there is no way I can let go of this rock. Already, my fingers slip from the pull of water lauvan. I grit my teeth and dig in. And what would March be able to do?

I'm on my own.

My fingers lose their grasp and I am sucked away to bang against the rocky bottom. Where are they taking me? And why? I shout incantations through my regulator, but the garbled words have no effect. The chain around my neck only prevents me from falling into a trance and hearing the voices, not from lauvan trapping me.

The water swirls me up from the rock bottom, my only hope of a handhold now lost to me. I twist in circles, caught in a whirlpool deep underwater. Glittering threads of water lauvan twist around me in a long funnel, so thick I can scarcely see out. The voices grow louder despite my chain's barrier. I press my regulator to my mouth, terrified that I might lose my source of air.

Fish appear in the funnel, darting in and out of the strands, eyeing me curiously. Their silver bodies glint in the reflected light of the lauvan. A wolf eel emerges through the lauvan and swims around my body as we spin. I suck air from my regulator more rapidly than it can deliver and feel close to panic.

How can I get out of this alive? After all this time, will it be death by drowning? Death by spirits, more like. Perhaps they are a test that I cannot pass, a final limit to my abilities to survive.

And if I can't save myself, I don't have a hope for stopping the tsunami. Even now, March swims closer and closer to her goal. How many will die because of her greed? And there is nothing I can do to stop it.

The funnel parts briefly and the edge of the underwater cliff is clearly visible. Lauvan encircle my arms and pull me down past the edge, into the dark abyss that yawns with unfathomable depth below me. I'm sinking too deep, too quickly. I push the wolf eel out of the way to wrestle my console close to my face and watch the depth gauge. Seventy feet. Seventy-five. Eighty.

Too deep and I will never recover, assuming I ever make it to the surface. There is only one thing left to try. I fumble along the waistline of my BCD until I grasp a toggle in each hand. I take a breath, then yank forward.

My weights slide out of their pouches. I let them go and they sink forever into the darkness.

With the weights gone, I shoot upward. The lauvan

wrapped around my body break away with the shock of sudden movement. I rise with uncontrollable speed and release my breath in a steady stream to keep my lungs from bursting with expanding air. My legs and arms are spread like a sea star to slow my ascent. I hope I have enough time on the surface to fix my lauvan before decompression sickness takes over.

Darkness looms above, and with a start I realize the wreck of the *Minerva Louise* hangs over the cliff's edge. I have one small chance to avoid sickness. My arms reach out, and when the bowsprit passes by me, the long spar that extends from the vessel's bow, I grab it with all my might.

My arms wrench in their sockets from the sudden stop, but I stay put. Air in my dry suit flows to my feet and they rise until I dangle upside down by my hands with my legs straight above me.

I have a chance, now. If I fill my pockets with rocks and take immense care ascending, I might survive this.

I glance at the ship to my left. In the darkness of a jagged hole in the bow, something gleams. Is it metal, perhaps covered by multicolored lauvan? My heart thumps painfully. There it is, the grail. So close. Can I inch toward it, untangle the strands that tie it to the ship? Can I prevent the tsunami?

The dark sea below me boils with glittering light and rises rapidly toward me. Damn. I'm not in safe harbor yet.

The strands surround me in a moment, and the shouting increases in volume again. I am yanked from side to side, but I hold onto the bowsprit with white knuckles.

If I let go, I will shoot to the surface. If I make it to the top, I might not survive because of decompression sickness. The likelihood of the spirits being surprised by my sudden ascent twice is doubtful, however. They will capture me, drag me down to the bottom for their unknown reasons, and I will drown.

It is only a matter of time before March finds the grail. I think of Jen and Alejandro in Vancouver. Will they be safe from a tsunami where they are? I wish I hadn't been so confident. I wish I'd told them to flee to higher ground.

The lauvan pull harder, and my fingers ache with the strain. I am out of ideas, and finally out of time.

CHAPTER XXIX

Out of nowhere, March's words come to me.

You must let the spirits come to you and connect with you, let those connections form organically. It's about nurturing the connection, not forcing it.

Can I understand why the water spirits are attacking me, by connecting with them? I look at my own brown lauvan, tucked tightly around my body in defense. The water strands pluck at mine. What would happen if I stop fighting?

Do I have anything to lose?

With a released breath and immense will, I allow my lauvan to relax. My fingers continue to grip the bowsprit, but my threads float out from my body and fan into the water.

The water lauvan immediately entwine with mine. The force that pulls my legs lessens. The shouting voices that have been my constant companion this entire trip grow quiet. A few voices speak calmly, but because of the barrier of my chain are still too quiet to understand.

At this point, I really don't care what they say. With the lack of resistance, I manage to pull myself hand over hand toward the wreck. There are the remains of an anchor and heavy chain in the moldering rubble of the bow. I hang on with one hand while I use the other to pick up the chain and balance it on the gunwale. Now that the chain has lauvan from being on its precarious perch, it's a matter of moments to sever crucial threads to break the chain into pieces. I tuck a few loops of chain into each pocket—an awkward proposition with one hand, upside down—but eventually I drift to the deck of the old ship.

I take a moment to calm my breathing and adjust my buoyancy. My air gauge says I have only eight hundred psi left, almost time to head to the guideline. I'll have to run it dry today.

Now that I'm not fighting for my life, my eyes search for the object I glimpsed through the hole. It must be the grail. Below me lies rubble covered with a thick layer of silt. I dig my gloved hands into the mess and pry up rotten wood. The silt shoots up in thick clouds, reducing my visibility to almost nothing. I sink low and point my flashlight to the spot where I think I saw the grail and continue to feel around.

There. My hand connects to something rounded and unyielding. This is it. But what of the lauvan that might connect it to the ocean, that could cause a tsunami? I can't feel anything with my gloves on, so I strip them off and tuck them in my pocket with the chain pieces, careful to minimize my movements to avoid more silt. Slowly, the cloud dissipates, and my eyes can see what my fingers already feel.

It's a small stemless cup, covered in barnacles and lauvan of every conceivable color. The layer of strands is too thick, and the light is too dim, so I can't make out any details on the cup. Intertwined with the strands are glowing blue threads that twist together into cords. These descend through the ship to the depths far below.

It's this connection that I must break, somehow sever without causing a shockwave that will set off a wave of epic proportions.

How can I do this? My fingers gently prod the cords of water lauvan. I take one slender strand and snap it in the spirit of experimentation. A ripple passes through the water and blurs my vision for a moment. A dribble of water leaks into my mask from the pressure wave.

Breaking is not the solution. Can I untangle the threads? I examine the connection, and my heart sinks. There are so many knots, so many threads intertwined with each other, that it

211

would take me days to untangle them all. I have minutes, at most, until I run out of air or March finds me.

The voices murmur quietly in the background, and my thoughts turn to them. I can't hear them clearly, not with the charm still on, but they appear more benevolent than before. Can they help? How can I tell them what I want?

I relax and close my eyes, attempting to let my lauvan connect even more. My fingers slide into the strands that trap the grail, and I send my mind into them the way I do with the lauvan cables on land. It's surprisingly easy, although I've never tried it before. I sense infinite pathways that stretch ahead of me, beckoning me to explore, but instead I focus on communication.

I send a vision of my hands pulling apart the water's strands to release the grail, and then transporting it up to the surface. I project thoughts of calm waters and serene bays. Will the spirits understand me? Can they help?

Something slithers through my fingers. I open my eyes. The blue strands that hold the grail captive slide and twist, unknotting themselves from the multicolored lauvan with a speed I could never hope to match. Within a few short seconds, the grail is free.

Gratitude flows through me, but the lauvan cords have disappeared. I have no time to re-enter the cord to communicate my thanks, in any event. I pull out the replica cup from my pocket and tuck the real thing in its place. The replica rests on the rubble, and I throw a handful of silt on top for authenticity. It drifts down in a slow snowfall.

Five hundred psi left. I need to find March and return to the surface. I'm rather fond of breathing, and now that the spirits have stopped their attack, I would like to breathe fresh air again. Swimming has lost its appeal.

I kick my legs with powerful strokes of my fins and swim

slowly over the wreck to look for the gleam of March's flashlight.

Although the iron hull of the *Minerva Louise* is mostly intact, the wooden deck near the bow collapsed years ago and remains only as piles of anemone-covered rubble on the bottom. The stern, however, has retained some structure. Ghastly black holes gape like open maws in the green-tinged wood, but I must go in—March is nowhere else.

The largest jagged hole on the decking is the most likely place March has disappeared to. I aim my fin strokes to propel me past the rotting wood of the deck and into the darkness beyond. My flashlight illuminates very little—crawling crabs over steps, a cluster of tubeworms in a corner—but past a series of posts, another light flickers.

March is behind a stack of disintegrating crates. She pulls at one, the strips of wood that make up the box falling apart under her hands. She is completely engrossed in her task and does not notice my presence. I pull out my diving knife and rap my tank to create a loud clanging noise. March looks up in surprise, and I gesture for her to follow me. I put enough excitement into the movement that she follows immediately.

We swim to the bow and I point at the replica. March hovers above it, clearly reveling in the moment, then plucks it delicately from its rubble bed. She gazes at it then holds it up to me in triumph. Her eyes shine from behind her mask. I give her the "okay" hand signal, then point to my air gauge and indicate that we should ascend. She nods and follows me out of the wreck.

March takes the lead once we are in the open, and she follows her compass to the guideline. We ascend to fifteen feet and pause there for a few minutes to allow our bodies to acclimate to the decreased pressure. March examines the replica in her hand and I look as well.

What we see is a cup no taller than a handspan and covered in untarnished gold. Barnacles gather in white clusters around the lip beside pink bryozoans, which are encrusting creatures that look like lichen. I'm rather impressed with my skills at lauvan manipulation. In truth, it is a bottle of beer from my fridge that I transformed to look like an ancient grail, lost at sea.

After our three-minute wait, March gives the signal and floats up. I put some air in my BCD and follow. When my head breaks the surface, sound assaults me—frothing waves against the boat, seagulls crying, the wind across my hood—and it's a shock after the quiet of underwater. The sea is even rougher than when we descended, and I keep my regulator in my mouth to avoid choking on water splashing in my face by the waves and heavy rain. March kicks toward the aft of the boat without a backward glance and swims to a ladder that the captain must have put out for us. I latch onto the bottom rung while I wait to avoid being swept away by the mild but constant current. The waves roll in so high that I am partially lifted out of the water on every crest and sink below the surface in every trough. My pockets are still full of anchor chain, and I dump them to avoid awkward questions. The grail I carefully shuffle to one side.

After I climb up the ladder, hauling only the weight of my tank, I rip off my gloves, mask, and hood. March is already bereft of tank and helps me with mine, then unzips my dry suit.

"We found it, Merry." March's brisk, business-like movements contrast with the bubbling excitement in her voice. "The grail is ours." A flash of lightning and a rumble of thunder punctuate her words.

"That's incredible. Sorry I didn't keep up for a while. I lost track of you."

"Oh, I thought you were right behind me." March looks

214

surprised, but her lauvan show her usual calm. "I guess I was preoccupied. I'm glad you caught up." She turns for me to unzip her dry suit.

I don't mention the spirit attack, since she clearly didn't know it happened. I look more closely at her lauvan. They may look still, but they wriggle minutely with knowledge. Thoughts strike me with the force of blows. Did she see me hauled away by the spirits? She communicates with them—did she know what was going to happen?

"That was lucky the tsunami didn't occur," I say while I watch March. She shrugs and pulls her head out of the neck seal. I do likewise, and we shimmy out of our gear.

"It was only a remote possibility. And it didn't happen, so no harm done."

No harm done, thanks to me and the spirits. The rain pounds down and lightning flashes once more on the rolling deck. March slips out of her fleece suit then turns her attention to the bench between us. The replica cup is wedged between the strapped-down tanks. Its barnacle encrustation, which had looked mysterious underwater, now makes it look uncared for. I am curious to see my handiwork closer, and my hand darts out to clench around the bowl. Barnacles bite into my palm, feeling very authentic. The gold gleams dully in the dim light. Before I can take a closer look, March's front explodes.

A boiling mass of blue lauvan erupts from under her shirt and pours out toward me. The strands push away my own lauvan with a force that sends shooting pain up my arms. My fingers open with a spasm and the cup falls. March catches it with both hands.

"Sorry," she says, breathless. "I'm a little protective. This is too important to mess around with. So many lives will change after we get this safely home."

"No apologies needed. I understand."

215

March shrugs on a fleece coat hanging in the cabinet and tucks the cup in its roomy pocket. She leans over and reaches into the pocket of the closest BCD.

"I think I left my spare knife in here," she says.

My eyes widen with horror. Her hand is groping around the pocket of my vest, the one with the true grail inside.

"March," I begin. "Wait—"

She freezes. Her body shakes and her lauvan fan out in a wide cloud, electrified and vibrating. Her eyes roll back in her head.

What the hell is happening? Is she having a seizure? I hover to catch her if she falls.

The lauvan of the grail sneak out of the pocket and interweave with March's until she is surrounded by a multicolored cloud that looks like a stormy sky at a red sunrise.

Then, just as suddenly as they emerged, the grail's lauvan retreat to their source. March keeps her eyes closed, taking deep breaths, while her strands relax and drape around her body in limp exhaustion.

"March?" I venture. "Are you all right?"

She opens her eyes and looks at me. Her expression is confused, and the resemblance to her amnesiac sister has never been stronger.

"March," I say more urgently. "What happened?"

She shakes her head, visibly collecting herself. Lightning cracks overhead, and still she is silent. Frustration overcomes my concern, and I open my mouth to speak, but March interrupts me.

"I don't know."

"The other BCD is yours, by the way," I say, and she removes her hand from the pocket. I sigh in relief. "Are you all right?"

"I'm fine, Mer—Merry." She stumbles on my name.

216

"Whew! I'm a little giddy from our discovery and the exertion of the dive. Let's take apart the tanks and regulators then get to bed. I'll sort out the rest in the morning."

I stare at her for a few moments longer, but she turns to her regulator. I move to my own equipment, but I can feel her eyes glancing at me every so often.

What did the grail do to her? For once, I have no conjectures.

After we strap the equipment into the cabinet, I start to feel the effects of my inadvertent journey to the depths. Itchiness from my ears to my waist and a deep ache in my joints both point to the beginning of decompression sickness. I must fix my lauvan before I become seriously ill. Luckily, March doesn't want to be out here any longer than I do.

"Good enough for now." She waves away the gear. "Time enough for cleaning during our ride back tomorrow. Great work today, Merry. Now, go get some sleep." She gives me one last searching glance, then smiles and disappears with the replica into the main cabin. I give her a minute's head start then extract the true grail from my BCD's pocket and tuck it under my shirt. I walk directly to my cabin, shut the door, and collapse on the swaying bed. I avoid scratching my neck and torso with great difficulty and plunge fingers into my lauvan to alleviate the symptoms.

A half-hour's work removes most knots, and I idly pick at the remaining while I stare at the grail where it perches on the windowsill. Like the replica, it too is encrusted with barnacles. It is difficult to decipher any engravings on the outside, not only because of the sea life but because there are many multicolored lauvan swirling around the cup. It must have been swarming with them in its heyday, if there are this many after being lost at sea for over a century. Under the growth and lauvan there are stylized patterns of enamel in peacock blue, aquamarine, and rusty red. It's metalwork in the La Tène style, common in Britain before I was born. It's clearly older than me and used far before Arthur was around.

I wonder if it would have worked for March's ceremony. At least now, I won't find out.

CHAPTER XXX

The boat's motors rumble to life at daybreak. Ocean and distant shores pass by my window, but I feel no desire to get up yet. There is nothing to do except clean dive gear and make conversation with March, which I'm not in the mood for this early. I miss Alejandro, Jen, Minnie—I've grown used to their welcoming presence in my life. March is friendly on the outside, but prone to strange outbursts, intensity, and duplicity.

With nothing better to do, I doze until the banging of cupboards emerges from the direction of the galley. My stomach growls, and I consider that it might be worth facing March to eat some breakfast. She is never dull, I'll give her that.

I dress and amble to the galley, where March spreads peanut butter on toast. She looks startled when she sees me.

"Merry! Good morning. I thought you might sleep in."

"Too hungry. The scent of toast lured me here." I lean against the counter to support myself on our rolling journey through the waves. "Is there any to spare?"

March gazes at me for a moment then shakes herself.

"Here, I'll pop some down for you. Toast is all I could safely manage while we're moving." She pulls two slices of bread from a plastic bag and slides them into a toaster. The skin under her eyes is dark and bruised-looking.

"How did you sleep last night?" I ask. March gives me a wry smile.

"Woke up far too early. There is a lot to think about, and my brain insists that three in the morning is the best time to think. The curse of a middle-aged woman, I'm afraid."

I examine March's lauvan. Her normally sedate strands are as lively as anyone else's. What happened to her yesterday when she touched the grail?

My toast pops up, and I busy myself with spreading honey over it. March sips coffee and waits for me. Her eyes bore into the side of my head.

"All done." I hold up my plate. "Let's eat."

March hands me another cup of coffee and leads the way to the dining room. After a few minutes of silent eating, she leans back with her cup of coffee between both hands.

"So, Merry. Tell me more about yourself. We've been on quite an adventure together, but I don't know much about you. Apart from what my investigator could uncover, that is." She winks at me, entirely unabashed. "Tell me, have you always called Vancouver home?"

I'm not interested in playing twenty questions, but I can humor March for a while.

"No, I moved here five years ago. I traveled around for a few years before that. Received my PhD at the University of Lyon." Every time I change persona, I make sure my back story is airtight.

"That sounds fascinating," March says. She takes a sip of her coffee. "Are you French, originally? Because you speak English like a native, if so."

I laugh.

"No, I was born in Wales. I've had a lot of exposure to different languages over the years."

March gazes at me, a perplexed look on her face.

"Indeed," she murmurs. "Indeed."

What has her so confused? I decide to ignore her eccentricity and take a bite of my toast. The silence stretches until March breaks it.

"What did you think of Fiona, our resident guru of searching for past lives? I must admit, I was skeptical when I first approached her, but after a few sessions, she's really opened my mind to my past lives."

I make a non-committal noise.

"Do you believe in reincarnation?" she asks.

"I have yet to see proof, so I'll retain my skepticism for now. I'm always willing to be proven wrong."

March smiles with a wary look in her eyes but says nothing in reply. Her odd behavior is starting to irk me.

"When are we expected back in port?" I ask, hoping to inject a practical note into our conversation.

"Around noon," March says. "Thank you for coming, Merry. We successfully retrieved the grail—and on our first attempt, too—and I learned a lot. I appreciate having you along to witness retrieval of the grail. As you said, it is a historic moment. Now that we have it, we can begin preparations for the ceremony to bring the spirits to Earth. It's exciting times."

"Thanks for letting me tag along," I say. What did she learn? I feel very much in the dark, and I don't like it one bit. March pushes back from the table.

"I must speak with the captain. Enjoy the ride back, it's a beautiful day."

March walks out of the room and leaves me disquieted and uneasy, despite my triumph.

It takes me only a few minutes to pack my belongings in my satchel, so I head to the deck to enjoy the sun. My feet walk with practiced quiet on the carpeted floor, but I pause when I hear March's voice from her cabin. She must be on the phone, but with whom? Curiosity compels me to press my ear to the door.

"You wouldn't believe it, Anna. I don't know what

happened, some kind of aura disruption, surely from the grail itself, but it was incredible. I saw flashes of lives, past lives that I must have lived. It was so clear, much clearer than when Fiona delves into our pasts. We must recreate it for you. You'll be astonished, and enlightened." There's a pause, then, "No, it didn't seem to affect Merry. But there's something else you should know about him. I'll tell you tonight."

I back away silently from the door and tiptoe upstairs into the galley. Past lives? And what does she know about me? It's a good thing the true grail is safely in my satchel.

Disembarking is quick. March seems eager to leave with her prize and doesn't linger to chat. I drive my yellow Prius back home, my thoughts so preoccupied that I barely notice two people waving at me to pick them up in my taxi look-alike. I walk into my apartment, and Alejandro jumps up from the couch.

"Merlo, you're back."

"And you're still here and dry."

"You found the grail?" he says. I nod. Alejandro frowns. "But no tsunami?"

"I had a little help," I say, and drop my satchel against the wall. "The spirits almost killed me, but we finally met on common ground. They untangled the lauvan from the grail safely, and I put a replica in place for March to find."

Alejandro laughs in delighted disbelief.

"You have it? Really?"

"In my bag. Knock yourself out."

Alejandro dives for my satchel. When his fingers touch the cup, his whole body goes rigid. His green lauvan look

222

electrified, then he starts to shake.

"Alejandro!" I rush to his side, but his strands repel me. All I can do is watch in horror and fascination. Multicolored strands snake out of the satchel and around Alejandro's body. After a few moments, whatever hold the grail has on Alejandro fades, and its threads retreat into the satchel.

Alejandro slumps over with his hands on his knees. I take his shoulders and guide him to the couch.

"What happened?" I ask. "What did you feel?"

Alejandro's eyes are closed, and he takes a deep, shuddering breath.

"It was overwhelming. Like all the dreams I've ever had, and more, but in reverse and all at the same time. Flashes of you and me and others I've never seen except in dreams." He shakes his head. "I don't know. I'm okay now."

"March had something similar happen to her when she touched the grail." I walk over to the satchel and extract the cup. It looks grimy and uncared for. Perhaps I can clean it up later. "I don't understand what happened. I didn't feel anything."

"But you're different, Merlo," Alejandro says with a weak chuckle. "That grail must be very powerful."

"But what sort of power?" I say. "Perhaps you shouldn't touch it for now."

"Good advice." He sits up and looks at the cup, then at me with shining eyes. "You did it, you really did. You took the grail away from Potestas."

"Where was your faith?" I say.

"I knew you would do it." Alejandro beams at me. It's infectious. "This is worth celebrating. Beer, Merlo?"

"I'd love one. Are you in a rush? I might wash off the salt water first."

"Take your time."

223

When I emerge from my bedroom, showered and in fresh clothes, there is a knock at the door. It opens, and Jen steps in. She looks at me in expectation.

"Well?"

I shrug.

"You're dry, and there's a dirty old cup on my coffee table. Success all around?"

CHAPTER XXXI

Jen joins us on the balcony. Alejandro passes around the beers, and I tell them what transpired on my trip. They are a good audience—both suitably horrified at my brush with death—and Jen squeezes my arm when I come to the part when I released my weights.

"I made it," I say. "But when we got on the boat, and I grabbed the replica, lauvan from March's amulet came forth and knocked it from my hands. A protective measure, she said. She's too powerful for her own good, and she still wants more. And when March touched the true grail by accident, it was the strangest thing. Touching it affected her somehow, but when I asked, she pretended nothing had happened. She hasn't been the same since. And when Alejandro touched it, the same thing."

"Are you okay, Alejandro?" Jen gazes at him searchingly. When he nods, she turns back to me. "And you didn't feel anything?"

"No, not at all."

"Maybe you didn't hold it for long enough," Alejandro says.

"She reacted instantly," I say.

"Well, you are a bit different," says Jen. "Maybe it's that." I look at her with a raised eyebrow and she giggles, then sobers. "Now what? About the grail, I mean? Where do we keep it, so March can't find it?"

"I'll hide it here," I say. "I can't let them have it, but it seems a shame to destroy something that's obviously older than me. It's a survivor, this cup."

"But what about when Anna comes waltzing back here, wiggling her hips and batting her eyelashes?" says Jen. She gives me a stern look. "You're gullible when it comes to her."

"Give me a little credit," I say. Jen raises her eyebrows. "I'm well and truly over Anna. She won't fool me again, I promise. And anyway, I will protect it here, with lauvan. No one will be able to find it except me."

Jen nods slowly. I look at her and Alejandro and notice something that I hadn't before.

"What's been happening while I've been gone? Anything you two want to tell me?"

Both turn red as one. I laugh.

"It's your lauvan. The ones that connect you two are very thick now, far more than when I left."

"That is not fair," Alejandro mutters. "Are no secrets sacred?"

"Not from me," I say.

"We're dating now," says Jen with her chin up. "That's what's happening."

I raise my glass in a toast.

"To things that should have happened earlier. Congrats."

Jen kicks me.

"Don't be a pain, Merry."

"But what about you, Alejandro?" I say. "Are you able to stay in Vancouver?"

"The embassy is processing my visa right now, but my job at the ESL school should help. I have a lead on an apartment, too. Your neighbor Gary helped me out there, his daughter was moving and needed to fill a sublet. I'll be able to stay for a while, at least." He reaches out and touches Jen's hand, and she squeezes his with a happy smile.

"That's great," I say. "I'm glad you're sticking around." I am sincerely happy he's staying, since it has been a treat to have someone who knows all of me, and we get on well. I have mixed feelings about him leaving my apartment. I suspect it will feel rather empty and quiet when he's gone, and I don't look forward to that.

But he and Jen are finally together. I've been predicting it since they first met, so I'm glad they finally figured it out. I told Jen once that she could do better than me, and I believe Alejandro fits the bill.

"Speaking of relationships," Jen says. "You've been around a while."

"Small understatement," I say. Jen waves me off.

"Have you ever been married before?"

"Fourteen times."

"What?" Jen looks flabbergasted. "That's—surprising."

"Hey," I protest. "What does that mean?"

"You don't seem the type to commit, that's all."

"At the moment, and that's for a good reason," I say. "It took me about thirty years to get over my last wife's death. I have no interest in doing that again, not soon, possibly not ever. I can't handle the loss anymore."

Jen bites her lip.

"Sorry, Merry. Yes, I get that." She looks past the edge of the balcony while Alejandro sips his beer, then she turns to me.

"Wait a minute, how many children did you have?" Jen asks, then her face drops in horror. "Oh, gross, how did you avoid having sex with your great-great-granddaughter? Do you keep intensive family trees? Reliable contraception is a pretty new thing."

"Not for me, it isn't. Lauvan, remember?" I keep my tone casual while my heart squeezes as if in a vise. "I had three children, long ago. One died in a fire. One by drowning. And the last swept away in a hurricane. None lived past their fourth year. I stopped trying after that. It's bad enough to say goodbye to a lover who has lived a long, full life. But to your own child, taken far before their time? I couldn't do that again."

Tears fill Jen's eyes, and we are all silent for a long while.

"I was thinking," Alejandro eventually says in a contemplative tone. "Do you want to hear what the water spirits say?"

"Yes," I say, surprised at myself for not remembering it before. "I do. But I don't fancy the helpless trance."

"That's where I can help," Alejandro says. He leans forward. "You turn on the tap, or whatever you need to do, listen for a bit, then I'll turn off the water."

"That's a great idea," Jen says with an adoring smile. Alejandro grins back. I nod slowly.

"I agree. A bath would be best. Immerse myself for full connection."

"What about the pool?" Jen points out the window.

"Then you'd have to drag me out at the end. In here, you can simply pull the plug." I stand and walk into the apartment, stripping my shirt off as I go.

"Umm, maybe I'd better stay out here," Jen says. I flash her a grin.

"Don't want to be tempted away from your new fling? I understand."

"Don't flatter yourself," she snaps, but her eyes laugh.

"If I don't, who will? Don't worry, I'll keep my underclothes on."

In the bathroom, I turn the water on full blast. The voices start, but they are calm and muted with my gold chain on. Alejandro follows me in.

"How long do you want?" he asks.

"I'm not sure. Shall we start with three minutes? You can pull the plug early if I seem in distress."

Alejandro nods in determination. When the bath is full, I turn off the tap. We both look at the agitated water for a moment in the quiet.

"Can you hear them yet?" Jen asks from the doorway.

"Quietly, yes. I'll take my chain off once I'm in the bath." I take a deep breath then step into the tub and lower myself into the tepid water. I reach around my neck to unfasten the gold chain and look at Alejandro.

"Three minutes?"

"Yes." He holds his wristwatch aloft. I remove the chain and lie back in the water with my eyes closed.

For a moment, all is quiet, as if the spirits don't believe that I'm finally listening. In the pause, I reflect. What do I want to ask? What will they say? Then, a few voices speak, as clearly as I've ever heard them, but still garbled together.

"He's here."

"It's time…"

"Is he the son? Is he listening?"

"One at a time," I say aloud. "I can't understand you when you're all talking at the same time. Who are you? Why are you trying to speak to me?"

There is a pause, during which water lauvan wrap their tendrils around my loose cloud of threads. It tickles.

"Who we are does not matter," says a sibilant voice slowly. "We are what you would call water elementals. We have been sent to find the truth."

"The truth about what?"

"We wish to find the son."

"What son? Whose son?" I say with a hint of exasperation coloring my voice. These spirits are not very forthcoming. I am quickly losing my awe and wonder.

"The son of our comrade's predecessor. He is the only one. We think he might be you. How long have you walked this Earth?"

I can't find a reason to lie, but I don't want to give these spirits more information than they need.

"Why don't you tell me how old this son is supposed to be?"

"The Earth has traveled over fifteen hundred journeys around the sun since the son was born. Is that you?"

"Perhaps."

"And the son was conceived in a place now called Wales."

I am silent. If there is another immortal born a millennium and a half ago in Wales, then I have been supremely unlucky not to have met him before. The son, whatever they mean by that, must be me. The spirits take my silence for confirmation and jabber all at once. If they're getting what they want, then I want answers too.

"How are you talking to me? Centuries without a whisper, and now I can't make you stop. How?"

The excited chattering tapers off, and the sibilant voice speaks.

"We have been allowed into this existence by a group of humans. They opened the gates between worlds enough for part of ourselves to extend through. We have limited capabilities in this form, but one day we hope to join with this group to enter the physical world once more."

"Once more? When has this happened before?"

"Long before you were, we came and went as we pleased."

This is fascinating, but I must find out who they were sent by.

"You said my father was your comrade's predecessor. Who was my father? What happened to him? Was he like me?"

"Your father is no more," the voice says without emotion. "His successor is our leader, but he needs our help to be free of his cage. We will tell him about your presence. We expect he will contact you soon. He is very interested in you. Farewell."

"Wait," I shout. "Why were you trying to kill me?"

"Kill you? No, we wished only to talk, but you were resistant. We have so few options at our disposal. We did what we could to make you listen. Now, we must say farewell."

"Come back. Where is the successor? Where can I find him?"

There is only silence, and my lauvan are no longer wrapped in water lauvan. My eyes pop open as I am released from my trance, and I sit up with a gasp. Alejandro grips the side of the tub with wide eyes.

"Only two minutes," he says breathlessly. "What happened?"

"More questions than answers." I stand and grab my towel to rub my hair. "Someone sent them to check my identity, someone who knew my father. My unknown father, who is apparently dead." I pause my toweling to let that sink in. So long an enigma, so many years searching—could he really have been around all this time, and never looked for me? And I never found him? A child's sense of unfairness wells up in me, but experience quickly dampens it down. For good or ill, he had his reasons. No one is a saint, and I can't expect him to be one. Perhaps he was a devil, as the legends say. I suppress a smile and continue to towel dry.

"Unfortunately, they left before I could ask more questions," I continue. "Not the most obliging set, spirits."

"Why were they trying to kill you?" Jen asks.

"Their way of getting my attention, apparently. It worked." I step out of the tub. "Let me dry off."

After I've toweled off and found dry clothes, I rejoin Jen and Alejandro in the living room. Alejandro wordlessly hands me another beer, and I smile at his foresight before I take a deep draft.

"Always with the beer," Jen says. She drinks some of her own and grimaces. "I prefer sweeter drinks. Or water."

231

"It was rare to drink water regularly until the last century," I say. "Not safe, too many waterborne diseases. Beer is comfortable to me."

There is a knock at the door.

"Who could that be?" I say. Jen walks to the door.

"It's probably Wayne. I texted him to say you were home. He wants to hear the story too, I bet."

I follow Jen to the door. She flings it open. Wayne and Liam stand in the hallway, laughing together over something Liam said. I shake my head in bemusement. Liam has a knack for making friends, just like Alejandro. Even I like him.

"Hi, guys," says Jen and steps aside with a smile. "Come in."

"I lose track," I whisper to Alejandro. "Does Liam know about the lauvan?"

"Yes," he whispers back. "He's in. And I'm not going to say sorry, because you won't regret it."

I raise my eyebrows at Alejandro, but inwardly congratulate his brazen confidence. And I do trust Alejandro, now. I believe that if he says Liam can be trusted, he can.

"You'd better fetch beers for these fine gentlemen," I say in my usual voice, and Wayne claps me on the back.

"Well said, Merry."

Before I close the door, there is the sound of a cleared throat across the threshold. My neighbor Gary holds a plate of cookies and has a perplexed look under his bushy gray eyebrows.

"I don't mean to disturb you, Merry. I thought you were sick, since you missed our chess game yesterday. The missus made cookies for you."

"Thursday!" I say with regret. "It completely slipped my mind. So sorry, Gary. But come in and bring your cookies. It seems that we're having an impromptu party, and you're most welcome, especially bearing gifts."

I usher Gary into the living room, where Jen greets him with a warm smile and Alejandro presses a beer into his hand. Wayne takes two cookies with a pat on Gary's back then hands one to a laughing Liam.

I gaze at all these people, old friends and new acquaintances alike, and marvel at how easy they are together, how right they seem all in the same room despite their differences in age and personality. I look down at my center. My brown lauvan extend toward each person: wrapped with golden strands for Jen, dark green for Alejandro, rust for Wayne, even a deep violet charcoal for Gary and a surprising loam-brown for Liam. My throat constricts, and my heart feels too large in my chest. For now, at least, I have a community. It feels fantastic.

The phone in my pocket vibrates. It's a text from Minnie, and I can't help but smile.

How are you feeling? Want to walk me home from work tomorrow?

I text back with an immediate yes. Navy blue strands intertwine with my chocolate brown ones, pointing to the northwest.

None of this will last, but I can enjoy it while it's here. I step forward into my circle of friends.

"Alejandro, we need music if we're having a party. And where are those cookies?"

The impromptu party lasts until the beer runs out. Gary heads off first, citing the missus, and the rest drift off for various engagements. Alejandro and Jen leave last, hand in hand, for a date to the movies. By nightfall I am alone, but not lonely. The promise of connection tomorrow sustains me, and the threads that link me to my friends are strong.

CHAPTER XXXII

Dreaming

Gawaine pulls up his horse at the crest of a hill, where a small clearing affords a view of the surrounding forest. On his mount, he looks even taller and broader than he usually does. He rubs his close-cropped brown hair with an absent gesture as he scans the countryside.

"No sign of a fire," he says. His gruff voice sounds disappointed, as if he wishes for a skirmish with a Saxon scout. His voice brightens when he says, "They might be at the river crossing. We should check there next."

Elian stops his own horse beside Gawaine's, where the animal takes the opportunity to crop a nearby tuft of grass. Elian pushes his hood of undyed wool from his brown curls. His eyes, a strange clear gray, follow Gawaine's gaze, and he touches his stubbled chin in contemplation.

"Perhaps the rumors aren't true. Perhaps Cedric's brother will not join his attack on our people."

"Doubtful," I say. "I have it on very good authority. Their reinforcements may be late, or more likely we have missed the scout."

"Where do you find your information, Merlin?" Elian says with interest. "You are always so well-informed."

Gawaine and I glance at each other. Gawaine has known about my abilities since he and Arthur were barely men, and he often helps us plan my spy missions into Saxon camps. Few others are aware of the truth, which I prefer. I expected I'll have to tell Elian soon, since his inquisitiveness is matched only by his determination. I'm not too worried about his reaction. He is easy-going, and most things slide off his back

235

without affecting his easy smile.

"That's a tale for another time," I say. Gawaine looks at me with surprise but refrains from comment. "Let's check the river crossing for the scout."

I kick my horse into motion, and it ambles down the shallow hill, back into the trees. The others follow.

After a while in the woods, the path flattens. We follow a curve, and on the trail before us a figure appears. He is dressed all in green: green hood, green shirt peeking between the fastenings of a green cape, even green trousers. His mouth and nose are hidden by a scrap of green cloth tied around his head, and his eyes are in shadow from the hood. He has a broadsword at the ready. Gawaine, Elian, and I glance at each other, then Gawaine dismounts and passes Elian his reins. He approaches the man in green with open hands held out.

"We wish to pass. Stand aside, for we have no quarrel with you."

"You must best me to pass," says the man in green, in a deep, emotionless voice.

"Why?" I ask. "What is your purpose here? Are you a Saxon scout?"

Is that a flash of anger from those masked eyes? Perhaps I imagined it, for his voice is as flat as before.

"I will give you no reason. You must best me to pass."

"We heard you the first time," Gawaine mutters, but he throws his cape to one side and unsheathes his broadsword from his back. It's an impressive weapon that reaches from the ground to my waist and is sharp and shining with care. Gawaine is a dedicated warrior, backed by long practice and experience, and it doesn't hurt that he's a head taller and broader than most men I've seen. The man in green won't be an opponent for long.

Gawaine doesn't hesitate, nor does he bother with any

talking or flourishes. He strikes hard and fast, but the man in green is ready with a parry and a swift counterstrike. Gawaine is quicker than his size would indicate, and he sidesteps with ease then brings his sword across in a powerful side slice that would have cut through the man in green if he didn't leap back. The man in green charges forward and the two swords meet with a clash of steel.

Their fighting is ferocious and well-matched. Gawaine sweats, and the mask of the man in green grows damp as time passes. With a final burst, Gawaine slices against the other's blade near the guard and the jolt loosens the man in green's grip. His sword flies through the air and clatters to a halt at the base of a tree. The man pauses then puts his hands up in defeat. His shoulders heave with gulping breaths.

"Do you concede defeat?" Gawaine's voice pushes past his own haggard breathing.

"I do. You may pass." The man steps to one side.

"What did you hope to achieve from this little demonstration?" I ask. "Out of curiosity."

The man doesn't answer. I shake my head. What a waste of time, for no discernable purpose. I wave at Gawaine to get on his horse again. Elian, who trotted forward as soon as the man in green was defeated, comes back in a hurry.

"The scouts are ahead, I'm sure of it."

"Quick, Gawaine," I say. "Let's capture the bastards."

We leave the man in green standing silently on the side of the path and follow Elian's horse. Before a small rise, Elian dismounts and motions us to do the same. We leave the horses eating grass and creep over the hill. Elian peers from between trees, and his eyes widen.

"What?" I hiss.

He opens his mouth to speak, but a shout interrupts him. Elian has been seen.

"Seven of them!" Elian says loudly. There is no need to hide now. The pounding of booted feet on hard-packed earth is unmistakable. "Prepare yourself!"

Gawaine and I throw our cloaks to the ground and unsheathe our swords. Gawaine hefts his two-handed broadsword into readiness, and I grip my shorter spatha in my right hand while my left-hand fingers flex, eager to grasp foreign lauvan. Elian joins us, and we stand in a defensive line.

"Two each, plus a bonus treat for whoever finishes theirs off first," Gawaine says with a grin.

"You think he'll be yours, don't you?" I say. "We'll see about that."

Then the Saxons are on us. Their long hair sweeps behind them, and their beards shake with braids. Each one wears a belt around his tunic with a sheathed seax attached, the knife that all Saxons wear, but it's the swords that are prominent. One particularly burly man hefts a lance straight toward Gawaine.

Gawaine roars and raises his broadsword to sweep downward in a powerful stroke. I parry one Saxon's blow to my chest and slash at another, drawing blood. His lauvan loosen with his pain and I snatch my opportunity. With a yank at a handful of his floating strands, the man drops to the ground in agony and I whirl away from the blows of the other. In the second I have before my Saxon comes at me again, I see Elian bearing down on his attacker, and Gawaine yelling in fury as he swings his sword in a great arc.

We drop three of the Saxons to the ground, but four still fight valiantly on. They are formidable opponents, even for us. We hold our own—Gawaine has two at the end of his broadsword—but I can't find an opening in my opponent's defense. His lauvan are too tight for me to easily grasp, and his sword keeps me far enough away to not have a chance.

Through the clangs and shouts, another sound reaches my

238

ears. I risk a glance behind us. Two more Saxons charge through the trees, their faces grim with determination. My heart sinks. Six against three, and two of the attackers are fresh. The odds are not in our favor.

I don't have time to contemplate our fate, because my opponent renews his attack with vigor once he sees his fellows approach. He shouts with gladness and pushes me back toward the newcomers.

"Gawaine, Elian! There are more, behind us," I shout. Elian glances briefly, his expression resigned, and continues to engage his opponent. Gawaine doesn't spare a look. He is fully occupied with his two attackers, neither of which has let up for a moment. The big man sweats profusely, but he doesn't hesitate.

A few moments more is all we have before the others are on us. I grit my teeth and prepare for the worst.

A great roar bursts out from behind me. My opponent pauses and looks confused. I use his momentary lapse to slash his open chest. The blow slides along rib bones without breaking them, but a line of bright red blood wells up in a diagonal line across his woolen tunic. He gasps and falls back, and I look behind me.

The man in green has appeared from nowhere and now engages with the two newcomers. He is as fierce as when he fought Gawaine, perhaps more so. The two Saxons fall back from the onslaught of blows that rain down on them from his broadsword. Before long, the sword arm of one hangs uselessly from his shoulder, and the other limps from a wound to the thigh. Neither are in a condition to attack, and the man in green turns to the rest of the Saxons.

Between Gawaine, the man in green, and myself, Gawaine's opponents are quickly dispatched, dead or too wounded to fight more. Elian disarms his own attacker shortly after, and we all stand, panting, amid the bodies. Once I catch my breath, I turn to the man in green.

"Thank you for your assistance. Our foes were many." I edge closer to the man under the pretext of cleaning my sword on some grass underfoot. The man nods in acknowledgement. I reach out, swift as a snake, and rip off the cloth that covers his face.

He steps back immediately, but the damage is done. Despite the lack of beard, his face is clearly Saxon. Gawaine growls and swings his sword up into position, and even calm Elian tenses. I narrow my eyes.

"What do you want, Saxon?" I ask. "Why did you help us? Are you a spy?"

"No," he snarls. His lauvan bristle at the notion, and I'm inclined to believe him.

"He looks like one," says Elian. "I say we bring him back to Arthur and he can decide."

"Fine by me," says Gawaine. "I'll tie up those who can walk, and we'll be on our way." He addresses the man in green. "Will you come quietly, or must we subdue you?"

The man in green's shoulders slump.

"I will come. I hope your lord is more willing to speak than you are."

"He usually is," I say and sheath my sword. "Come, it's not far."

We enter the camp with a line of four stumbling Saxons tied together with rope. The man in green walks quietly beside me. He has made no attempt to run. I glance at his lauvan from time to time, and they always tell the same story: he's nervous and

240

resigned, hopeful and stoic all at once. I wonder what he wants, but I don't question him. Better to leave that to silver-tongued Arthur, whose diplomacy is much more effective than mine.

Arthur breaks away from a group of men near a cooking fire and approaches us.

"I see that your mission was successful," he says. "Have you questioned the scouts yet?"

"We left that for you," says Elian. "You always make them talk. And if you can't, Merlin can."

Arthur flashes a grin at me.

"We'll try my way first, shall we?" He waves at the green man. "But who is this?"

"We're not sure," I say. "He insisted on fighting Gawaine before he let us pass. Gawaine bested him, of course, but then when we were overtaken by the Saxon raiding party—I believe there were nine, all told—he sprang out of nowhere and helped us defeat them."

"He's an excellent fighter," Gawaine added.

"High praise from you," Arthur says with a nod to Gawaine. He looks at the man in green. "What's your name?"

"I am Gareth." The man does not elaborate further. Arthur sighs.

"That's not a very Saxon name. Nothing else? Where are you from? Don't the Saxons usually mention who their father is?"

Gareth spits at the ground.

"My father was some Saxon whoreson who raped my mother. I want nothing to do with him. Unfortunately, he gave me his face. My mother's people are from Ergyng."

Understanding clears Arthur's face.

"It must have been difficult, living there, looking as you do."

Gareth nods with a grimace.

241

"I left as soon as I could. I've been a mercenary on the mainland for years, but I tire of that life. I want to come home, although home doesn't want me. All I wish for is a place in a household here, one in need of a sword. That is my specialty, after all."

"Why did you hide your face?" I ask. "And why fight us? It seems a roundabout way of getting what you want."

"I needed to prove myself first, show my skills, before I was judged for my face. Please, give me a chance. Let me fight for you against the Saxons you seek. I will not let you down." Gareth's face is open and pleading, and his lauvan float loose with a yearning gesture toward us. Arthur gazes at him for a minute, then turns to me.

"Does he speak from the heart, Merlin?"

I nod.

"He does. I see no guile in him."

Arthur puts out his hand. Gareth grasps his wrist with hesitation, as if he can't believe his luck.

"Fight well in the battles to come, and you are welcome in my house, Gareth. I hope you are ready to fight, because we do a lot of it in the borderlands. There are always Saxons trying to take what is not theirs."

Gareth smiles widely. His broad face is transformed, and a grin looks very much at home there.

"I am always ready to fight. I promise, you will not regret this."

"So be it," Arthur says, and pats Gareth's shoulder in a friendly fashion. "Come, everyone, cook has made a stew. Someone bind up the Saxons' wounds and feed them, will you? It's easier to get information from those who are well-cared for."

It doesn't take Arthur long to get the truth from the Saxons. Once they are patched up and sup from bowls of broth, I accompany him to watch for signs that they speak lies, but I find none. We rejoin the men around one of the cookfires, where Gareth is already proving his worth as entertainment. The men listen to a tale from some misadventure on the mainland.

"And then I found it in his saddlebag!" Gareth finishes, and the men roar with laughter. Arthur grins at me as we take seats on a log near the flames.

"He seems to be fitting in."

"Gareth the green warrior," I say slowly. "I think he'll fit in nicely indeed. Does he know about the peace treaty with Guinevere's father? I hope that isn't a problem. He may look Saxon, but it's clear he is a staunch Briton. I don't want him to defect to Morgan."

"Yes, I did mention it," Arthur assures me. "He was surprised at first, but then seemed relieved that he would not be the only one at the villa with golden hair. Less to explain."

"Good." I lean back. "Gawaine, Elian, and now Gareth—you have some very loyal friends."

"And you," Arthur says with a smile. "Last but not least."

"And me. Always."

I hide in the shade of an arched doorway and look at the market in the square. Brightly colored awnings cover sturdy wooden stalls filled with a dizzying plethora of goods: silks from China, ivory from Africa, glassware from the Iberian Peninsula. Trade is strong with Kufa, this dazzling city near the river Euphrates.

I'm enamored with this region. It's the grandest, most enlightened and civilized place I've seen in all my three hundred and fifty-odd years. Certainly, it smells the best. I sniff appreciatively at the air, scented with cinnamon and ginger from a nearby spice merchant. And with my swarthy skin and black hair, it only takes a few tweaks of the lauvan to blend in with the locals.

I watch a perfume merchant pour liquid into a small glass vial while I consider my plan. In this city of scientific and philosophic learning, there is one man above all whom I wish to meet. Jabir ibn Hayyan is known throughout the region for his prolific treatises on subjects of all description: astronomy, geography, physics, pharmacy, and many others. But it is his studies of alchemy that pique my interest. Alchemy is the search for a compound that will grant endless youth and life.

I don't need it for myself, of course—with skill and luck, I've preserved my own endless youth for centuries—but my hope is that Jabir, as such a learned man in this subject and with so many connections in the alchemic community, would have heard of a place where people like me live. Perhaps he knows where my father came from, where I could find him now. I've searched for centuries with ever-decreasing hope, but Jabir's work infused me with fresh purpose. Perhaps now, finally, I may find some answers.

My mind is made up, and I grasp the necessary lauvan to transform. A brief sojourn into nothingness, and I reform as a messenger boy in loose trousers and a light shirt. Jabir is notoriously closeted in his laboratory, and his interaction with other great minds is by written correspondence instead of visits in person. The best way to gain his presence is with a letter.

I slip into the bustling crowd. No one glances at me. Jabir lives in this part of Kufa, but I don't know in which house. My small fingers tug at the sleeve of a portly man in long robes and a white turban when he takes a breath from advertising his wares, jars of golden honey that glow in the hot sun like amber.

He looks down in surprise.

"What do you want, boy?" he asks, not unkindly. I hold up a folded piece of paper tied with a ribbon.

"Please, do you know the house of Jabir ibn Hayyan? I must deliver this for my master."

The man nods, then points a beefy finger toward a nearby street that leads away from the busy market square.

"Pass the fruit seller and travel west. Turn right on the second road crossing, then follow that road. It will turn three times. Jabir's house has a grand-looking arch over the doorway. There is none else like it on that road. I often deliver honey there. Now, be off with you."

He aims a swat at my head in a friendly fashion. I duck with a grin, murmur my thanks, then take off through the marketplace.

It's crowded with men and slave-women, and I dart between them with ease in my lithe boy's body. A woman above a certain rank would never dream of exposing herself to the vulgarities of the market, and no self-respecting husband or father would allow her to. The dearth of visible women is my only complaint against Kufa—otherwise, it is unparalleled.

I bend under a raised arm and twist past a group of chatting men to reach the fruit seller. Out of the market it is quieter, although shoppers spill into the adjoining streets. This main thoroughfare is lined with baked brick houses covered with stucco and is peaceful and refined despite the busyness. In the distance, the huge dome of a nearby mosque looms on the skyline.

At the second road crossing, I wait for a rubbish-collecting donkey cart to rattle by then slip into a shady street. It's narrow and winding, filled on either side by tall dwellings. There is an air of wealth here, and the stucco surrounding each doorway is fancifully carved.

The third twist in the road reveals an arched doorway with a solid wooden door beneath. Jabir's house, if the honey merchant was not mistaken. I run to it on bare feet and knock loudly on the wood. A whistling man strolls behind me, but the street is otherwise quiet.

A man answers the door, his bare feet and simple dress betraying him for a servant.

"Yes, boy?" he says in a haughty tone. I prefer the automatic respect being a grown man affords but hide my displeasure under servile demeanor.

"I have a letter for Jabir ibn Hayyan, please. I must deliver it to him."

"I will take it." The servant reaches out his hand, but I snatch the folded paper back.

"I must give it to him directly. My master will whip me if I do not. Please."

The man sighs but waves me inside.

"You'd best be quick. My master does not like to be disturbed."

The man leads me through blissfully cool hallways lined with patterned tile. He stops at a doorway, hesitates, then knocks and swings the door open.

"Master, there is a messenger boy with a letter for you," he says with deference.

I slip inside under the arm of the servant and grab hold of a few of his lauvan on the way. He frowns at me but says nothing. I rub the lauvan and concentrate on his desire to leave the room. He frowns again but this time in confusion, then he backs away and closes the door. I smile and turn to survey the room.

Large windows, open to an inner garden beyond, spread ample light into the large space. Three long tables stand in rows. Two are covered with thick layers of papers, maps, and codices. The third houses instruments of alchemy. I recognize a retort, as well as two vessels connected with a narrow tube called an alembic. There are beakers and cups of various sizes and materials, sharp knives and tweezers, crucibles, candles, and all manner of equipment.

Jabir leans over this table with his back to me. He is immersed in swirling a beaker full of a colorless liquid. I take this opportunity to revert to my usual form, then I clear my throat.

"Yes, yes, wait a moment," he says with an absent air. When a few more swirls of the beaker do not produce an effect, he sighs and places the beaker on the table. With a swirl of his red robes, he faces me. His black beard has streaks of gray, and his face is lined, but his eyes are sharp and glitter with intelligence.

"You are not a messenger boy," he says.

"No, I am not," I agree in a pleasant tone.

"I'm not in the habit of receiving visitors," he says. "They waste valuable time and rarely have anything of interest to relate. Nothing that will further my work, at any rate. Who are you? What do you want?"

"My name is Malin. What I want is your knowledge."

"You can read my treatises," he says with impatience. "There are enough of them to keep you busy for a while."

"I have read them all," I say calmly. Jabir's eyebrows raise in surprise. There are many—it took me days of solid reading. "All of the alchemic ones. And yet, they do not describe what I hope to find. How does your work progress in that subject?"

As I suspected, Jabir's face animates at the prospect of an interested audience.

"You understand my work! You are a student of the alchemical school. My search for the al-iksir is close to fruition. It will allow me to rearrange the qualities of one metal, transform it into another. Already I have seen promising signs with copper. To purify the metal, what a feat! I am so close. Look at my recent findings." He takes a rough piece of paper from the table and pushes it toward me. It is covered with notes in an angular script and sketches of laboratory equipment. I don't take the offered paper.

"And what of your study of takwin, the creation of artificial life? You write of it, but have you succeeded?"

"Ah, the ultimate goal." Jabir's sharp eyes turn inward in contemplation, and he slowly puts the paper on the table again. "Much of what I do furthers that goal. The al-iksir is to purify metal, but if I can achieve that, think how much closer I will be to purifying the soul, then to creating one."

I want to hear that he is closer, that he knows more, but his lauvan indicate that he hides nothing. It's time to let him in on some knowledge of my own.

"So, you have not yet succeeded in finding the al-iksir to create or prolong life," I say. "But in all your studies, all your research, have you ever come across a land of men who have succeeded themselves? Have you any evidence that it is possible?"

"The theories are sound, and just because it hasn't been done yet doesn't mean that I cannot be the first," he says, his shoulders stiffening with indignation. Then his eyes widen. "A land of men? What do you mean? What have you heard?"

I pause for effect.

"I know of one who has achieved this goal," I speak of my father, although the same words could be applied to myself. "I had hoped he had contacted you, given your interest in the subject. Your treatises indicate good progress, and I wondered if that might be why."

Jabir's eyes bulge, and he grips the table with a shaking hand.

"It has been done? It is possible? This, this is astonishing news! Where can I find this man? I must speak with him, examine him. This is astounding!"

"I wish to find him myself, hence my visit here today." Disappointment squeezes my gut. Over three hundred years of searching, and nothing. My final hope has evaporated into the breeze. Jabir leans forward to ask more questions, but I'm not in the mood to humor him any longer.

"Please, tell me more. Think of how my work could be furthered by leaps and bounds by even the smallest knowledge of this man!"

Outside the door, footsteps echo down the hallway. I take my chance.

"Who is at the door?" I say. When Jabir turns, distracted, I leap to the nearest window. It's the only one that faces the street instead of the courtyard garden. The laboratory is on the first floor, so I dive over the sill and roll onto the ground below. A few quick pulls of my lauvan, and I am a messenger boy once more. I run back down the road and risk one quick glance back. Jabir hangs out of the window and scans the street.

For my own sanity, I should stop looking. I must lay the mystery of my father to rest and accept that I will never know the truth. It is a bitter potion, but I'm tired of the disappointment that follows every failed lead. I will never know the truth.

It's an uncommonly warm spring day, and I'm visiting Nimue at her mountain home. Dappled light flickers through the waving leaves of freshly budded trees, and birds trill with exuberance. We lie on damp moss beside a bubbling stream,

249

ten paces apart. I lean my head over the water until my lips almost touch the surface.

"Hello, Nimue, my love," I whisper.

I glance downstream to Nimue, whose hand drifts in the current. A moment later, she smiles and meets my gaze.

"Hello, Merlin," she calls out. "Say something that I wouldn't guess."

I think for a moment then bend my head once more.

"Nimue has beautiful eyes, a big smile, and can't ride a horse to save her life."

Nimue closes her eyes to listen then bursts into laughter. She hits the water to send a spray in my direction. I shield my face with my hand and grin.

"You'll just have to teach me, won't you?" she says.

I crawl over to where Nimue sits and lay down on the moss beside her. She smiles when my fingers tickle the crook of her elbow gently.

"This afternoon, I promise." I sit up and place my hands in the stream. "Are you thirsty?"

Without waiting for a reply, I pluck a few water lauvan out of the stream. An arc rises, glittering in the sunlight, and splashes back into the water. Nimue leans forward and sips at the jet. When she finishes, I allow the water to subside.

"How do your abilities work?" I ask once she leans against my chest. We watch a spring butterfly flitter past. "How do you know what I say without hearing it?"

"I hear whispers, echoes of your words. It's not your voice, it's many different voices. I can't tell if they are male or female. Perhaps neither, perhaps it's the water itself talking. The whispers fill my mind until I have a sense of what is said."

"Can you hear everything said in water? What if some lout splashes about in a distant lake, cursing and shouting? Would you hear it?"

Nimue laughs lightly, and the sound melds into the warm freshness of the spring day.

"I must touch the same water source, and the sound can't be too far away. The voices sometimes come unbidden, but if I truly want to try, I simply relax and open my mind to them."

I stroke her fingers one by one.

"Why do you have this power, I wonder?"

She shrugs.

"It runs in my family. There are legends that say our ancestors long ago were blessed by the spirits of the elements, blessed with powers much stronger than what I have. Over time, they have been diluted and only appear in a weakened state." She bends her neck to look up at me. "What about your abilities? They are very strong, and not restricted to a particular element."

It is my turn to shrug.

"I don't know. My mother had nothing like it, so I suppose it must have come from my father, if anywhere. I would like to find him one day. I want to know why I am the way I am, where he came from. I want to know if there are more like me in the world. But do you know what I want more than any of that?"

"What?"

"To be with you."

Nimue twists to face me with a smile on her lips, a smile that I soon cover with a kiss.

CHAPTER XXXIII

Minnie walks out of her office into the warm evening sunshine. She wears pressed gray trousers and a pastel blue blouse, her professional work attire, and it suits her well. When she sees me, a relieved smile lights up her face.

"Merry. I'm glad you could make it. I'm going this way." She points down the road.

I fall into step beside her.

"I must admit, I'm surprised you texted. Our last date was a show-stopper, and not in a good way."

"I told you, I'm not going anywhere," she says and takes my hand. "I meant it."

I squeeze her hand in reply. We walk in silence for a few moments, although it is a comfortable quiet.

"How are you doing?" Minnie asks after the pause. "With the voices, I mean."

"Much better," I say. Ever since my conversation with the spirits, they have left me alone. Left me with plenty to think about, but I can think in peace and quiet. I try to mollify Minnie. "I was very tired that day, lots going on. Things are much better now, and I figured some important things out."

"What's been happening?" She looks at me with concern.

"Not today, if that's all right. My life is very tumultuous right now, and you're an oasis of calm that I can enjoy. One day I'll tell you about it, but you can't expect me to bare my soul after a few dates." I give her a half-smile and she nudges my shoulder.

"Okay, I can be your oasis. And if you want to talk, I'm always here. Did you get my referral for the evaluation?"

"Yes, I did. Thank you." I don't elaborate, since I have no intention of following up. After a searching glance, Minnie

252

leaves it alone. To change the subject, I say, "How was your day?"

"Clients, the usual. Of course, nothing I can discuss. Oh, but I went paddle boarding at lunch, and a seal swam up to me, so close I could have touched it with my paddle! And…"

I listen to Minnie chatter and give the appropriate responses, but my attention is on the shifting expressions of her face, the way she lights up, then frowns with a sweet crease of confusion that is then erased by a gentle laugh. We're comfortable together, which is strange after only three dates, but I suppose it's because of our therapy history. Whatever the reason, I'm enjoying it. Our lauvan dance around each other and gently touch.

Too soon, we reach Minnie's apartment.

"This is me," she says with an awkward wave. "Would you like to come up for a drink? You can see the ocean from the balcony."

It's unclear from her body language and her lauvan whether she truly wants me to come up. The threads that were dancing with mine are suddenly stiff, either from awkwardness at what I might expect should I come up, or excitement of what she wants to happen. I'm unsure myself. Somehow, through the most trying behavior on my part and against the advice of her friends, she still wants to know me better. It won't last, but I don't want to cut our relationship short by pushing too quickly before it has a chance to develop. A few months would be nice. I don't want to rush things and truncate the dating dance before it blossoms, and I have time to spare.

"I would love to sit on your balcony with you. Can I take a rain check? I have a large stack of papers to mark before tomorrow morning. The students will be frothing mad if I don't deliver."

While it's true I have papers to mark—my sojourn to the

Minerva Louise used up more time than I had expected—I wouldn't let that stop me if I had decided to accept Minnie's invitation. She looks disappointed but understanding.

"Of course. We must prevent you from becoming a headline: 'Instructor mowed down in student rampage.'"

I laugh, but before I finish, Minnie leans in and presses her mouth to mine. Her lips are soft and so sweet, I can't breathe for a moment. I respond immediately with a passion that surprises me. All the feelings that appeared when we danced at the wedding surge up in me now, and I place my hands around her waist to draw her close. She doesn't resist and presses herself against my chest.

It's only a moment, then she stops the kiss and steps back. Her cheeks are flushed, and her eyes are bright.

"Thanks for the walk, Merry. I'll see you soon."

She turns before I can manage a coherent response and disappears through her building's front door. I take a deep breath and examine the lauvan that connect us, chocolate brown and navy blue entwined together in a cord that moves upward as Minnie climbs the stairs inside her building. A smile covers my face and I can't help whistling when I walk away.

ALSO BY EMMA SHELFORD

Immortal Merlin
Ignition
Winded
Floodgates
Buried
Possessed
Unleashed
Worshiped

Nautilus Legends
Free Dive
Caught
Surfacing

Breenan Series
Mark of the Breenan
Garden of Last Hope
Realm of the Forgotten

ACKNOWLEDGEMENTS

My tireless editing team were ready again: Gillian Brownlee, Wendy and Chris Callendar, and Kathryn Humphries. As always, my heartfelt thanks for your fresh eyes and keen story sense. Deranged Doctor Designs produced another exciting cover. And, of course, the support of Steven Shelford buoys me in my author's journey.

ABOUT THE AUTHOR

Emma Shelford feels that life is only complete with healthy doses of magic, history, and science. Since these aren't often found in the same place, she creates her own worlds where they happily coexist. If you catch her in person, she will eagerly discuss Lord of the Rings ad nauseam, why the ancient Sumerians are so cool, and the important role of phytoplankton in the ocean.

Apart from the Immortal Merlin books, Emma is the author of the Nautilus Legends (a marine biologist discovers that mythical sea creatures are real) and the Breenan Series (a young woman follows a mysterious stranger into an enchanting Otherworld).

Printed in Great Britain
by Amazon

23839901R00148